Joh

The Journal of John Woolman

Anatiposi

John G. Whittier

The Journal of John Woolman

Reprint of the original.

1st Edition 2023 | ISBN: 978-3-38210-610-2

Anatiposi Verlag is an imprint of Outlook Verlagsgesellschaft mbH.

Verlag (Publisher): Outlook Verlag GmbH, Zeilweg 44, 60439 Frankfurt, Deutschland
Vertretungsberechtigt (Authorized to represent): E. Roepke, Zeilweg 44, 60439 Frankfurt, Deutschland
Druck (Print): Books on Demand GmbH, In de Tarpen 42, 22848 Norderstedt, Deutschland

THE JOURNAL OF JOHN WOOLMAN

WITH AN INTRODUCTION BY

JOHN G. WHITTIER

"The work of righteousness shall be peace; and the effect of righteousness, quietness and assurance forever." — ISAIAH.

BOSTON AND NEW YORK
HOUGHTON MIFFLIN COMPANY
The Riverside Press Cambridge

NINETEENTH IMPRESSION

CONTENTS.

CHAPTER IV.

1757, 1758.

CHAPTER V.

1757, 1758.

CHAPTER VI.

1758, 1759.

CHAPTER VII.

1760.

CHAPTER VIII.

1761, 1762.

CHAPTER IX.

1763 - 1769.

CHAPTER X.

1769, 1770.

CHAPTER XI.

1772.

CHAPTER XII.

1772.

APPENDIX.

INTRODUCTION.

TO those who judge by the outward appearance, nothing is more difficult of explanation than the strength of moral influence often exerted by obscure and uneventful lives. Some great reform which lifts the world to a higher level, some mighty change for which the ages have waited in anxious expectancy, takes place before our eyes, and, in seeking to trace it back to its origin, we are often surprised to find the initial link in the chain of causes to be some comparatively obscure individual, the divine commission and significance of whose life were scarcely understood by his contemporaries, and perhaps not even by himself. The little one has become a thousand; the handful of corn shakes like Lebanon. "The kingdom of God cometh not by observation"; and the only solution of the mystery is in the reflection that through the humble instrumentality Divine power was manifested, and that the Everlasting Arm was beneath the human one.

The abolition of human slavery now in process of consummation throughout the world furnishes one of the most striking illustrations of this truth. A far-reaching moral, social, and political revolution, undoing the evil work of centuries, unquestionably owes much of its original impulse to the life and labors of a poor, unlearned workingman of New Jersey, whose very existence was scarcely known beyond the narrow circle of his religious society.

It is only within a comparatively recent period that the journal and ethical essays of this remarkable man have attracted the attention to which they are manifestly entitled. In one of my last interviews with William Ellery Channing, he expressed his very great surprise that they were so little known. He had himself just read the book for the first time, and I shall never forget how his countenance lighted up as he pronounced it beyond comparison the sweetest and purest autobiography in the language. He wished to see it placed within the reach of all classes of readers; it was not a light to be hidden under the bushel of a sect. Charles Lamb, probably from his friends, the Clarksons, or from Bernard Barton, became acquainted with it, and on more than one occasion, in his letters and Essays of Elia, refers to it with warm commendation. Edward Irving pronounced it a godsend. Some idea of the lively interest which the fine literary circle gathered around the hearth of Lamb felt in the beautiful simplicity of Woolman's pages may be had from the Diary of Henry Crabb Robinson, one of their number, himself a man of wide and varied culture, the intimate friend of Goethe, Wordsworth, and Coleridge. In his notes for First Month, 1824, he says, after a reference to a sermon of his friend Irving, which he feared would deter rather than promote belief: "How different this from John Woolman's Journal I have been reading at the same time! A perfect gem! His is a *schöne Seele*, a beautiful soul. An illiterate tailor, he writes in a style of the most exquisite purity and grace. His moral qualities are transferred to his writings. Had he not been so very humble, he would have written a still better book; for, fearing to indulge in vanity, he conceals the events in which he was a great actor. His religion was love. His whole existence and all his passions were love. If one could venture to impute to his creed, and not to his personal character, the delightful frame of mind he exhibited, one could not hesitate to be a convert. His Christianity is most inviting, — it is fascinating!" One of the leading British reviews a few years ago, referring to this Journal, pronounced its author the man who, in all the centuries since the advent of Christ, lived nearest to the Divine pattern. The author of The Patience of Hope,* whose authority in devotional literature is unquestioned, says of him: "John Woolman's

* It will be interesting to the thousands in this country who have learned to admire and love this remarkable writer to learn that she has in preparation an appreciative review of the life and character of Woolman, which, it is to be hoped, will soon be published.

gift was love, — a charity of which it does not enter into the natural heart of man to conceive, and of which the more ordinary experiences, even of renewed nature, give but a faint shadow. Every now and then, in the world's history, we meet with such men, the kings and priests of Humanity, on whose heads this precious ointment has been so poured forth that it has run down to the skirts of their clothing, and extended over the whole of the visible creation; men who have entered, like Francis of Assisi, into the secret of that deep amity with God and with his creatures which makes man to be in league with the stones of the field, and the beasts of the field to be at peace with him. In this pure, universal charity there is nothing fitful or intermittent, nothing that comes and goes in showers and gleams and sunbursts. Its springs are deep and constant, its rising is like that of a mighty river, its very overflow calm and steady, leaving life and fertility behind it."

After all, anything like personal eulogy seems out of place in speaking of one who in the humblest self-abasement sought no place in the world's estimation, content to be only a passive instrument in the hands of his Master; and who, as has been remarked, through modesty concealed the events in which he was an actor. A desire to supply in some sort this deficiency in his Journal is my especial excuse for this introductory paper.

It is instructive to study the history of the moral progress of individuals or communities; to mark the gradual development of truth, to watch the slow germination of its seed sown in simple obedience to the command of the Great Husbandman, while yet its green promise, as well as its golden fruition, was hidden from the eyes of the sower; to go back to the well-springs and fountain-heads, tracing the small streamlet from its hidden source, and noting the tributaries which swell its waters, as it moves onward, until it becomes a broad river, fertilizing and gladdening our present humanity. To this end it is my purpose, as briefly as possible, to narrate the circumstances attending the relinquishment of slaveholding by the Society of Friends, and to hint at the effect of that act of justice and humanity upon the abolition of slavery throughout the world.

At an early period after the organization of the Society, members of it emigrated to the Maryland, Carolina, Virginia, and New England colonies. The act of banishment enforced against dissenters under Charles II. consigned others of the sect to the West Indies, where their frugality, temperance, and thrift transmuted their intended punishment into a blessing. Andrew Marvell, the inflexible republican statesman, in some of the sweetest and tenderest lines in the English tongue, has happily described their condition: —

"'What shall we do but sing His praise
Who led us through the watery maze,
Unto an isle so long unknown,
And yet far kinder than our own?
He lands us on a grassy stage,

Safe from the storms and prelates' rage;
He gives us this eternal spring,
Which here enamels everything,
And sends the fowls to us in care,
On daily visits through the air.
He hangs in shades the orange bright,
Like golden lamps, in a green night,
And doth in the pomegranate close
Jewels more rich than Ormus shows.

. . . . .

And in these rocks for us did frame
A temple where to sound His name.
Oh! let our voice His praise exalt,
Till it arrive at Heaven's vault,
Which then, perhaps rebounding, may
Echo beyond the Mexic bay.'

So sang they in the English boat,
A holy and a cheerful note;
And all the way, to guide their chime,
With falling oars they kept the time."

Unhappily, they very early became owners of slaves, in imitation of the colonists around them. No positive condemnation of the evil system had then been heard in the British islands. Neither English prelates nor expounders at dissenting conventicles had aught to say against it. Few colonists doubted its entire compatibility with Christian profession and conduct. Saint and sinner, ascetic and worldling, united in its practice. Even the extreme Dutch saints of Bohemia Manor on the Delaware, the pietists of John de Labadie, sitting at meat with hats on, and pausing ever and anon with suspended mouthfuls to hear a brother's or sister's exhortation, and sandwiching prayers between the courses, were waited upon by negro slaves. Everywhere men were contending with each other upon matters of faith, while, so far as their slaves were concerned, denying the ethics of Christianity itself.

Such was the state of things when, in 1671, George Fox visited Barbadoes. He was one of those men to whom it is given to discern through the mists of custom and prejudice something of the lineaments of absolute truth, and who, like the Hebrew lawgiver, bear with them, from a higher and purer atmosphere, the shining evidence of communion with the Divine Wisdom. He saw slavery in its mildest form among his friends, but his intuitive sense of right condemned it. He solemnly admonished those who held slaves to bear in mind that they were brethren, and to train them up in the fear of God. "I desired, also," he says, "that they would cause their overseers to deal gently and mildly with their negroes, and not use cruelty towards them as the manner of some hath been and is; and that, after certain years of servitude, they should make them free."

In 1675, the companion of George Fox, William Edmundson, revisited Barbadoes, and once more bore testimony against the unjust treatment of slaves. He was accused of endeavoring to excite an insurrection among the blacks, and was brought before the Governor on the charge. It was probably during this journey that he addressed a remonstrance to friends in Maryland and Virginia on the subject of holding slaves. It is one of the first emphatic and decided testimonies on record against negro slavery as incompatible with Christianity, if we except the Papal bulls of Urban and Leo the Tenth.

Thirteen years after, in 1688, a meeting of German Quakers, who had emigrated from Kriesheim, and settled at Germantown, Pennsylvania, addressed a memorial against "the buying and keeping of negroes" to the Yearly Meeting for the Pennsylvania and New Jersey colonies. That meeting took the subject into consideration, but declined giving judgment in the case. In 1696, the Yearly Meeting advised against "bringing in any more negroes." In 1714, in its Epistle to London Friends, it expresses a wish that Friends would be "less concerned in buying or selling slaves." The Chester Quarterly Meeting, which had taken a higher and clearer view of the matter, continued to press the Yearly Meeting to adopt some decided measure against any traffic in human beings.

The Society gave these memorials a cold reception. The love of gain and power was too strong, on the part of the wealthy and influential planters and merchants who had become slaveholders, to allow the scruples of the Chester meeting to take the shape of discipline. The utmost that could be obtained of the Yearly Meeting was an expression of opinion adverse to the importation of negroes, and a desire that "Friends generally do, as much as may be, avoid buying such negroes as shall hereafter be brought in, rather than offend any

Friends who are against it; yet this is only caution, and not censure."

In the mean time the New England Yearly Meeting was agitated by the same question. Slaves were imported into Boston and Newport, and Friends became purchasers, and in some instances were deeply implicated in the foreign traffic. In 1716, the monthly meetings of Dartmouth and Nantucket suggested that it was "not agreeable to truth to purchase slaves and keep them during their term of life." Nothing was done in the Yearly Meeting, however, until 1727, when the practice of importing negroes was censured. That the practice was continued notwithstanding, for many years afterwards, is certain. In 1758, a rule was adopted prohibiting Friends within the limits of New England Yearly Meeting from engaging in or countenancing the foreign slave-trade.

In the year 1742 an event, simple and inconsiderable in itself, was made the instrumentality of exerting a mighty influence upon slavery in the Society of Friends. A small storekeeper at Mount Holly,* in New Jersey, a member of the Society,

* Mount Holly is a village lying in the western part of the long, narrow township of Northampton, on Rancocas Creek, a tributary of the Delaware. In John Woolman's day it was almost entirely a settlement of Friends. A very few of the old houses with their quaint stoops or porches are left. That occupied by John Woolman was a small, plain, two-story structure, with two windows in each story in front, a four-barred fence enclosing the grounds, with the trees he planted and loved to cultivate. The house was not painted, but

sold a negro woman, and requested the young man in his employ to make a bill of sale of her. On taking up his pen, the young clerk felt a sudden and strong scruple in his mind. The thought of writing an instrument of slavery for one of his fellow-creatures oppressed him. God's voice against

whitewashed. The name of the place is derived from the highest hill in the county, rising two hundred feet above the sea, and commanding a view of a rich and level country, of cleared farms and woodlands. Here, no doubt, John Woolman often walked under the shadow of its holly-trees, communing with nature and musing on the great themes of life and duty.

When the excellent Joseph Sturge was in this country, some thirty years ago, on his errand of humanity, he visited Mount Holly, and the house of Woolman, then standing. He describes it as a very "humble abode." But one person was then living in the town who had ever seen its venerated owner. This aged man stated that he was at Woolman's little farm in the season of harvest, when it was customary among farmers to kill a calf or sheep for the laborers. John Woolman, unwilling that the animal should be slowly bled to death, as the custom had been, and to spare it unnecessary suffering, had a smooth block of wood prepared to receive the neck of the creature, when a single blow terminated its existence. Nothing was more remarkable in the character of Woolman than his concern for the well-being and comfort of the brute creation. "What is religion?" asks the old Hindoo writer of the Vishnu Sarman. "Tenderness toward all creatures." Or, as Woolman expresses it, "Where the love of God is verily perfected, a tenderness towards all creatures made subject to our will is experienced, and a care felt that we do not lessen that sweetness of life in the animal creation which the Creator intends for them under our government."

the desecration of his image spoke in his soul. He yielded to the will of his employer, but, while writing the instrument, he was constrained to declare, both to the buyer and the seller, that he believed slave-keeping inconsistent with the Christian religion. This young man was John Woolman. The circumstance above named was the starting-point of a life-long testimony against slavery. In the year 1746 he visited Maryland, Virginia, and North Carolina. He was afflicted by the prevalence of slavery. It appeared to him, in his own words, "as a dark gloominess overhanging the land." On his return, he wrote an essay on the subject, which was published in 1754. Three years after, he made a second visit to the Southern meetings of Friends. Travelling as a minister of the gospel, he was compelled to sit down at the tables of slaveholding planters, who were accustomed to entertain their friends free of cost, and who could not comprehend the scruples of their guest against receiving as a gift food and lodging which he regarded as the gain of oppression. He was a poor man, but he loved truth more than money. He therefore either placed the pay for his entertainment in the hands of some member of the family, for the benefit of the slaves, or gave it directly to them, as he had opportunity.*

* The tradition is that he travelled mostly on foot during his journeys among slaveholders. Brissot, in his New Travels in America, published in 1788, says: "John Woolman, one of the most distinguished of men in the cause of humanity, travelled much as a minister of his sect, but always on foot,

Wherever he went, he found his fellow-professors entangled in the mischief of slavery. Elders and ministers, as well as the younger and less high in profession, had their house servants and field hands. He found grave drab-coated apologists for the slave-trade, who quoted the same Scriptures, in support of oppression and avarice, which have since been cited by Presbyterian doctors of divinity, Methodist bishops, and Baptist preachers for the same purpose. He found the meetings generally in a low and evil state. The gold of original Quakerism had become dim, and the fine gold changed. The spirit of the world prevailed among them, and had wrought an inward desolation. Instead of

and without money, in imitation of the Apostles, and in order to be in a situation to be more useful to poor people and the blacks. He hated slavery so much that he could not taste food provided by the labor of slaves." That this writer was on one point misinformed is manifest from the following passage from the Journal: "When I expected soon to leave a friend's house where I had entertainment, if I believed that I should not keep clear from the gain of oppression without leaving money, I spoke to one of the heads of the family privately, and desired them to accept of pieces of silver, and give them to such of their negroes as they believed would make the best use of them; and at other times I gave them to the negroes myself, as the way looked clearest to me. Before I came out, I had provided a large number of small pieces for this purpose, and thus offering them to some who appeared to be wealthy people was a trial both to me and them. But the fear of the Lord so covered me at times that my way was made easier than I expected; and few, if any, manifested any resentment at the offer, and most of them, after some conversation, accepted of them."

meekness, gentleness, and heavenly wisdom, he found "a spirit of fierceness and love of dominion." In love, but at the same time with great faithfulness, he endeavored to convince the masters of their error, and to awaken a degree of sympathy for the enslaved.

At this period, or perhaps somewhat earlier, a remarkable personage took up his residence in Pennsylvania. He was by birthright a member of the Society of Friends, but having been disowned in England for some extravagances of conduct and language, he spent some years in the West Indies, where he became deeply interested in the condition of the slaves. His violent denunciations of the practice of slaveholding excited the anger of the planters, and he was compelled to leave the island. He came to Philadelphia, but, contrary to his expectations, he found the same evil existing there. He shook off the dust of the city, and took up his abode in the country, a few miles distant. His dwelling was a natural cave, with some slight addition of his own making. His drink was the spring-water flowing by his door; his food, vegetables alone. He persistently refused to wear any garment or eat any food purchased at the expense of animal life, or which was in any degree the product of slave labor. Issuing from his cave, on his mission of preaching "deliverance to the captive," he was in the habit of visiting the various meetings for worship and bearing his testimony against slaveholders, greatly to their disgust and indignation.

On one occasion he entered the Market Street Meeting, and a leading Friend requested some one to take him out. A burly blacksmith volunteered to do it, leading him to the gate and thrusting him out with such force that he fell into the gutter of the street. There he lay until the meeting closed, telling the bystanders that he did not feel free to rise himself. "Let those who cast me here raise me up. It is their business, not mine."

His personal appearance was in remarkable keeping with his eccentric life. A figure only four and a half feet high, hunchbacked, with projecting chest, legs small and uneven, arms longer than his legs; a huge head, showing only beneath the enormous white hat large, solemn eyes and a prominent nose; the rest of his face covered with a snowy semicircle of beard falling low on his breast,—a figure to recall the old legends of troll, brownie, and kobold. Such was the irrepressible prophet who troubled the Israel of slaveholding Quakerism, clinging like a rough chestnut-burr to the skirts of its respectability and settling like a pertinacious gad-fly on the sore places of its conscience.

On one occasion, while the annual meeting was in session at Burlington, N. J., in the midst of the solemn silence of the great assembly, the unwelcome figure of Benjamin Lay, wrapped in his long white overcoat, was seen passing up the aisle. Stopping midway, he exclaimed, "You slaveholders! Why don't you throw off your Quaker coats as I do mine, and show yourselves as you are?" Casting off as he spoke his outer garment, he disclosed to the astonished assembly a military coat underneath and a sword dangling at his heels. Holding in one hand a large book, he drew his sword with the other. "In the sight of God," he cried, "you are as guilty as if you stabbed your slaves to the heart, as I do this book!" suiting the action to the word, and piercing a small bladder filled with the juice of poke-weed (*phytolacca decandra*), which he had concealed between the covers, and sprinkling as with fresh blood those who sat near him. John Woolman makes no mention of this circumstance in his Journal, although he was probably present, and it must have made a deep impression on his sensitive spirit. The violence and harshness of Lay's testimony, however, had nothing in common with the tender and sorrowful remonstrances and appeals of the former, except the sympathy which they both felt for the slave himself.*

Still later, a descendant of the persecuted French Protestants, Anthony Benezet, a man of uncommon tenderness of feeling, began to write and speak

* Lay was well acquainted with Dr. Franklin, who sometimes visited him. Among other schemes of reform he entertained the idea of converting all mankind to Christianity. This was to be done by three witnesses,—himself, Michael Lovell, and Abel Noble, assisted by Dr. Franklin. But on their first meeting at the Doctor's house, the three "chosen vessels" got into a violent controversy on points of doctrine, and separated in ill-humor. The philosopher, who had been an amused listener, advised the three sages to give up the project of converting the world until they had learned to tolerate each other.

against slavery. How far, if at all, he was moved thereto by the example of Woolman is not known, but it is certain that the latter found in him a steady friend and coadjutor in his efforts to awaken the slumbering moral sense of his religious brethren. The Marquis de Chastellux, author of *De la Félicité Publique*, describes him as a small, eager-faced man, full of zeal and activity, constantly engaged in works of benevolence, which were by no means confined to the blacks. Like Woolman and Lay, he advocated abstinence from intoxicating spirits. The poor French neutrals who were brought to Philadelphia from Nova Scotia, and landed penniless and despairing among strangers in tongue and religion, found in him a warm and untiring friend, through whose aid and sympathy their condition was rendered more comfortable than that of their fellow-exiles in other colonies.*

The annual assemblage of the Yearly Meeting in 1758 at Philadelphia must ever be regarded as one of the most important religious convocations in the history of the Christian church. The labors of

* The reader of Evangeline will recall in this connection the words of the poet: —

"In that delightful land which is washed by the Delaware's waters,
Guarding in sylvan shades the name of Penn the apostle,
Stands on the banks of its beautiful stream the city he founded.
There from the troubled sea had Evangeline landed, an exile,
Finding among the children of Penn a home and a country.
There old René Leblanc had died; and when he departed,

Woolman and his few but earnest associates had not been in vain. A deep and tender interest had been awakened; and this meeting was looked forward to with varied feelings of solicitude by all parties. All felt that the time had come for some definite action; conservative and reformer stood face to face in the Valley of Decision. John Woolman, of course, was present, — a man humble and poor in outward appearance, his simple dress of undyed homespun cloth contrasting strongly with the plain but rich apparel of the representatives of the commerce of the city and of the large slave-stocked plantations of the country. Bowed down by the weight of his concern for the poor slaves and for the well-being and purity of the Society, he sat silent during the whole meeting, while other matters were under discussion. "My mind," he says, "was frequently clothed with inward prayer; and I could say with David that 'tears were my meat and drink, day and night.' The case of slave-keeping lay heavy upon me; nor did I find any engagement to speak directly to any other matter before

Saw at his side only one of all his hundred descendants.
Something at least there was in the friendly streets of the city,
Something that spake to her heart, and made her no longer a stranger;
And her ear was pleased with the Thee and Thou of the Quakers,
For it recalled the past, the old Acadian country,
Where all men were equal, and all were brothers and sisters."

the meeting." When the important subject came up for consideration many faithful Friends spoke with weight and earnestness. No one openly justified slavery as a system, although some expressed a concern lest the meeting should go into measures calculated to cause uneasiness to many members of the Society. It was also urged that Friends should wait patiently until the Lord in his own time should open a way for the deliverance of the slave. This was replied to by John Woolman. "My mind," he said, "is led to consider the purity of the Divine Being, and the justice of his judgments; and herein my soul is covered with awfulness. I cannot forbear to hint of some cases where people have not been treated with the purity of justice, and the event has been most lamentable. Many slaves on this continent are oppressed, and their cries have entered into the ears of the Most High. Such are the purity and certainty of his judgments, that he cannot be partial in our favor. In infinite love and goodness he hath opened our understandings from one time to another, concerning our duty towards this people; and it is not a time for delay. Should we now be sensible of what he requires of us, and through a respect to the private interest of some persons, or through a regard to some friendships which do not stand upon an immutable foundation, neglect to do our duty in firmness and constancy, still waiting for some extraordinary means to bring about their deliverance, God may by terrible things in righteousness answer us in this matter."

This solemn and weighty appeal was responded to by many in the assembly, in a spirit of sympathy and unity. Some of the slaveholding members expressed their willingness that a strict rule of discipline should be adopted against *dealing* in slaves for the future. To this it was answered, that the root of the evil would never be reached effectually until a searching inquiry was made into the circumstances and motives of such as *held* slaves. At length the truth in a great measure triumphed over all opposition ; and, without any public dissent, the meeting agreed that the injunction of our Lord and Saviour to do to others as we would that others should do to us should induce Friends who held slaves "to set them at liberty, making a Christian provision for them," and four Friends — John Woolman, John Scarborough, Daniel Stanton, and John Sykes — were approved of as suitable persons to visit and treat with such as kept slaves, within the limits of the Meeting.

This painful and difficult duty was faithfully performed. In that meekness and humility of spirit which has nothing in common with the "fear of man, which bringeth a snare," the self-denying followers of their Divine Lord and Master "went about doing good." In the city of Philadelphia, and among the wealthy planters of the country, they found occasion often to exercise a great degree of patience, and to keep a watchful guard over their feelings. In his Journal for this important period of his life John Woolman says but little of his own services. How arduous and delicate they were may be readily understood. The number of slaves held by members of the Society was very large. Isaac Jackson, in his report of his labors among slaveholders in a single Quarterly Meeting, states that he visited the owners of more than *eleven hundred* slaves. From the same report may be gleaned some hints of the difficulties which presented themselves. One elderly man says he has well brought up his eleven slaves, and "now they must work to maintain him." Another owns it is all wrong, but "cannot release his slaves; his tender wife under great concern of mind" on account of his refusal. A third has fifty slaves, knows it to be wrong, but can't see his way clear out of it. "Perhaps," the report says, "interest dims his vision." A fourth is full of "excuses and reasonings." "Old Jos. Richison has forty, and is determined to keep them." Another man has fifty, and "means to keep them." Robert Ward "wants to release his slaves, but his wife and daughters hold back." Another "owns it is wrong, but says he will not part with his negroes, — no, not while he lives." The far greater number, however, confess the wrong of slavery and agree to take measures for freeing their slaves.*

* An incident occurred during this visit of Isaac Jackson which impressed him deeply. On the last evening, just as he was about to turn homeward, he was told that a member of the Society whom he had not seen owned a very old slave who was happy and well cared for. It was a case which it was thought might well be left to take care of itself. Isaac

An extract or two from the Journal at this period will serve to show both the nature of the service in

Jackson, sitting in silence, did not feel his mind quite satisfied; and as the evening wore away, feeling more and more exercised, he expressed his uneasiness, when a young son of his host eagerly offered to go with him and show him the road to the place. The proposal was gladly accepted. On introducing the object of their visit, the Friend expressed much surprise that any uneasiness should be felt in the case, but at length consented to sign the form of emancipation, saying, at the same time, it would make no difference in their relations, as the old man was perfectly happy. At Isaac Jackson's request the slave was called in and seated before them. His form was nearly double, his thin hands were propped on his knees, his white head was thrust forward, and his keen, restless, inquiring eyes gleamed alternately on the stranger and on his master. At length he was informed of what had been done; that he was no longer a slave, and that his master acknowledged his past services entitled him to a maintenance so long as he lived. The old man listened in almost breathless wonder, his head slowly sinking on his breast. After a short pause, he clasped his hands, then spreading them high over his hoary head, slowly and reverently exclaimed, "Oh, goody Gody, oh!" — bringing his hands again down on his knees. Then raising them as before, he twice repeated the solemn exclamation, and with streaming eyes and a voice almost too much choked for utterance, he continued, "*I thought I should die a slave, and now I shall die a free man!*"

It is a striking evidence of the divine compensations which are sometimes graciously vouchsafed to those who have been faithful to duty, that, on his death-bed this affecting scene was vividly revived in the mind of Isaac Jackson. At that supreme moment, when all other pictures of time were fading out, that old face, full of solemn joy and devout thanksgiving, rose before him, and comforted him as with the blessing of God.

which he was engaged and the frame of mind in which he accomplished it.

"In the beginning of the 12th month I joined in company with my friends, John Sykes and Daniel Stanton, in visiting such as had slaves. Some, whose hearts were rightly exercised about them, appeared to be glad of our visit, but in some places our way was more difficult. I often saw the necessity of keeping down to that root from whence our concern proceeded, and have cause in reverent thankfulness humbly to bow down before the Lord who was near to me, and preserved my mind in calmness under some sharp conflicts, and begat a spirit of sympathy and tenderness in me towards some who were grievously entangled by the spirit of this world."

"1st month, 1759.—Having found my mind drawn to visit some of the more active members of society at Philadelphia who had slaves, I met my friend John Churchman there by agreement, and we continued about a week in the city. We visited some that were sick, and some widows and their families; and the other part of the time was mostly employed in visiting such as had slaves. It was a time of deep exercise; but looking often to the Lord for assistance, he in unspeakable kindness favored us with the influence of that spirit which crucifies to the greatness and splendor of this world, and enabled us to go through some heavy labors, in which we found peace."

These labors were attended with the blessing of

the God of the poor and oppressed. Dealing in slaves was almost entirely abandoned, and many who held slaves set them at liberty. But many members still continuing the practice, a more emphatic testimony against it was issued by the Yearly Meeting in 1774; and two years after the subordinate meetings were directed to *deny the right of membership to such as persisted in holding their fellow men as property.*

A concern was now felt for the temporal and religious welfare of the emancipated slaves and, in 1779 the Yearly Meeting came to the conclusion that some reparation was due from the masters to their former slaves for services rendered while in the condition of slavery. The following is an extract from an epistle on this subject: —

"We are united in judgment that the state of the oppressed people who have been held by any of us, or our predecessors, in captivity and slavery, calls for a deep inquiry and close examination how far we are clear of withholding from them what under such an exercise may open to view as their just right; and therefore we earnestly and affectionately entreat our brethren in religious profession to bring this matter home, and that all who have let the oppressed go free may attend to the further openings of duty.

"A tender Christian sympathy appears to be awakened in the minds of many who are not in religious profession with us, who have seriously considered the oppressions and disadvantages under which those people have long labored; and whether a pious care extended to their offspring is not justly due from us to them is a consideration worthy our serious and deep attention."

Committees to aid and advise the colored people were accordingly appointed in the various Monthly Meetings. Many former owners of slaves faithfully paid the latter for their services, submitting to the award and judgment of arbitrators as to what justice required at their hands. So deeply had the sense of the wrong of slavery sunk into the hearts of Friends!

John Woolman, in his Journal for 1769, states, that having some years before, as one of the executors of a will, disposed of the services of a negro boy belonging to the estate until he should reach the age of thirty years, he became uneasy in respect to the transaction, and, although he had himself derived no pecuniary benefit from it, and had simply acted as the agent of the heirs of the estate to which the boy belonged, he executed a bond, binding himself to pay the master of the young man for four years and a half of his unexpired term of service.

The appalling magnitude of the evil against which he felt himself especially called to contend was painfully manifest to John Woolman. At the outset, all about him, in every department of life and human activity, in the state and the church, he saw evidences of its strength, and of the depth and extent to which its roots had wound their way among the foundations of society. Yet he seems never to have doubted for a moment the power of simple truth to eradicate it, nor to have hesitated as to his own duty in regard to it. There was no groping like Samson in the gloom; no feeling in blind wrath and impatience for the pillars of the temple of Dagon. "The candle of the Lord shone about him," and his path lay clear and unmistakable before him. He believed in the goodness of God that leadeth to repentance; and that love could reach the witness for itself in the hearts of all men, through all entanglements of custom and every barrier of pride and selfishness. No one could have a more humble estimate of himself; but as he went forth on his errand of mercy he felt the Infinite Power behind him, and the consciousness that he had known a preparation from that Power "to stand as a trumpet through which the Lord speaks." The event justified his confidence; wherever he went hard hearts were softened, avarice and love of power and pride of opinion gave way before his testimony of love.

The New England Yearly Meeting then, as now, was held in Newport, on Rhode Island. In the year 1760 John Woolman, in the course of a religious visit to New England, attended that meeting. He saw the horrible traffic in human beings, — the slave-ships lying at the wharves of the town, — the sellers and buyers of men and women and children thronging the market-place. The same abhorrent scenes which a few years after stirred the spirit of the excellent Hopkins to denounce the slave-trade and slavery as hateful in the sight of God to his congregation at Newport were enacted in the full view and hearing of the annual convocation of Friends, many of whom were themselves partakers in the shame and wickedness. "Understanding," he says, "that a large number of slaves had been imported from Africa into the town, and were then on sale by a member of our Society, my appetite failed; I grew outwardly weak, and had a feeling of the condition of Habakkuk: 'When I heard, my belly trembled, my lips quivered; I trembled in myself, that I might rest in the day of trouble.' I had many cogitations, and was sorely distressed." He prepared a memorial to the Legislature, then in session, for the signatures of Friends, urging that body to take measures to put an end to the importation of slaves. His labors in the Yearly Meeting appear to have been owned and blessed by the Divine Head of the church. The London Epistle for 1758, condemning the unrighteous traffic in men, was read, and the substance of it embodied in the discipline of the meeting; and the following query was adopted, to be answered by the subordinate meetings:—

"Are Friends clear of importing negroes, or buying them when imported; and do they use those well, where they are possessed by inheritance or otherwise, endeavoring to train them up in principles of religion?"

At the close of the Yearly Meeting, John Woolman requested those members of the Society who held slaves to meet with him in the chamber of the house for worship, where he expressed his concern for the well-being of the slaves, and his sense of the iniquity of the practice of dealing in or holding them as property. His tender exhortations were not lost upon his auditors; his remarks were kindly received, and the gentle and loving spirit in which they were offered reached many hearts.

In 1769, at the suggestion of the Rhode Island Quarterly Meeting, the Yearly Meeting expressed its sense of the wrongfulness of holding slaves, and appointed a large committee to visit those members who were implicated in the practice. The next year this committee reported that they had completed their service, "and that their visits mostly seemed to be kindly accepted. Some Friends manifested a disposition to set such at liberty as were suitable; some others, not having so clear a sight of such an unreasonable servitude as could be desired, were unwilling to comply with the advice given them at present, yet seemed willing to take it into consideration; a few others manifested a disposition to keep them in continued bondage."

It was stated in the Epistle to London Yearly Meeting of the year 1772, that a few Friends had freed their slaves from bondage, but that others "have been so reluctant thereto that they *have been disowned* for not complying with the advice of this meeting."

In 1773 the following minute was made: "It

is our sense and judgment that truth not only requires the young of capacity and ability, but likewise the aged and impotent, and also all in a state of infancy and nonage, among Friends, to be discharged and set free from a state of slavery, that we do no more claim property in the human race, as we do in the brutes that perish."

In 1782 no slaves were known to be held in the New England Yearly Meeting. The next year it was recommended to the subordinate meetings to appoint committees to effect a proper and just *settlement between the manumitted slaves and their former masters, for their past services.* In 1784 it was concluded by the Yearly Meeting that any former slaveholder who refused to comply with the award of these committees should, after due care and labor with him, be disowned from the Society. This was effectual; settlements without disownment were made to the satisfaction of all parties, and every case was disposed of previous to the year 1787.

In the New York Yearly Meeting, slave-trading was prohibited about the middle of the last century. In 1771, in consequence of an epistle from the Philadelphia Yearly Meeting, a committee was appointed to visit those who held slaves, and to advise with them in relation to emancipation. In 1776 it was made a disciplinary offence to buy, sell, or hold slaves upon any condition. In 1784 but one slave was to be found in the limits of the meeting. In the same year, by answers from the several subordinate meetings, it was ascertained that an equitable settlement for past services had been effected between the emancipated negroes and their masters in all save three cases.

In the Virginia Yearly Meeting slavery had its strongest hold. Its members, living in the midst of slaveholding communities, were necessarily exposed to influences adverse to emancipation. I have already alluded to the epistle addressed to them by William Edmondson, and to the labors of John Woolman while travelling among them. In 1757 the Virginia Yearly Meeting condemned the foreign slave-trade. In 1764 it enjoined upon its members the duty of kindness towards their servants, of educating them, and carefully providing for their food and clothing. Four years after, its members were strictly prohibited from purchasing any more slaves. In 1773 it earnestly recommended the immediate manumission of all slaves held in bondage, after the females had reached eighteen and the males twenty-one years of age. At the same time it was advised that committees should be appointed for the purpose of instructing the emancipated persons in the principles of morality and religion, and for advising and aiding them in their temporal concerns.

I quote a single paragraph from the advice sent down to the subordinate meetings, as a beautiful manifestation of the fruits of true repentance: —

"It is the solid sense of this meeting, that we of the present generation are under strong obligations to express our love and concern for the offspring of those people who by their labors have greatly contributed towards the cultivation of these colonies under the afflictive disadvantage of enduring a hard bondage; and many amongst us are enjoying the benefit of their toil."

In 1784 the different Quarterly Meetings having reported that many still held slaves, notwithstanding the advice and entreaties of their friends, the Yearly Meeting directed, that where *endeavors* to convince those offenders of their error proved ineffectual, the Monthly Meetings should proceed to disown them. We have no means of ascertaining the precise number of those actually disowned for slaveholding in the Virginia Yearly Meeting, but it is well known to have been very small. In almost all cases the care and assiduous labors of those who had the welfare of the Society and of humanity at heart were successful in inducing offenders to manumit their slaves, and confess their error in resisting the wishes of their friends, and bringing reproach upon the cause of truth.

So ended slavery in the Society of Friends. For three quarters of a century the advice put forth in the meetings of the Society at stated intervals, that Friends should be "careful to maintain their testi mony against slavery" has been adhered to so far as owning, or even hiring, a slave is concerned. Apart from its first-fruits of emancipation, there is a perennial value in the example exhibited of the power of truth, urged patiently and in earnest love, to overcome the difficulties in the way of the eradication of an evil system, strengthened by long habit, entangled with all the complex relations of society, and closely allied with the love of power, the pride of family, and the lust of gain.

The influence of the life and labors of John Woolman has by no means been confined to the religious society of which he was a member. It may be traced wherever a step in the direction of emancipation has been taken in this country or in Europe. During the war of the Revolution many of the noblemen and officers connected with the French army became, as their journals abundantly testify, deeply interested in the Society of Friends, and took back to France with them something of its growing antislavery sentiment. Especially was this the case with Jean Pierre Brissot, the thinker and statesman of the Girondists, whose intimacy with Warner Mifflin, a friend and disciple of Woolman, so profoundly affected his whole after life. He became the leader of the "Friends of the Blacks," and carried with him to the scaffold a profound hatred of slavery. To his efforts may be traced the proclamation of Emancipation in Hayti by the commissioners of the French convention, and indirectly the subsequent uprising of the blacks and their successful establishment of a free government. The same influence reached Thomas Clarkson and stimulated his early efforts for the abolition of the slave-trade; and in after life the volume of the New Jersey Quaker was the cherished companion of himself and his amiable helpmate. It was in a degree, at least, the influence of Stephen Grellet and William Allen, men deeply imbued with the spirit of Woolman, and upon whom it might almost be said his mantle had fallen, that drew the attention of Alexander I. of Russia to the importance of taking measures for the abolition of serfdom, an object the accomplishment of which the wars during his reign prevented, but which, left as a legacy of duty, has been peaceably effected by his namesake, Alexander II. In the history of Emancipation in our own country evidences of the same original impulse of humanity are not wanting. In 1790 memorials against slavery from the Society of Friends were laid before the first Congress of the United States. Not content with clearing their own skirts of the evil, the Friends of that day took an active part in the formation of the abolition societies of New England, New York, Pennsylvania, Maryland, and Virginia. Jacob Lindley, Elisha Tyson, Warner Mifflin, James Pemberton, and other leading Friends, were known throughout the country as unflinching champions of Freedom. One of the earliest of the class known as modern abolitionists was Benjamin Lundy, a pupil in the school of Woolman, through whom William Lloyd Garrison became interested in the great work to which his life has been so faithfully and nobly devoted. Looking back to the humble workshop at Mount Holly from the stand-point of the Proclamation of President Lincoln, how has the seed sown in weakness been raised up in power!

The larger portion of Woolman's writings are devoted to the subjects of slavery, uncompensated labor, and the excessive toil and suffering of the many to support the luxury of the few. The argument running through them is searching, and in its conclusions uncompromising, but a tender love for the wrong-doer as well as the sufferer underlies all. They aim to convince the judgment and reach the heart without awakening prejudice and passion. To the slaveholders of his time they must have seemed like the voice of conscience speaking to them in the cool of the day. One feels, in reading them, the tenderness and humility of a nature redeemed from all pride of opinion and self-righteousness, sinking itself out of sight, and intent only upon rendering smaller the sum of human sorrow and sin by drawing men nearer to God and to each other. The style is that of a man unlettered, but with natural refinement and delicate sense of fitness, the purity of whose heart enters into his language. There is no attempt at fine writing, not a word or phrase for effect; it is the simple unadorned diction of one to whom the temptations of the pen seem to have been wholly unknown. He wrote as he believed from an inward spiritual prompting; and with all his unaffected humility he evidently felt that his work was done in the clear radiance of

> "The light which never was on land or sea."

It was not for him to outrun his Guide, or, as Sir Thomas Browne expresses it, to "order the finger of the Almighty to his will and pleasure, but to sit still under the soft showers of Providence." Very wise are these essays, but their wisdom is not altogether that of this world. They lead one away from all the jealousies, strifes, and competitions of luxury, fashion, and gain, out of the close air of parties and sects, into a region of calmness, —

> "The haunt
> Of every gentle wind whose breath can teach
> The wild to love tranquillity," —

a quiet habitation where all things are ordered in what he calls "the pure reason"; a rest from all self-seeking, and where no man's interest or activity conflicts with that of another. Beauty they certainly have, but it is not that which the rules of art recognize; a certain indefinable purity pervades them, making one sensible, as he reads, of a sweetness as of violets. "The secret of Woolman's purity of style," said Dr. Channing, "is that his eye was single, and that conscience dictated his words."

Of course we are not to look to the writings of such a man for tricks of rhetoric, the free play of imagination, or the unscrupulousness of epigram and antithesis. He wrote as he lived, conscious of "the great Task-master's eye." With the wise heathen Marcus Aurelius Antoninus he had learned to "wipe out imaginations, to check desire, and let the spirit that is the gift of God to every man, as his guardian and guide, bear rule."

I have thought it inexpedient to swell the bulk of this volume with the entire writings appended to the old edition of the Journal, inasmuch as they mainly refer to a system which happily on this continent is no longer a question at issue. I content myself with throwing together a few passages from them which touch subjects of present interest; and in the Appendix at the close of this volume will be found one of the last written and longest of his papers, — "A Word of Remembrance and Caution to the Rich."

"Selfish men may possess the earth: it is the meek alone who inherit it from the Heavenly Father free from all defilements and perplexities of unrighteousness."

"Whoever rightly advocates the cause of some, thereby promotes the good of the whole."

"If one suffer by the unfaithfulness of another, the mind, the most noble part of him that occasions the discord, is thereby alienated from its true happiness."

"There is harmony in the several parts of the Divine work in the hearts of men. He who leads them to cease from those gainful employments which are carried on in the wisdom which is from beneath delivers also from the desire of worldly greatness, and reconciles to a life so plain that a little suffices."

"After days and nights of drought, when the sky hath grown dark, and clouds like lakes of water have hung over our heads, I have at times beheld with awfulness the vehement lightning accompanying the blessings of the rain, a messenger from

Him to remind us of our duty in a right use of his benefits."

"The marks of famine in a land appear as humbling admonitions from God, instructing us by gentle chastisements, that we may remember that the outward supply of life is a gift from our Heavenly Father, and that we should not venture to use or apply that gift in a way contrary to pure reason."

"Oppression in the extreme appears terrible; but oppression in more refined appearances remains to be oppression. To labor for a perfect redemption from the spirit of it is the great business of the whole family of Jesus Christ in this world."

"In the obedience of faith we die to self-love, and, our life being 'hid with Christ in God,' our hearts are enlarged towards mankind universally; but many in striving to get treasures have departed from this true light of life and stumbled on the dark mountains. That purity of life which proceeds from faithfulness in following the pure spirit of truth, that state in which our minds are devoted to serve God, and all our wants are bounded by his wisdom, has often been opened to me as a place of retirement for the children of the light, in which we may be separated from that which disordereth and confuseth the affairs of society, and may have a testimony for our innocence in the hearts of those who behold us."

"There is a principle which is pure, placed in the human mind, which in different places and ages hath had different names; it is, however, pure, and proceeds from God. *It is deep and inward, confined to no forms of religion nor excluded from any, when the heart stands in perfect sincerity.* In whomsoever this takes root and grows, they become brethren."

"The necessity of an inward stillness hath appeared clear to my mind. In true silence strength is renewed, and the mind is weaned from all things, save as they may be enjoyed in the Divine will; and a lowliness in outward living, opposite to worldly honor, becomes truly acceptable to us. In the desire after outward gain the mind is prevented from a perfect attention to the voice of Christ; yet being weaned from all things, except as they may be enjoyed in the Divine will, the pure light shines into the soul. Where the fruits of the spirit which is of this world are brought forth by many who profess to be led by the Spirit of truth, and cloudiness is felt to be gathering over the visible church, the sincere in heart, who abide in true stillness, and are exercised therein before the Lord for his name's sake, have knowledge of Christ in the fellowship of his sufferings; and inward thankfulness is felt at times, that through Divine love our own wisdom is cast out, and that forward, active part in us is subjected, which would rise and do something without the pure leadings of the spirit of Christ.

"While aught remains in us contrary to a perfect resignation of our wills, it is like a seal to the book wherein is written 'that good and acceptable and perfect will of God' concerning us. But when our minds entirely yield to Christ, that silence is known which followeth the opening of the last of the seals. In this silence we learn to abide in the Divine will, and there feel that we have no cause to promote except that alone in which the light of life directs us."

Occasionally, in "Considerations on the Keeping of Negroes," the intense interest of his subject gives his language something of passionate elevation, as in the following extract:—

"When trade is carried on productive of much misery, and they who suffer by it are many thousand miles off, the danger is the greater of not laying their sufferings to heart. In procuring slaves on the coast of Africa, many children are stolen privately; wars are encouraged among the negroes, but all is at a great distance. Many groans arise from dying men which we hear not. Many cries are uttered by widows and fatherless children which reach not our ears. Many cheeks are wet with tears, and faces sad with unutterable grief, which we see not. Cruel tyranny is encouraged. The hands of robbers are strengthened.

"Were we, for the term of one year only, to be eye-witnesses of what passeth in getting these slaves; were the blood that is there shed to be sprinkled on our garments; were the poor captives, bound with thongs, and heavily laden with elephants' teeth, to pass before our eyes on their way to the sea; were their bitter lamentations, day after day, to ring in our ears, and their mournful cries in the night to hinder us from sleeping, — were we to behold and hear these things, what pious heart would not be deeply affected with sorrow!"

"It is good for those who live in fulness to cultivate tenderness of heart, and to improve every opportunity of being acquainted with the hardships and fatigues of those who labor for their living, and thus to think seriously with themselves: Am I influenced by true charity in fixing all my demands? Have I no desire to support myself in expensive customs, because my acquaintances live in such customs?

"If a wealthy man, on serious reflection, finds a witness in his own conscience that he indulges himself in some expensive habits, which might be omitted, consistently with the true design of living, and which, were he to change places with those who occupy his estate, he would desire to be discontinued by them; whoever is thus awakened will necessarily find the injunction binding, 'Do ye even so to them.' Divine Love imposeth no rigorous or unreasonable commands, but graciously points out the spirit of brotherhood and the way to happiness, in attaining which it is necessary that we relinquish all that is selfish.

"Our gracious Creator cares and provides for all his creatures; his tender mercies are over all his works, and so far as true love influences our minds, so far we become interested in his workmanship, and feel a desire to make use of every opportunity to lessen the distresses of the afflicted, and to increase the happiness of the creation. Here we have a prospect of one common interest from which our own is inseparable, so that to turn all we possess into the channel of universal love becomes the business of our lives."

His liberality and freedom from "all narrowness as to sects and opinions" are manifest in the following passages:—

"Men who sincerely apply their minds to true virtue, and find an inward support from above, by which all vicious inclinations are made subject; who love God sincerely, and prefer the real good of mankind universally to their own private interest,—though these, through the strength of education and tradition, may remain under some great speculative errors, it would be uncharitable to say that therefore God rejects them. The knowledge and goodness of Him who creates, supports, and gives understanding to all men, are superior to the various states and circumstances of his creatures, which to us appear the most difficult. Idolatry indeed is wickedness; but it is the thing, not the name, which is so. Real idolatry is to pay that adoration to a creature which is known to be due only to the true God.

"He who professeth to believe in one Almighty Creator, and in his Son Jesus Christ, and is yet more intent on the honors, profits, and friendships of the world than he is, in singleness of heart, to stand faithful to the Christian religion, is in the channel of idolatry; while the Gentile, who, notwithstanding some mistaken opinions, is established in the true principle of virtue, and humbly adores an Almighty Power, may be of the number that fear God and work righteousness."

Nowhere has what is called the "Labor Question," which is now agitating the world, been discussed more wisely and with a broader humanity than in these essays. His sympathies were with the poor man, yet the rich too are his brethren, and he warns them in love and pity of the consequences of luxury and oppression:—

"Every degree of luxury, every demand for money inconsistent with the Divine order, hath connection with unnecessary labors."

"To treasure up wealth for another generation, by means of the immoderate labor of those who in some measure depend upon us, is doing evil at present, without knowing that wealth thus gathered may not be applied to evil purposes when we are gone. To labor hard, or cause others to do so, that we may live conformably to customs which our Redeemer discountenanced by his example, and which are contrary to Divine order, is to manure a soil for propagating an evil seed in the earth."

"When house is joined to house, and field laid to field, until there is no place, and the poor are thereby straitened, though this is done by bargain and purchase, yet so far as it stands distinguished from universal love, so far that woe predicted by the prophet will accompany their proceedings. As He who first founded the earth was then the true proprietor of it, so he still remains, and though he hath given it to the children of men, so that multitudes of people have had their sustenance from it while they continued here, yet he hath never alienated it, but his right is as good as at first; nor can any apply the increase of their possessions contrary to universal love, nor dispose of lands in a way which they know tends to exalt some by oppressing others, without being justly chargeable with usurpation."

It will not lessen the value of the foregoing extracts in the minds of the true disciples of our Divine Lord, that they are manifestly not written to subserve the interests of a narrow sectarianism. They might have been penned by Fénélon in his time, or Robertson in ours, dealing as they do with Christian practice, — the life of Christ manifesting itself in purity and goodness, — rather than with the dogmas of theology. The underlying thought of all is simple obedience to the Divine word in the soul. "Not every one that saith unto me Lord, Lord, shall enter into the kingdom of heaven, but he that *doeth the will of my Father* in heaven." In the preface to an English edition, published some years ago, it is intimated that objections had been raised to the Journal on the ground that it had so little to say of doctrines and so much of duties. One may easily understand that this objection might have been forcibly felt by the slaveholding religious professors of his day, and that it may still be entertained by a class of persons who, like the Cabalists, attach a certain mystical significance to words, names, and titles, and who, in consequence, question the piety which hesitates to flatter the Divine ear by "vain repetitions" and formal enumeration of sacred attributes, dignities, and offices. Every instinct of his tenderly sensitive nature shrank from the wordy irreverence of noisy profession. His very silence is significant. The husks of emptiness rustle in every wind; the full corn in the ear holds up its golden fruit noiselessly to the Lord of the harvest. John Woolman's faith, like the Apostle's, is manifested by his labors, standing not in words but in the demonstration of the spirit, — a faith that works by love to the purifying of the heart. The entire outcome of this faith was love manifested in reverent waiting upon God, and in that untiring benevolence, that quiet but deep enthusiasm of humanity, which made his daily service to his fellow-creatures a hymn of praise to the common Father.

However the intellect may criticise such a life, whatever defects it may present to the trained eyes of theological adepts, the heart has no questions to ask, but at once owns and reveres it. Shall we regret that he who had so entered into fellowship of suffering with the Divine One, walking with him under the cross, and dying daily to self, gave to the faith and hope that were in him this testimony of a life, rather than any form of words, however sound? A true life is at once interpreter and proof of the gospel, and does more to establish its truth in the hearts of men than all the "Evidences" and "Bodies of Divinity" which have perplexed the world with more doubts than they solved. Shall we venture to account it a defect in his Christian character, that, under an abiding sense of the goodness and long-suffering of God, he wrought his work in gentleness and compassion, with the delicate tenderness which comes of a deep sympathy with the trials and weaknesses of our nature, never allowing himself to indulge in heat or violence, persuading rather than threatening? Did he overestimate that immeasurable Love, the manifestation of which in his own heart so reached the hearts of others, revealing everywhere unsuspected fountains of feeling and secret longings after purity, as the rod of the diviner detects sweet, cool water-springs under the parched surfaces of a thirsty land? And, looking at the purity, wisdom, and sweetness of his life, who shall say that his faith in the teaching of the Holy Spirit — the interior guide and light — was a mistaken one? Surely it was no illusion by which his feet were so guided that all who saw him felt that, like Enoch, he walked with God. "Without the actual inspiration of the Spirit of Grace, the inward teacher and soul of our souls," says Fénélon, "we could neither do, will, nor believe good. We must silence every creature, we must silence ourselves also, to hear in a profound stillness of the soul this inexpressible voice of Christ. The outward word of the gospel itself without this living efficacious word within would be but an empty sound." * "Thou Lord," says Augustine in his Meditations, "communicatest thyself to all: thou teachest the heart without words; thou speakest to it without articulate sounds." Never was this divine principle more fully tested than by John Woolman; and the result is seen in a life of such rare excellence that the world is still better and richer for its sake, and the fragrance of it comes down to us through a century, still sweet and precious.

It will be noted throughout the Journal and essays that in his life-long testimony against wrong he never lost sight of the oneness of humanity, its common responsibility, its fellowship of suffering and communion of sin. Few have ever had so profound a conviction of the truth of the Apostle's declaration that no man liveth and no man dieth to himself. Sin was not to him an isolated fact, the responsibility of which began and ended with the individual transgressor; he saw it as a part of a vast network and entanglement, and traced the lines of influence converging upon it in the underworld of causation. Hence the wrong and discord which pained him called out pity, rather than indig-

* "However, I am sure that there is a common spirit that plays within us, and that is the Spirit of God. Whoever feels not the warm gale and gentle ventilation of this Spirit, I dare not say he lives; for truly without this to me there is no heat under the tropic, nor any light though I dwelt in the body of the sun." — *Sir Thomas Browne's Religio Medici.*

nation. The first inquiry which they awakened was addressed to his own conscience. How far am I in thought, word, custom, responsible for this? Have none of my fellow-creatures an equitable right to any part which is called mine? Have the gifts and possessions received by me from others been conveyed in a way free from all unrighteousness? "Through abiding in the law of Christ," he says, "we feel a tenderness towards our fellow-creatures, and a concern so to walk that our conduct may not be the means of strengthening them in error." He constantly recurs to the importance of a right example in those who profess to be led by the spirit of Christ, and who attempt to labor in his name for the benefit of their fellow-men. If such neglect or refuse themselves to act rightly, they can but "entangle the minds of others and *draw a veil over the face of righteousness.*" His eyes were anointed to see the common point of departure from the Divine harmony, and that all the varied growths of evil had their underlying root in human selfishness. He saw that every sin of the individual was shared in greater or less degree by all whose lives were opposed to the Divine order, and that pride, luxury, and avarice in one class gave motive and temptation to the grosser forms of evil in another. How gentle, and yet how searching, are his rebukes of self-complacent respectability, holding it responsible, in spite of all its decent seemings, for much of the depravity which it condemned with Pharisaical harshness! In his "Considerations on the True Harmony of Mankind," he dwells with great earnestness upon the importance of possessing "the mind of Christ," which removes from the heart the desire of superiority and worldly honors, incites attention to the Divine Counsellor and awakens an ardent engagement to promote the happiness of all. "*This state*," he says, "*in which every motion from the selfish spirit yieldeth to pure love, I may acknowledge with gratitude to the Father of Mercies, is often opened before me as a pearl to seek after.*"

"At times when I have felt true love open my heart towards my fellow-creatures, and have been engaged in weighty conversation in the cause of righteousness, the instructions I have received under these exercises in regard to the true use of the outward gifts of God have made deep and lasting impressions on my mind. I have beheld how the desire to provide wealth and to uphold a delicate life has grievously entangled many, and has been like a snare to their offspring; and though some have been affected with a sense of their difficulties, and have appeared desirous at times to be helped out of them, yet for want of abiding under the humbling power of truth they have continued in these entanglements; expensive living in parents and children hath called for a large supply, and in answering this call the 'faces of the poor' have been ground away, and made thin through hard dealing.

"There is balm; there is a physician! and O what

longings do I feel that we may embrace the means appointed for our healing; may know that removed which now ministers cause for the cries of many to ascend to Heaven against their oppressors; and that thus we may see the true harmony restored!—a restoration of that which was lost at Babel, and which will be, as the prophet expresses it, 'the returning of a pure language!'"

It is easy to conceive how unwelcome this clear spiritual insight must have been to the superficial professors of his time busy in tithing mint, anise, and cummin. There must have been something awful in the presence of one endowed with the gift of looking through all the forms, shows, and pretensions of society, and detecting with certainty the germs of evil hidden beneath them; a man gentle and full of compassion, clothed in "the irresistible might of meekness," and yet so wise in spiritual discernment,

> "Bearing a touchstone in his hand
> And testing all things in the land
> By his unerring spell.
>
> "Quick births of transmutation smote
> The fair to foul, the foul to fair;
> Purple nor ermine did he spare,
> Nor scorn the dusty coat."

In bringing to a close this paper, the preparation of which has been to me a labor of love, I am not unmindful of the wide difference between the appreciation of a pure and true life and the living of it, and am willing to own that in delineating a character of such moral and spiritual symmetry I have felt something like rebuke from my own words. I have been awed and solemnized by the presence of a serene and beautiful spirit redeemed of the Lord from all selfishness, and I have been made thankful for the ability to recognize and the disposition to love him. I leave the book with its readers. They may possibly make large deductions from my estimate of the author; they may not see the importance of all his self-denying testimonies; they may question some of his scruples, and smile over passages of childlike simplicity;—but I believe they will all agree in thanking me for introducing them to the Journal of John Woolman.

J. G. W.

AMESBURY, 20th 1st mo., 1871.

THE

JOURNAL OF JOHN WOOLMAN.

CHAPTER I.

1720-1742.

His Birth and Parentage. — Some Account of the Operations of Divine Grace on his Mind in his Youth. — His first Appearance in the Ministry. — And his Considerations, while Young, on the Keeping of Slaves.

I HAVE often felt a motion of love to leave some hints in writing of my experience of the goodness of God, and now, in the thirty-sixth year of my age, I begin this work.

I was born in Northampton, in Burlington County, West Jersey, in the year 1720. Before I was seven years old I began to be acquainted with the operations of Divine love. Through the care of my parents, I was taught to read nearly as soon as I was capable of it; and as I went from school one day, I remember that while my companions were playing by the way, I went forward out of sight, and, sitting down, I read the twenty-second chapter of Revelation: "He showed me a pure river of water of life, clear as crystal, proceeding out of the throne of God and of the Lamb, &c."

In reading it, my mind was drawn to seek after that pure habitation which I then believed God had prepared for his servants. The place where I sat, and the sweetness that attended my mind, remain fresh in my memory. This, and the like gracious visitations, had such an effect upon me that when boys used ill language it troubled me; and, through the continued mercies of God, I was preserved from that evil.

The pious instructions of my parents were often fresh in my mind, when I happened to be among wicked children, and were of use to me. Having a large family of children, they used frequently, on first-days, after meeting, to set us one after another to read the Holy Scriptures, or some religious books, the rest sitting by without much conversation; I have since often thought it was a good practice. From what I had read and heard, I believed there had been, in past ages, people who walked in uprightness before God in a degree exceeding any that I knew or heard of now living: and the apprehension of there being less steadiness and firmness amongst people in the present age often troubled me while I was a child.

I may here mention a remarkable circumstance that occurred in my childhood. On going to a neighbor's house, I saw on the way a robin sitting on her nest, and as I came near she went off; but having young ones, she flew about, and with many cries expressed her concern for them. I stood and threw stones at her, and one striking her she fell down dead. At first I was pleased with the exploit, but after a few minutes was seized with horror, at having, in a sportive way, killed an innocent creature while she was careful for her young. I beheld her lying dead, and thought those young ones, for which she was so careful, must now perish for want of their dam to nourish them. After some painful considerations on the subject, I climbed up the tree, took all the young birds, and killed them, supposing that better than to leave them to pine away and die miserably. In this case I believed that Scripture proverb was fulfilled, "The tender mercies of the wicked are cruel." I then went on my errand, and for some hours could think of little else but the cruelties I had committed, and was much troubled. Thus He whose tender mercies are over all his works hath placed a principle in the human mind, which incites to exercise goodness towards every living creature; and this being singly attended to, people become tender-hearted and sympathizing; but when frequently and totally rejected, the mind becomes shut up in a contrary disposition.

About the twelfth year of my age, my father being abroad, my mother reproved me for some misconduct, to which I made an undutiful reply. The next first-day, as I was with my father returning from meeting, he told me that he understood I had behaved amiss to my mother, and advised me to be more careful in future. I knew myself blamable, and in shame and confusion remained silent. Being thus awakened to a sense of my wickedness, I felt remorse in my mind, and on getting home I retired and prayed to the Lord to forgive me, and I do not remember that I ever afterwards spoke unhandsomely to either of my parents, however foolish in some other things.

Having attained the age of sixteen years, I began to love wanton company; and though I was preserved from profane language or scandalous conduct, yet I perceived a plant in me which produced much wild grapes; my merciful Father did not, however, forsake me utterly, but at times, through his grace, I was brought seriously to consider my ways; and the sight of my backslidings affected me with sorrow, yet for want of rightly attending to the reproofs of instruction, vanity was added to vanity, and repentance to repentance. Upon the whole, my mind became more and more alienated from the truth, and I hastened toward destruction. While I meditate on the gulf towards which I travelled, and reflect on my youthful disobedience, for these things I weep, mine eye runneth down with water.

Advancing in age, the number of my acquaintance increased, and thereby my way grew more difficult. Though I had found comfort in reading the Holy Scriptures and thinking on heavenly things, I was now estranged therefrom. I knew I was going from the flock of Christ and had no resolution to return, hence serious reflections were uneasy to me, and youthful vanities and diversions were my greatest pleasure. In this road I found many like myself, and we associated in that which is adverse to true friendship.

In this swift race it pleased God to visit me with sickness, so that I doubted of recovery; then did darkness, horror, and amazement with full force seize me, even when my pain and distress of body were very great. I thought it would have been better for me never to have had being, than to see the day which I now saw. I was filled with confusion, and in great affliction, both of mind and body, I lay and bewailed myself. I had not confidence to lift up my cries to God, whom I had thus offended; but in a deep sense of my great folly I was humbled before him. At length that word which is as a fire and a hammer broke and dissolved my rebellious heart; my cries were put up in contrition; and in the multitude of his mercies I found inward relief, and a close engagement that if he was pleased to restore my health I might walk humbly before him.

After my recovery this exercise remained with me a considerable time, but by degrees giving way to youthful vanities, and associating with wanton young people, I lost ground. The Lord had been very gracious, and spoke peace to me in the time of my distress, and I now most ungratefully turned again to folly; at times I felt sharp reproof, but I did not get low enough to cry for help. I was not so hardy as to commit things scandalous, but to exceed in vanity and to promote mirth was my chief study. Still I retained a love and esteem for pious people, and their company brought an awe upon me. My dear parents several times admonished me in the fear of the Lord, and their admonition entered into my heart and had a good effect for a season; but not getting deep enough to pray rightly, the tempter, when he came, found entrance. Once having spent a part of the day in wantonness, when I went to bed at night there lay in a window near my bed a Bible, which I opened, and first cast my eye on the text, "We lie down in our shame, and our confusion covereth us." This I knew to be my case, and meeting with so unexpected a reproof I was somewhat affected with it, and went to bed under remorse of conscience, which I soon cast off again.

Thus time passed on; my heart was replenished with mirth and wantonness, while pleasing scenes of vanity were presented to my imagination, till I attained the age of eighteen years, near which time I felt the judgments of God in my soul, like a consuming fire, and looking over my past life the prospect was moving. I was often sad, and longed to be delivered from those vanities; then again my heart was strongly inclined to them, and there was in me a sore conflict. At times I turned to folly, and then again sorrow and confusion took hold of me. In a while I resolved totally to leave off some of my vanities, but there was a secret reserve in my heart of the more refined part of them, and I was not low enough to find true peace. Thus for some months I had great troubles ; my will was unsubjected, which rendered my labors fruitless. At length, through the merciful continuance of heavenly visitations, I was made to bow down in spirit before the Lord. One evening I had spent some time in reading a pious author, and walking out alone I humbly prayed to the Lord for his help, that I might be delivered from all those vanities which so ensnared me. Thus being brought low, he helped me, and as I learned to bear the cross I felt refreshment to come from his presence, but not keeping in that strength which gave victory I lost ground again, the sense of which greatly affected me. I sought deserts and lonely places, and there with tears did confess my sins to God and humbly craved his help. And I may say with reverence, he was near to me in my troubles, and in those times of humiliation opened my ear to discipline. I was now led to look seriously at the means by which I was drawn from the pure truth, and learned that if I would live such a life as the faithful servants of God lived, I must not go into company as heretofore in my own will, but all the cravings of sense must be governed by a Divine principle. In times of sorrow and abasement these instructions were sealed upon me, and I felt the power of Christ prevail over selfish desires, so that I was preserved in a good degree of steadiness, and being young, and believing at that time that a single life was best for me, I was strengthened to keep from such company as had often been a snare to me.

I kept steadily to meetings; spent first-day afternoons chiefly in reading the Scriptures and other good books, and was early convinced in my mind that true religion consisted in an inward life, wherein the heart doth love and reverence God the Creator, and learns to exercise true justice and goodness, not only toward all men, but also toward the brute creatures; that, as the mind was moved by an inward principle to love God as an invisible, incomprehensible Being, so, by the same principle, it was moved to love him in all his manifestations in the visible world; that, as by his breath the flame of life was kindled in all animal sensible creatures, to say we love God as unseen, and at the same time exercise cruelty toward the least creature moving by his life, or by life derived from him, was a contradiction in itself. I found no narrowness respecting sects and opinions, but believed that sincere, upright-hearted people, in every society, who truly love God, were accepted of him.

As I lived under the cross, and simply followed the opening of truth, my mind, from day to day, was more enlightened, my former acquaintance were left to judge of me as they would, for I found it safest for me to live in private, and keep these things sealed up in my own breast. While I silently ponder on that change wrought in me, I find no language equal to convey to another a clear idea of it. I looked upon the works of God in this visible creation, and an awfulness covered me. My heart was tender and often contrite, and universal love to my fellow-creatures increased in me. This will be understood by such as have trodden in the same path. Some glances of real beauty may be seen in their faces who dwell in true meekness. There is a harmony in the sound of that voice to which Divine love gives utterance, and some appearance of right order in their temper and conduct whose passions are regulated ; yet these do not fully show forth that inward life to those who have not felt it ; this white stone and new name is only known rightly by such as receive it.

Now, though I had been thus strengthened to bear the cross, I still found myself in great danger, having many weaknesses attending me, and strong temptations to wrestle with ; in the feeling whereof I frequently withdrew into private places, and often with tears besought the Lord to help me, and his gracious ear was open to my cry.

All this time I lived with my parents, and wrought on the plantation ; and having had schooling pretty well for a planter, I used to improve myself in winter evenings, and other leisure times. Being now in the twenty-first year of my age, with my father's consent I engaged with a man, in much business as a shop-keeper and baker, to tend shop and keep books. At home I had lived retired ; and now having a prospect of being much in the way of company, I felt frequent and fervent cries in my heart to God, the Father of Mercies, that he would preserve me from all taint and corruption ; that, in this more public employment, I might serve him, my gracious Redeemer, in that humility and self-denial which I had in a small degree exercised in a more private life.

The man who employed me furnished a shop in Mount Holly, about five miles from my father's house, and six from his own, and there I lived alone and tended his shop. Shortly after my settlement here I was visited by several young people, my former acquaintance, who supposed that vanities would be as agreeable to me now as ever. At these times I cried to the Lord in secret for wisdom and strength; for I felt myself encompassed with difficulties, and had fresh occasion to bewail the follies of times past, in contracting a familiarity with libertine people; and as I had now left my father's house outwardly, I found my Heavenly Father to be merciful to me beyond what I can express.

By day I was much amongst people, and had many trials to go through; but in the evenings I was mostly alone, and I may with thankfulness acknowledge, that in those times the spirit of supplication was often poured upon me; under which I was frequently exercised, and felt my strength renewed.

After a while, my former acquaintance gave over expecting me as one of their company, and I began to be known to some whose conversation was helpful to me. And now, as I had experienced the love of God, through Jesus Christ, to redeem me from many pollutions, and to be a succor to me through a sea of conflicts, with which no person was fully acquainted, and as my heart was often enlarged in this heavenly principle, I felt a tender compassion for the youth who remained entangled in snares like those which had entangled me. This love and tenderness increased, and my mind was strongly engaged for the good of my fellow-creatures. I went to meetings in an awful frame of mind, and endeavored to be inwardly acquainted with the language of the true Shepherd. One day, being under a strong exercise of spirit, I stood up and said some words in a meeting; but not keeping close to the Divine opening, I said more than was required of me. Being soon sensible of my error, I was afflicted in mind some weeks, without any light or comfort, even to that degree that I could not take satisfaction in anything. I remembered God, and was troubled, and in the depth of my distress he had pity upon me, and sent the Comforter. I then felt forgiveness for my offence; my mind became calm and quiet, and I was truly thankful to my gracious Redeemer for his mercies. About six weeks after this, feeling the spring of Divine love opened, and a concern to speak, I said a few words in a meeting, in which I found peace. Being thus humbled and disciplined under the cross, my understanding became more strengthened to distinguish the pure spirit which inwardly moves upon the heart, and which taught me to wait in silence sometimes many weeks together, until I felt that rise which prepares the creature to stand like a trumpet, through which the Lord speaks to his flock.

From an inward purifying, and steadfast abiding under it springs a lively operative desire for the good of others. All the faithful are not called to the public ministry; but whoever are, are called to minister of that which they have tasted and handled spiritually. The outward modes of worship are various; but whenever any are true ministers of Jesus Christ, it is from the operation of his Spirit upon their hearts, first purifying them, and thus giving them a just sense of the conditions of others. This truth was early fixed in my mind, and I was taught to watch the pure opening, and to take heed lest, while I was standing to speak, my own will should get uppermost, and cause me to utter words from worldly wisdom, and depart from the channel of the true gospel ministry.

In the management of my outward affairs, I may say with thankfulness, I found truth to be my support; and I was respected in my master's family, who came to live in Mount Holly within two years after my going there.

In a few months after I came here, my master bought several Scotchmen servants, from on board a vessel, and brought them to Mount Holly to sell, one of whom was taken sick and died. In the latter part of his sickness, being delirious, he used to curse and swear most sorrowfully; and the next night after his burial I was left to sleep alone in the chamber where he died. I perceived in me a timorousness; I knew, however, I had not injured the man, but assisted in taking care of him according to my capacity. I was not free to ask any one on that occasion to sleep with me. Nature was feeble; but every trial was a fresh incitement to give myself up wholly to the service of God, for I found no helper like him in times of trouble.

About the twenty-third year of my age, I had many fresh and heavenly openings, in respect to the care and providence of the Almighty over his creatures in general, and over man as the most noble amongst those which are visible. And being clearly convinced in my judgment that to place my whole trust in God was best for me, I felt renewed engagements that in all things I might act on an inward principle of virtue, and pursue worldly business no further than as truth opened my way.

About the time called Christmas I observed many people, both in town and from the country, resorting to public-houses, and spending their time in drinking and vain sports, tending to corrupt one another; on which account I was much troubled. At one house in particular there was much disorder; and I believed it was a duty incumbent on me to speak to the master of that house. I considered I was young, and that several elderly friends in town had opportunity to see these things; but though I would gladly have been excused, yet I could not feel my mind clear.

The exercise was heavy; and as I was reading what the Almighty said to Ezekiel, respecting his duty as a watchman, the matter was set home more clearly. With prayers and tears I besought the

Lord for his assistance, and He, in loving-kindness, gave me a resigned heart. At a suitable opportunity I went to the public-house; and seeing the man amongst much company, I called him aside, and in the fear and dread of the Almighty expressed to him what rested on my mind. He took it kindly, and afterwards showed more regard to me than before. In a few years afterwards he died, middle-aged; and I often thought that had I neglected my duty in that case it would have given me great trouble; and I was humbly thankful to my gracious Father, who had supported me herein.

My employer, having a negro woman,* sold her, and desired me to write a bill of sale, the man being waiting who bought her. The thing was sudden; and though I felt uneasy at the thoughts of writing an instrument of slavery for one of my fellow-creatures, yet I remembered that I was hired by the year, that it was my master who directed me to do it, and that it was an elderly man, a member of our

* The number of slaves in New Jersey at the commencement of Woolman's labors for emancipation was undoubtedly large. As late as 1800 there were 12,442. Perth Amboy was a place of deposit for the newly imported Africans, and long barracks were erected for their accommodation. In 1734, when Woolman was a lad of fourteen, an insurrection took place, which had for its object the massacre of the masters, and an alliance with the Indians and French. Some years later a negro convicted of crime was burned alive at Perth Amboy. An immense number of negroes, gathered from all the neighboring townships, were compelled to be witnesses of the slow torment of the victim.

Society, who bought her; so through weakness I gave way, and wrote it; but at the executing of it I was so afflicted in my mind, that I said before my master and the Friend that I believed slave-keeping to be a practice inconsistent with the Christian religion. This, in some degree, abated my uneasiness; yet as often as I reflected seriously upon it I thought I should have been clearer if I had desired to be excused from it, as a thing against my conscience; for such it was. Some time after this a young man of our Society spoke to me to write a conveyance of a slave to him, he having lately taken a negro into his house. I told him I was not easy to write it; for, though many of our meeting and in other places kept slaves, I still believed the practice was not right, and desired to be excused from the writing. I spoke to him in good-will; and he told me that keeping slaves was not altogether agreeable to his mind; but that the slave being a gift made to his wife he had accepted her.

CHAPTER II.

1743-1748.

His first Journey, on a Religious Visit, in East Jersey. — Thoughts on Merchandising, and Learning a Trade. — Second Journey into Pennsylvania, Maryland, Virginia, and North Carolina. — Third Journey through part of West and East Jersey. — Fourth Journey through New York and Long Island, to New England. — And his fifth Journey to the Eastern Shore of Maryland, and the Lower Counties on Delaware.

MY esteemed friend Abraham Farrington being about to make a visit to Friends on the eastern side of this province, and having no companion, he proposed to me to go with him; and after a conference with some elderly Friends I agreed to go. We set out on the 5th of ninth month, 1743; had an evening meeting at a tavern in Brunswick, a town in which none of our Society dwelt; the room was full, and the people quiet. Thence to Amboy, and had an evening meeting in the court-house, to which came many people, amongst whom were several members of Assembly, they being in town on the public affairs of the province. In both these meetings my ancient companion was engaged to preach largely in the love of the gospel. Thence we went to Woodbridge, Rahway, and Plainfield, and had six or seven meetings in places where Friends' meetings are not usually held, chiefly attended by Presbyterians, and my beloved companion was frequently strengthened to publish the word of life amongst them. As for me, I was often silent through the meetings, and when I spake it was with much care, that I might speak only what truth opened. My mind was often tender, and I learned some profitable lessons. We were out about two weeks.

Near this time, being on some outward business in which several families were concerned, and which was attended with difficulties, some things relating thereto not being clearly stated, nor rightly understood by all, there arose some heat in the minds of the parties, and one valuable friend got off his watch. I had a great regard for him, and felt a strong inclination, after matters were settled, to speak to him concerning his conduct in that case; but being a youth, and he far advanced in age and experience, my way appeared difficult; after some days' deliberation, and inward seeking to the Lord for assistance, I was made subject, so that I expressed what lay upon me in a way which became my youth and his years; and though it was a hard task to me it was well taken, and I believe was useful to us both.

Having now been several years with my employer, and he doing less in merchandise than heretofore, I was thoughtful about some other way of business, perceiving merchandise to be attended with much cumber in the way of trading in these parts.

My mind, through the power of truth, was in a good degree weaned from the desire of outward greatness, and I was learning to be content with real conveniences, that were not costly, so that a way of life free from much entanglement appeared best for me, though the income might be small. I had several offers of business that appeared profitable, but I did not see my way clear to accept of them, believing they would be attended with more outward care and cumber than was required of me to engage in. I saw that an humble man, with the blessing of the Lord, might live on a little, and that where the heart was set on greatness, success in business did not satisfy the craving; but that commonly with an increase of wealth the desire of wealth increased. There was a care on my mind so to pass my time that nothing might hinder me from the most steady attention to the voice of the true Shepherd.

My employer, though now a retailer of goods, was by trade a tailor, and kept a servant-man at that business; and I began to think about learning the trade, expecting that if I should settle I might by this trade and a little retailing of goods get a living in a plain way, without the load of great business. I mentioned it to my employer, and we soon agreed on terms, and when I had leisure from the affairs of merchandise I worked with his man. I believed the hand of Providence pointed out this business for me, and I was taught to be content with it, though I felt at times a disposition that would have sought for something greater; but through the revelation of Jesus Christ I had seen the happiness of humility, and there was an earnest desire in me to enter deeply into it; at times this desire arose to a degree of fervent supplication, wherein my soul was so environed with heavenly light and consolation that things were made easy to me which had been otherwise.

After some time my employer's wife died; she was a virtuous woman, and generally beloved of her neighbors. Soon after this he left shop-keeping, and we parted. I then wrought at my trade as a tailor; carefully attended meetings for worship and discipline; and found an enlargement of gospel love in my mind, and therein a concern to visit Friends in some of the back settlements of Pennsylvania and Virginia. Being thoughtful about a companion, I expressed it to my beloved friend, Isaac Andrews, who told me that he had drawings to the same places, and also to go through Maryland, Virginia, and Carolina. After a considerable time, and several conferences with him, I felt easy to accompany him throughout, if way opened for it. I opened the case in our Monthly Meeting, and, Friends expressing their unity therewith, we obtained certificates to travel as companions, — he from Haddonfield, and I from Burlington.

We left our province on the 12th of third month, 1746, and had several meetings in the upper part of Chester County, and near Lancaster; in some of which the love of Christ prevailed, uniting us together in his service. We then crossed the river Susquehanna, and had several meetings in a new settlement, called the Red Lands. It is the poorer sort of people that commonly begin to improve remote deserts; with a small stock they have houses to build, lands to clear and fence, corn to raise, clothes to provide, and children to educate, so that Friends who visit such may well sympathize with them in their hardships in the wilderness; and though the best entertainment that they can give may seem coarse to some who are used to cities or old settled places, it becomes the disciples of Christ to be therewith content. Our hearts were sometimes enlarged in the love of our Heavenly Father amongst these people, and the sweet influence of his Spirit supported us through some difficulties: to him be the praise.

We passed on to Manoquacy, Fairfax, Hopewell, and Shanando, and had meetings, some of which were comfortable and edifying. From Shanando, we set off in the afternoon for the old settlements of Friends in Virginia; the first night we, with our guide, lodged in the woods, our horses feeding near us; but he being poorly provided with a horse, and we young, and having good horses, were free the next day to part with him. In two days after we reached our friend John Cheagle's, in Virginia. We took the meetings in our way through Virginia; were in some degree baptized into a feeling sense of the conditions of the people, and our exercise in general was more painful in these old settlements than it had been amongst the back inhabitants; yet through the goodness of our Heavenly Father the well of living waters was at times opened to our encouragement, and the refreshment of the sincere-hearted. We went on to Perquimans, in North Carolina; had several large meetings, and found some openness in those parts, and a hopeful appearance amongst the young people. Afterwards we turned again to Virginia, and attended most of the meetings which we had not been at before, laboring amongst Friends in the love of Jesus Christ, as ability was given; thence went to the mountains, up James River to a new settlement, and had several meetings amongst the people, some of whom had lately joined in membership with our Society. In our journeying to and fro, we found some honest-hearted Friends, who appeared to be concerned for the cause of truth among a backsliding people.

From Virginia, we crossed over the river Potomac, at Hoe's Ferry, and made a general visit to the meetings of Friends on the western shore of Maryland, and were at their Quarterly Meeting. We had some hard labor amongst them, endeavoring to discharge our duty honestly as way opened, in the love of truth. Thence, taking sundry meetings in our way, we passed towards home, which, through the favor of Divine Providence, we reached the 16th of sixth month, 1746; and I may say, that through the assistance of the Holy Spirit, which mortifies selfish desires, my companion and I travelled in

unity of Friends, and in company with my beloved friend and neighbor Peter Andrews, brother to my companion before mentioned, and visited them in their meetings generally about Salem, Cape May, Great and Little Egg Harbor; we had meetings also at Barnagat, Manahockin, and Mane Squan, and so to the Yearly Meeting at Shrewsbury. Through the goodness of the Lord way was opened, and the strength of Divine love was sometimes felt in our assemblies, to the comfort and help of those who were rightly concerned before him. We were out twenty-two days, and rode, by computation, three hundred and forty miles. At Shrewsbury Yearly Meeting we met with our dear friends Michael Lightfoot and Abraham Farrington, who had good service there.

The winter following died my eldest sister, Elizabeth Woolman, of the small-pox, aged thirty-one years.

Of late I found drawings in my mind to visit Friends in New England, and having an opportunity of joining in company with my beloved friend Peter Andrews, we obtained certificates from our Monthly Meeting, and set forward on the 16th of third month, 1747. We reached the Yearly Meeting at Long Island, at which were our friends, Samuel Nottingham from England, John Griffith, Jane Hoskins, and Elizabeth Hudson from Pennsylvania, and Jacob Andrews from Chesterfield, several of whom were favored in their public exercise; and, through the goodness of the Lord, we had some edifying meetings. After this my companion and I visited Friends on Long Island; and through the mercies of God we were helped in the work.

Besides going to the settled meetings of Friends, we were at a general meeting at Setawket, chiefly made up of other societies; we had also a meeting at Oyster Bay in a dwelling-house, at which were many people. At the former there was not much said by way of testimony, but it was, I believe, a good meeting; at the latter, through the springing up of living waters, it was a day to be thankfully remembered. Having visited the island, we went over to the main, taking meetings in our way, to Oblong, Nine-partners, and New Milford. In these back settlements we met with several people who, through the immediate workings of the Spirit of Christ on their minds, were drawn from the vanities of the world to an inward acquaintance with him. They were educated in the way of the Presbyterians. A considerable number of the youth, members of that society, used often to spend their time together in merriment, but some of the principal young men of the company, being visited by the powerful workings of the Spirit of Christ, and thereby led humbly to take up his cross, could no longer join in those vanities. As these stood steadfast to that inward convincement, they were made a blessing to some of their former companions; so that through the power of truth several were brought into a close exercise concerning the eternal well-being of their souls. These young people continued for a time to frequent their public worship; and, besides that, had meetings of their own, which meetings were awhile allowed by their preacher, who sometimes met with them; but in time their judgment in matters of religion disagreeing with some of the articles of the Presbyterians their meetings were disapproved by that society; and such of them as stood firm to their duty, as it was inwardly manifested, had many difficulties to go through. In a while their meetings were dropped; some of them returned to the Presbyterians, and others joined to our religious society.

I had conversation with some of the latter to my help and edification, and believe several of them are acquainted with the nature of that worship which is performed in spirit and in truth. Amos Powel, a friend from Long Island, accompanied me through Connecticut, which is chiefly inhabited by Presbyterians, who were generally civil to us. After three days' riding, we came amongst Friends in the colony of Rhode Island, and visited them in and about Newport, Dartmouth, and generally in those parts; we then went to Boston, and proceeded eastward as far as Dover. Not far from thence we met our friend Thomas Gawthrop, from England, who was then on a visit to these provinces. From Newport we sailed to Nantucket; were there nearly a week; and from thence came over to Dartmouth. Having finished our visit in these parts, we crossed the Sound from New London to Long Island, and taking some meetings on the island proceeded towards home, which we reached the 13th of seventh month, 1747, having rode about fifteen hundred miles, and sailed about one hundred and fifty.

In this journey, I may say in general, we were sometimes in much weakness, and labored under discouragements, and at other times, through the renewed manifestations of Divine love, we had seasons of refreshment wherein the power of truth prevailed. We were taught by renewed experience to labor for an inward stillness; at no time to seek for words, but to live in the spirit of truth, and utter that to the people which truth opened in us. My beloved companion and I belonged both to one meeting, came forth in the ministry near the same time, and were inwardly united in the work. He was about thirteen years older than I, bore the heaviest burden, and was an instrument of the greatest use.

Finding a concern to visit Friends in the lower counties of Delaware, and on the eastern shore of Maryland, and having an opportunity to join with my well-beloved ancient friend, John Sykes, we obtained certificates, and set off the 7th of eighth month, 1748, were at the meetings of Friends in the lower counties, attended the Yearly Meeting at Little Creek, and made a visit to most of the meetings on the eastern shore, and so home by the way of Nottingham. We were abroad about six weeks, and rode, by computation, about five hundred and fifty miles.

Our exercise at times was heavy, but through the goodness of the Lord we were often refreshed, and I may say by experience "he is a stronghold in the day of trouble." Though our Society in these parts appeared to me to be in a declining condition, yet I believe the Lord hath a people amongst them who labor to serve him uprightly, but they have many difficulties to encounter.

CHAPTER III.

1749-1756.

His Marriage. — The Death of his Father. — His Journeys into the upper part of New Jersey, and afterwards into Pennsylvania. — Considerations on keeping Slaves, and Visits to the Families of Friends at several times and places. — An Epistle from the General Meeting. — His journey to Long Island. — Considerations on Trading and on the Use of Spirituous Liquors and Costly Apparel. — Letter to a Friend.

ABOUT this time, believing it good for me to settle, and thinking seriously about a companion, my heart was turned to the Lord with desires that he would give me wisdom to proceed therein agreeably to his will, and he was pleased to give me a well-inclined damsel, Sarah Ellis, to whom I was married the 18th of eighth month, 1749.

In the fall of the year 1750 died my father, Samuel Woolman, of a fever, aged about sixty years. In his lifetime he manifested much care for us his children, that in our youth we might learn to fear the Lord; and often endeavored to imprint in our minds the true principles of virtue, and particularly to cherish in us a spirit of tenderness, not only towards poor people, but also towards all creatures of which we had the command.

After my return from Carolina in 1746, I made

some observations on keeping slaves, which some time before his decease I showed to him; he perused the manuscript, proposed a few alterations, and appeared well satisfied that I found a concern on that account. In his last sickness, as I was watching with him one night, he being so far spent that there was no expectation of his recovery, though he had the perfect use of his understanding, he asked me concerning the manuscript, and whether I expected soon to proceed to take the advice of friends in publishing it? After some further conversation thereon, he said, "I have all along been deeply affected with the oppression of the poor negroes; and now, at last, my concern for them is as great as ever."

By his direction I had written his will in a time of health, and that night he desired me to read it to him, which I did; and he said it was agreeable to his mind. He then made mention of his end, which he believed was near; and signified that though he was sensible of many imperfections in the course of his life, yet his experience of the power of truth, and of the love and goodness of God from time to time, even till now, was such that he had no doubt that on leaving this life he should enter into one more happy.

The next day his sister Elizabeth came to see him, and told him of the decease of their sister Anne, who died a few days before; he then said, "I reckon Sister Anne was free to leave this world?" Elizabeth said she was. He then said, "I also am free to leave it"; and being in great weakness of body said, "I hope I shall shortly go to rest." He continued in a weighty frame of mind, and was sensible till near the last.

Second of ninth month, 1751.—Feeling drawings in my mind to visit Friends at the Great Meadows, in the upper part of West Jersey, with the unity of our Monthly Meeting, I went there, and had some searching laborious exercise amongst Friends in those parts, and found inward peace therein.

Ninth month, 1753.—In company with my well-esteemed friend, John Sykes, and with the unity of Friends, I travelled about two weeks, visiting Friends in Buck's County. We labored in the love of the gospel, according to the measure received; and through the mercies of Him who is strength to the poor who trust in him, we found satisfaction in our visit. In the next winter, way opening to visit Friends' families within the compass of our Monthly Meeting, partly by the labors of two Friends from Pennsylvania, I joined in some part of the work, having had a desire some time that it might go forward amongst us.

About this time, a person at some distance lying sick, his brother came to me to write his will. I knew he had slaves, and, asking his brother, was told he intended to leave them as slaves to his children. As writing is a profitable employ, and as offending sober people was disagreeable to my inclination, I was straitened in my mind; but as I looked to the Lord, he inclined my heart to his testimony. I told the man that I believed the practice of continuing slavery to this people was not right, and that I had a scruple in my mind against doing writings of that kind; that though many in our Society kept them as slaves, still I was not easy to be concerned in it, and desired to be excused from going to write the will. I spake to him in the fear of the Lord, and he made no reply to what I said, but went away; he also had some concerns in the practice, and I thought he was displeased with me. In this case I had fresh confirmation that acting contrary to present outward interest, from a motive of Divine love and in regard to truth and righteousness, and thereby incurring the resentments of people, opens the way to a treasure better than silver, and to a friendship exceeding the friendship of men.

The manuscript before mentioned having laid by me several years, the publication of it rested weightily upon me, and this year I offered it to the revisal of my friends, who, having examined and made some small alterations in it, directed a number of copies thereof to be published and dispersed amongst members of our Society.*

In the year 1754 I found my mind drawn to join in a visit to Friends' families belonging to Chesterfield Monthly Meeting, and having the approbation of our own, I went to their Monthly Meeting in order to confer with Friends, and see

* This pamphlet bears the imprint of Benjamin Franklin, 1754.

if way opened for it. I had conference with some of their members, the proposal having been opened before in their meeting, and one Friend agreed to join with me as a companion for a beginning; but when meeting was ended, I felt great distress of mind, and doubted what way to take, or whether to go home and wait for greater clearness. I kept my distress secret, and going with a friend to his house, my desires were to the great Shepherd for his heavenly instruction. In the morning I felt easy to proceed on the visit, though very low in my mind. As mine eye was turned to the Lord, waiting in families in deep reverence before him, he was pleased graciously to afford help, so that we had many comfortable opportunities, and it appeared as a fresh visitation to some young people. I spent several weeks this winter in the service, part of which time was employed near home. And again in the following winter I was several weeks in the same service; some part of the time at Shrewsbury, in company with my beloved friend, John Sykes; and I have cause humbly to acknowledge that through the goodness of the Lord our hearts were at times enlarged in his love, and strength was given to go through the trials which, in the course of our visit, attended us.

From a disagreement between the powers of England and France, it was now a time of trouble on this continent, and an epistle to Friends went forth from our general spring meeting, which I thought good to give a place in this Journal.

An Epistle from our general Spring Meeting of ministers and elders for Pennsylvania and New Jersey, held at Philadelphia, from the 29th of the third month to the 1st of the fourth month inclusive, 1755.

TO FRIENDS ON THE CONTINENT OF AMERICA:—

DEAR FRIENDS,—In an humble sense of Divine goodness, and the gracious continuation of God's love to his people, we tenderly salute you, and are at this time therein engaged in mind, that all of us who profess the truth, as held forth and published by our worthy predecessors in this latter age of the world, may keep near to that Life which is the light of men, and be strengthened to hold fast the profession of our faith without wavering, that our trust may not be in man, but in the Lord alone, who ruleth in the army of heaven and in the kingdoms of men, before whom the earth is "as the dust of the balance, and her inhabitants as grasshoppers." (Isa. xl. 22.)

Being convinced that the gracious design of the Almighty in sending his Son into the world was to repair the breach made by disobedience, to finish sin and transgression, that his kingdom might come, and his will be done on earth as it is in heaven, we have found it to be our duty to cease from those national contests which are productive of misery and bloodshed, and submit our cause to him, the Most High, whose tender love to his children exceeds the most warm affections of natural parents, and who hath promised to his seed throughout the earth, as to one individual, "I will never leave thee, nor forsake thee." (Heb. xiii. 5.) And we, through the gracious dealings of the Lord our God, have had experience of that work which is carried on, not by earthly might, nor by power, but by my Spirit, saith the Lord of Hosts." (Zech. iv. 6.) By which operation that spiritual kingdom is set up, which is to subdue and break in pieces all kingdoms that oppose it, and shall stand forever. In a deep sense thereof, and of the safety, stability, and peace that are in it, we are desirous that all who profess the truth may be inwardly acquainted with it, and thereby be qualified to conduct ourselves in all parts of our life as becomes our peaceable profession; and we trust as there is a faithful continuance to depend wholly upon the almighty arm, from one generation to another, the peaceable kingdom will gradually be extended "from sea to sea, and from the river to the ends of the earth" (Zech. ix. 10), to the completion of those prophecies already begun, that "nation shall not lift up a sword against nation, nor learn war any more." (Isa. ii. 4. Micah iv. 3.)

And, dearly beloved friends, seeing that we have these promises, and believe that God is beginning to fulfil them, let us constantly endeavor to have our minds sufficiently disentangled from the surfeiting cares of this life, and redeemed from the love of the world, that no earthly possessions nor enjoyments may bias our judgments, or turn us from that resignation and entire trust in God to which his blessing is most surely annexed; then may we say, "Our Redeemer is mighty, he will plead our cause for us." (Jer. l. 34.) And if, for the further promoting of his most gracious purposes in the earth, he should give us to taste of that bitter cup of which his faithful ones have often partaken, O that we might be rightly prepared to receive it!

And now, dear friends, with respect to the commotions and stirrings of the powers of the earth at this time near us, we are desirous that none of us may be moved thereat, but repose ourselves in the munition of that rock which all these shakings shall not move, even in the knowledge and feeling of the eternal power of God, keeping us subjectly given up to his heavenly will, and feeling it daily to mortify that which remains in any of us which is of this world; for the worldly part in any is the changeable part, and that is up and down, full and empty, joyful and sorrowful, as things go well or ill in this world. For as the truth is but one, and many are made partakers of its spirit, so the world is but one, and many are made partakers of the spirit of it; and so many as do partake of it, so many will be straitened and perplexed with it. But they who are single to the truth, waiting daily to feel the life and virtue of it in their hearts, shall rejoice in the midst of adversity, and have to experience with the prophet, that, "although the fig-tree shall not blossom, neither shall fruit be in the vines; the labor of the olive shall fail, and the fields shall yield no meat; the flock shall be cut off from the fold, and there shall be no herd in the stalls; yet will they rejoice in the Lord, and joy in the God of their salvation." (Hab. iii. 17, 18.)

If, contrary to this, we profess the truth, and, not living under the power and influence of it, are producing fruits disagreeable to the purity thereof, and trust to the strength of man to support ourselves, our confidence therein will be vain. For he who removed the hedge from his vineyard, and gave it to be trodden under foot by reason of the wild grapes it produced (Isa. v. 6), remains unchangeable; and if, for the chastisement of wickedness and the further promoting of his own glory, he doth arise, even to shake terribly the earth, who then may oppose him, and prosper?

We remain, in the love of the gospel, your friends and brethren.

(Signed by fourteen Friends.)

Scrupling to do writings relative to keeping slaves has been a means of sundry small trials to me, in which I have so evidently felt my own will set aside that I think it good to mention a few of them. Tradesmen and retailers of goods, who depend on their business for a living, are naturally inclined to keep the good-will of their customers; nor is it a pleasant thing for young men to be under any necessity to question the judgment or honesty of elderly men, and more especially of such as have a fair reputation. Deep-rooted customs, though wrong, are not easily altered; but it is the duty of all to be firm in that which they certainly know is right for them. A charitable, benevolent man, well acquainted with a negro, may, I believe, under some circumstances, keep him in his family as a servant, on no other motives than the negro's good; but man, as man, knows not what shall be after him, nor hath he any assurance that his children will attain to that perfection in wisdom and goodness necessary rightly to exercise such power; hence it is clear to me, that I ought not to be the scribe where wills are drawn in which some children are made ales masters over others during life.

About this time an ancient man of good esteem in the neighborhood came to my house to get his will written. He had young negroes, and I asked him privately how he purposed to dispose of them. He told me; I then said, "I cannot write thy will without breaking my own peace," and respectfully gave him my reasons for it. He signified that he had a choice that I should have written it, but as I could not, consistently with my conscience, he did not desire it, and so he got it written by some other person. A few years after, there being great alterations in his family, he came again to get me to write his will. His negroes were yet young, and his son, to whom he intended to give them, was, since he first spoke to me, from a libertine become a sober young man, and he supposed that I would have been free on that account to write it. We had much friendly talk on the subject, and then deferred it. A few days after he came again and directed their freedom, and I then wrote his will.

Near the time that the last-mentioned Friend first spoke to me, a neighbor received a bad bruise in his body and sent for me to bleed him, which having done, he desired me to write his will. I took notes, and amongst other things he told me to which of his children he gave his young negro. I considered the pain and distress he was in, and knew not how it would end, so I wrote his will, save only that part concerning his slave, and carrying it to his bedside read it to him. I then told him in a friendly way that I could not write any instruments by which my fellow-creatures were made slaves, without bringing trouble on my own mind. I let him know that I charged nothing for what I had done, and desired to be excused from doing the other part in the way he proposed. We then had a serious conference on the subject; at length, he agreeing to set her free, I finished his will.

Having found drawings in my mind to visit Friends on Long Island, after obtaining a certificate from our Monthly Meeting, I set off 12th of fifth month, 1756. When I reached the island, I lodged the first night at the house of my dear friend, Richard Hallett. The next day being the first of the week, I was at the meeting in New Town, in which we experienced the renewed manifestations of the love of Jesus Christ to the comfort of the honest-hearted. I went that night to Flushing, and the next day I and my beloved friend, Matthew Franklin, crossed the ferry at White Stone; were at three meetings on the main, and then returned to the island, where I spent the remainder of the week in visiting meetings. The Lord, I believe, hath a people in those parts who are honestly inclined to serve him; but many I fear, are too much clogged with the things of this life, and do not come forward bearing the cross in such faithfulness as he calls for.

My mind was deeply engaged in this visit, both in public and private, and at several places where I was, on observing that they had slaves, I found myself under a necessity, in a friendly way, to labor with them on that subject; expressing, as way opened, the inconsistency of that practice with the purity of the Christian religion, and the ill effects of it manifested amongst us.

The latter end of the week their Yearly Meeting began; at which were our friends, John Scarborough, Jane Hoskins, and Susannah Brown, from Pennsylvania. The public meetings were large, and measurably favored with Divine goodness. The exercise of my mind at this meeting was chiefly on account of those who were considered as the foremost rank in the Society; and in a meeting of ministers and elders way opened for me to express in some measure what lay upon me; and when Friends were met for transacting the affairs of the church, having sat awhile silent, I felt a weight on my mind, and stood up; and through the gracious regard of our Heavenly Father strength was given fully to clear myself of a burden which for some days had been increasing upon me.

Through the humbling dispensations of Divine Providence, men are sometimes fitted for his service. The messages of the prophet Jeremiah were so disagreeable to the people, and so adverse to the spirit they lived in, that he became the object of their reproach, and in the weakness of nature he thought of desisting from his prophetic office ; but saith he, "His word was in my heart as a burning fire shut up in my bones ; and I was weary with forbearing, and could not stay." I saw at this time that if I was honest in declaring that which truth opened in me, I could not please all men ; and I labored to be content in the way of my duty, however disagreeable to my own inclination. After this I went homeward, taking Woodbridge and Plainfield in my way, in both which meetings the pure influence of Divine love was manifested, in an humbling sense whereof I went home. I had been out about twenty-four days, and rode about three hundred and sixteen miles.

While I was out on this journey my heart was much affected with a sense of the state of the churches in our southern provinces ; and believing the Lord was calling me to some further labor amongst them, I was bowed in reverence before him, with fervent desires that I might find strength to resign myself to his heavenly will.

Until this year, 1756, I continued to retail goods,

besides following my trade as a tailor; about which time I grew uneasy on account of my business growing too cumbersome. I had begun with selling trimmings for garments, and from thence proceeded to sell cloths and linens; and at length, having got a considerable shop of goods, my trade increased every year, and the way to large business appeared open, but I felt a stop in my mind.

Through the mercies of the Almighty, I had, in a good degree, learned to be content with a plain way of living. I had but a small family; and, on serious consideration, believed truth did not require me to engage much in cumbering affairs. It had been my general practice to buy and sell things really useful. Things that served chiefly to please the vain mind in people, I was not easy to trade in; seldom did it; and whenever I did I found it weaken me as a Christian.

The increase of business became my burden; for though my natural inclination was toward merchandise, yet I believed truth required me to live more free from outward cumbers; and there was now a strife in my mind between the two. In this exercise my prayers were put up to the Lord, who graciously heard me, and gave me a heart resigned to his holy will. Then I lessened my outward business, and, as I had opportunity, told my customers of my intentions, that they might consider what shop to turn to; and in a while I wholly laid down merchandise, and followed my trade as a tailor by myself, having no apprentice. I also had a nursery of apple-trees, in which I employed some of my time in hoeing, grafting, trimming, and inoculating.* In merchandise it is the custom where I lived to sell chiefly on credit, and poor people often get in debt; when payment is expected, not having wherewith to pay, their creditors often sue for it at law. Having frequently observed occurrences of this kind, I found it good for me to advise poor people to take such goods as were most useful, and not costly.

In the time of trading I had an opportunity of seeing that the too liberal use of spirituous liquors and the custom of wearing too costly apparel led some people into great inconveniences; and that

* He seems to have regarded agriculture as the business most conducive to moral and physical health. He thought "if the leadings of the Spirit were more attended to, more people would be engaged in the sweet employment of husbandry, where labor is agreeable and healthful." He does not condemn the honest acquisition of wealth in other business free from oppression; even "merchandising," he thought, *might* be carried on innocently and in pure reason. Christ does not forbid the laying up of a needful support for family and friends; the command is, "Lay not up for YOURSELVES treasures on earth." From his little farm on the Rancocas he looked out with a mingled feeling of wonder and sorrow upon the hurry and unrest of the world; and especially was he pained to see luxury and extravagance overgrowing the early plainness and simplicity of his own religious society. He regarded the merely rich man with unfeigned pity. With nothing of his scorn, he had all of Thoreau's commiseration, for people who went about bowed down with the weight of broad acres and great houses on their backs.

these two things appear to be often connected with each other. By not attending to that use of things which is consistent with universal righteousness. there is an increase of labor which extends beyond what our Heavenly Father intends for us. And by great labor, and often by much sweating, there is even among such as are not drunkards a craving of liquors to revive the spirits; that partly by the luxurious drinking of some, and partly by the drinking of others (led to it through immoderate labor), very great quantities of rum are every year expended in our colonies; the greater part of which we should have no need of, did we steadily attend to pure wisdom.

When men take pleasure in feeling their minds elevated with strong drink, and so indulge their appetite as to disorder their understandings, neglect their duty as members of a family or civil society, and cast off all regard to religion, their case is much to be pitied. And where those whose lives are for the most part regular, and whose examples have a strong influence on the minds of others, adhere to some customs which powerfully draw to the use of more strong liquor than pure wisdom allows, it hinders the spreading of the spirit of meekness, and strengthens the hands of the more excessive drinkers. This is a case to be lamented.

Every degree of luxury hath some connection with evil; and if those who profess to be disciples of Christ, and are looked upon as leaders of the people, have that mind in them which was also in

Christ, and so stand separate from every wrong way, it is a means of help to the weaker. As I have sometimes been much spent in the heat and have taken spirits to revive me, I have found by experience, that in such circumstances the mind is not so calm, nor so fitly disposed for Divine meditation, as when all such extremes are avoided. I have felt an increasing care to attend to that Holy Spirit which sets right bounds to our desires, and leads those who faithfully follow it to apply all the gifts of Divine Providence to the purposes for which they were intended. Did those who have the care of great estates attend with singleness of heart to this heavenly Instructor, which so opens and enlarges the mind as to cause men to love their neighbors as themselves, they would have wisdom given them to manage their concerns, without employing some people in providing the luxuries of life, or others in laboring too hard; but for want of steadily regarding this principle of Divine love, a selfish spirit takes place in the minds of people, which is attended with darkness and manifold confusions in the world.

Though trading in things useful is an honest employ, yet through the great number of superfluities which are bought and sold, and through the corruption of the times, they who apply to merchandise for a living have great need to be well experienced in that precept which the Prophet Jeremiah laid down for his scribe: "Seekest thou great things for thyself? seek them not."

In the winter this year I was engaged with friends in visiting families, and through the goodness of the Lord we oftentimes experienced his heart-tendering presence amongst us.

A Copy of a Letter written to a Friend.

"In this, thy late affliction, I have found a deep fellow-feeling with thee, and have had a secret hope throughout that it might please the Father of Mercies to raise thee up and sanctify thy troubles to thee; that thou being more fully acquainted with that way which the world esteems foolish, mayst feel the clothing of Divine fortitude, and be strengthened to resist that spirit which leads from the simplicity of the everlasting truth.

"We may see ourselves crippled and halting, and from a strong bias to things pleasant and easy find an impossibility to advance forward; but things impossible with men are possible with God; and our wills being made subject to his, all temptations are surmountable.

"This work of subjecting the will is compared to the mineral in the furnace, which, through fervent heat, is reduced from its first principle: 'He refines them as silver is refined; he shall sit as a refiner and purifier of silver.' By these comparisons we are instructed in the necessity of the melting operation of the hand of God upon us, to prepare our hearts truly to adore him, and manifest that adoration by inwardly turning away from that spirit, in all its workings, which is not of him. To forward this work the all-wise God is sometimes pleased, through outward distress, to bring us near the gates of death; that life being painful and afflicting, and the prospect of eternity opened before us, all earthly bonds may be loosened, and the mind prepared for that deep and sacred instruction which otherwise would not be received. If kind parents love their children and delight in their happiness, then he who is perfect goodness in sending abroad mortal contagions doth assuredly direct their use. Are the righteous removed by it? their change is happy. Are the wicked taken away in their wickedness? the Almighty is clear. Do we pass through with anguish and great bitterness, and yet recover? He intends that we should be purged from dross, and our ear opened to discipline.

"And now, as thou art again restored, after thy sore affliction and doubts of recovery, forget not Him who hath helped thee, but in humble gratitude hold fast his instructions, and thereby shun those by-paths which lead from the firm foundation. I am sensible of that variety of company to which one in thy business must be exposed; I have painfully felt the force of conversation proceeding from men deeply rooted in an earthly mind, and can sympathize with others in such conflicts, because much weakness still attends me.

"I find that to be a fool as to worldly wisdom, and to commit my cause to God, not fearing to offend men, who take offence at the simplicity of truth, is the only way to remain unmoved at the sentiments of others.

"The fear of man brings a snare. By halting in our duty, and giving back in the time of trial, our hands grow weaker, our spirits get mingled with the people, our ears grow dull as to hearing the language of the true Shepherd, so that when we look at the way of the righteous, it seems as though it was not for us to follow them.

"A love clothes my mind while I write, which is superior to all expression; and I find my heart open to encourage to a holy emulation, to advance forward in Christian firmness. Deep humility is a strong bulwark, and as we enter into it we find safety and true exaltation. The foolishness of God is wiser than man, and the weakness of God is stronger than man. Being unclothed of our own wisdom, and knowing the abasement of the creature, we find that power to arise which gives health and vigor to us."

CHAPTER IV.

1757, 1758.

Visit to the Families of Friends at Burlington. — Journey to Pennsylvania, Maryland, Virginia, and North Carolina. — Considerations on the State of Friends there, and the Exercise he was under in Travelling among those so generally concerned in keeping Slaves, with some Observations on this Subject. — Epistle to Friends at New Garden and Crane Creek. — Thoughts on the Neglect of a Religious Care in the Education of the Negroes.

THIRTEENTH fifth month, 1757. — Being in good health, and abroad with Friends visiting families, I lodged at a Friend's house in Burlington. Going to bed about the time usual with me, I awoke in the night, and my meditations, as I lay, were on the goodness and mercy of the Lord, in a sense whereof my heart was contrited. After this I went to sleep again; in a short time I awoke; it was yet dark, and no appearance of day or moonshine, and as I opened mine eyes I saw a light in my chamber, at the apparent distance of five feet, about nine inches in diameter, of a clear, easy brightness, and near its centre the most radiant. As I lay still looking upon it without any surprise, words were spoken to my inward ear, which filled my whole inward man. They were not the effect of thought, nor any conclusion in relation to the appearance, but as the language of the Holy One spoken in my mind. The words were, CERTAIN EVIDENCE OF DIVINE TRUTH. They were again repeated exactly in the same manner, and then the light disappeared.

Feeling the exercise in relation to a visit to the Southern Provinces to increase upon me, I acquainted our Monthly Meeting therewith, and obtained their certificate. Expecting to go alone, one of my brothers who lived in Philadelphia, having some business in North Carolina, proposed going with me part of the way; but as he had a view of some outward affairs, to accept of him as a companion was some difficulty with me, whereupon I had conversation with him at sundry times. At length feeling easy in my mind, I had conversation with several elderly Friends of Philadelphia on the subject, and he obtaining a certificate suitable to the occasion, we set off in the fifth month, 1757. Coming to Nottingham week-day meeting, we lodged at John Churchman's, where I met with our friend, Benjamin Buffington, from New England, who was returning from a visit to the Southern Provinces. Thence we crossed the river Susquehanna, and lodged at William Cox's in Maryland.

Soon after I entered this province a deep and painful exercise came upon me, which I often had some feeling of, since my mind was drawn toward these parts, and with which I had acquainted my brother before we agreed to join as companions. As the people in this and the Southern Provinces live much on the labor of slaves, many of whom are used hardly, my concern was that I might attend with singleness of heart to the voice of the true Shepherd, and be so supported as to remain unmoved at the faces of men.

As it is common for Friends on such a visit to have entertainment free of cost, a difficulty arose in my mind with respect to saving my money by kindness received from what appeared to me to be the gain of oppression. Receiving a gift, considered as a gift, brings the receiver under obligations to the benefactor, and has a natural tendency to draw the obliged into a party with the giver. To prevent difficulties of this kind, and to preserve the minds of judges from any bias, was that Divine prohibition: "Thou shalt not receive any gift; for a gift blindeth the wise, and perverteth the words of the righteous." (Exod. xxiii. 8.) As the disciples were sent forth without any provision for their journey, and our Lord said the workman is worthy of his meat, their labor in the gospel was considered as a reward for their entertainment, and therefore not received as a gift; yet, in regard to my present journey, I could not see my way clear in that respect. The difference appeared thus: the entertainment the disciples met with was from them whose hearts God had opened to receive them, from a love to them and the truth they published; but we, considered as members of the same religious society, look upon it as a piece of civility to receive each other in such visits; and such reception, at times, is partly in regard to reputation, and not from an inward unity of heart and spirit. Conduct is more convincing than language, and where people, by their actions, manifest that the slave-trade is not so disagreeable to their principles but that it may be encouraged, there is not a sound uniting with some Friends who visit them.

The prospect of so weighty a work, and of being so distinguished from many whom I esteemed before myself, brought me very low, and such were the conflicts of my soul that I had a near sympathy with the Prophet, in the time of his weakness, when he said: "If thou deal thus with me, kill me, I pray thee, if I have found favor in thy sight." (Num. xi. 15.) But I soon saw that this proceeded from the want of a full resignation to the Divine will. Many were the afflictions which attended me, and in great abasement, with many tears, my cries were to the Almighty for his gracious and fatherly assistance, and after a time of deep trial I was favored to understand the state mentioned by the Psalmist more clearly than ever I had done before; to wit: "My soul is even as a weaned child." (Psalm cxxxi. 2.) Being thus helped to sink down into resignation, I felt a deliverance from that tempest in which I had been sorely exercised, and in calmness of mind went forward, trusting that the Lord Jesus Christ, as I faithfully attended to him, would be a counsellor to me in all difficulties, and that by his strength I should be enabled even to leave money with the members of society where I had entertainment, when I found that omitting it would obstruct that work to which I believed he had called me. As I copy this after my return, I may here add, that oftentimes I did so under a sense of duty. The way in which I did it was thus: when I expected soon to leave a Friend's house where I had entertainment, if I believed that I should not keep clear from the gain of oppression without leaving money, I spoke to one of the heads of the family privately, and desired them to accept of those pieces of silver, and give them to such of their negroes as they believed would make the best use of them; and at other times I gave them to the negroes myself, as the way looked clearest to me. Before I came out, I had provided a large number of small pieces for this purpose and thus offering them to some who appeared to be wealthy people was a trial both to me and them. But the fear of the Lord so covered me at times that my way was made easier than I expected; and few, if any, manifested any resentment at the offer, and most of them, after some conversation, accepted of them.

Ninth of fifth month. — A Friend at whose house we breakfasted setting us a little on our way, I had conversation with him, in the fear of the Lord, concerning his slaves, in which my heart was tender; I used much plainness of speech with him, and he appeared to take it kindly. We pursued our journey without appointing meetings, being pressed in my mind to be at the Yearly Meeting in Virginia. In my travelling on the road, I often felt a cry rise from the centre of my mind, thus: "O Lord, I am a stranger on the earth, hide not thy face from me." On the 11th, we crossed the rivers Patowmack and Rapahannock, and lodged at Port Royal. On the way we had the company of a colonel of the militia, who appeared to be a thoughtful man. I took occasion to remark on the difference in general betwixt a people used to labor moderately for their living, training up their children in frugality and business, and those who live on the labor of slaves; the former, in my view, being the most happy life. He concurred in the remark, and mentioned the trouble arising from the untoward, slothful disposition of the negroes, adding that one of our laborers would do as much in a day as two of their slaves. I replied, that free men, whose minds were properly on their business, found a satisfaction in improving, cultivating, and providing for their families; but negroes, laboring to support others who claim them as their property, and expecting nothing but slavery during life, had not the like inducement to be industrious.

After some further conversation I said, that men having power too often misapplied it; that though we made slaves of the negroes, and the Turks made slaves of the Christians, I believed that liberty was the natural right of all men equally. This he did not deny, but said the lives of the negroes were so wretched in their own country that many of them lived better here than there. I replied, "There is great odds in regard to us on what principle we act"; and so the conversation on that subject ended. I may here add that another person, some time afterwards, mentioned the wretchedness of the negroes, occasioned by their intestine wars, as an argument in favor of our fetching them away for slaves. To which I replied, if compassion for the Africans, on account of their domestic troubles, was the real motive of our purchasing them, that spirit of tenderness being attended to, would incite us to use them kindly, that, as strangers brought out of affliction, their lives might be happy among us. And as they are human creatures, whose souls are as precious as ours, and who may receive the same help and comfort from the Holy Scriptures as we do, we could not omit suitable endeavors to instruct them therein; but that while we manifest by our conduct that our views in purchasing them are to advance ourselves, and while our buying captives taken in war animates those parties to push on the war, and increase desolation amongst them, to say they live unhappily in Africa is far from being an argument in our favor. I further said, the present circumstances of these provinces to me appear difficult; the slaves look like a burdensome stone to such as burden themselves with them; and that if the white people retain a resolution to prefer their outward prospects of gain to all other considerations, and do not act conscientiously toward them as fellow-creatures, I believe that burden will grow heavier and heavier, until times change in a way disagreeable to us. The person appeared very serious, and owned that in considering their condition and the manner of their treatment in these provinces he had sometimes thought it might be just in the Almighty so to order it.

Having travelled through Maryland, we came amongst Friends at Cedar Creek in Virginia, on the 12th; and the next day rode, in company with several of them, a day's journey to Camp Creek. As I was riding along in the morning, my mind was deeply affected in a sense I had of the need of Divine aid to support me in the various difficulties which attended me, and in uncommon distress of mind I cried in secret to the Most High, "O Lord be merciful, I beseech thee, to thy poor afflicted creature!" After some time, I felt inward relief, and, soon after, a Friend in company began to talk in support of the slave-trade, and said the negroes were understood to be the offspring of Cain, their blackness being the mark which God set upon him after he murdered Abel his brother; that it was the design of Providence they should be slaves, as a condition proper to the race of so wicked a man as Cain was. Then another spake in support of what had been said. To all which I replied in substance as follows: that Noah and his family were all who survived the flood, according to Scripture; and as Noah was of Seth's race, the family of Cain was wholly destroyed. One of them said that after the flood Ham went to the land of Nod and took a wife; that Nod was a land far distant, inhabited by Cain's race, and that the flood did not reach it; and as Ham was sentenced to be a servant of servants to his brethren, these two families, being thus joined, were undoubtedly fit only for slaves. I replied, the flood was a judgment upon the world for their abominations, and it was granted that Cain's stock was the most wicked, and therefore unreasonable to suppose that they were spared. As to Ham's going to the land of Nod for a wife, no time being fixed, Nod might be inhabited by some of Noah's family before Ham married a second time; moreover the text saith "That all flesh died that moved upon the earth." (Gen. vii. 21.) I further reminded them how the prophets repeatedly declare "that the son shall not suffer for the iniquity of the father, but every one be answerable for his own sins." I was troubled to perceive the darkness of their imaginations, and in some pressure of spirit said, "The love of ease and gain are the motives in general of keeping slaves, and men are wont to take hold of weak arguments to support a cause which is unreasonable. I have no interest on either side, save only the interest which I desire to have in the truth. I believe liberty is their right, and as I see they are not only deprived of it, but treated in other respects with inhumanity in many places, I believe He who is a refuge for the oppressed will, in his own time, plead their cause, and happy will it be for such as walk in uprightness before him." And thus our conversation ended.

Fourteenth of fifth month. — I was this day at Camp Creek Monthly Meeting, and then rode to the mountains up James River, and had a meeting at a Friend's house, in both which I felt sorrow of heart, and my tears were poured out before the Lord, who was pleased to afford a degree of strength by which way was opened to clear my mind amongst Friends in those places. From thence I went to Fork Creek, and so to Cedar Creek again, at which place I now had a meeting. Here I found a tender seed, and as I was preserved in the ministry to keep low with the truth, the same truth in their hearts answered it, that it was a time of mutual refreshment from the presence of the Lord. I lodged at James Standley's, father of William Standley, one of the young men who suffered imprisonment at Winchester last summer on account of their testimony against fighting, and I had some satisfactory conversation with him concerning it. Hence I went to the Swamp Meeting, and to Wayanoke Meeting, and then crossed James River, and lodged near Burleigh. From the time of my entering Maryland I have been much under sorrow, which of late so increased upon me that my mind was almost overwhelmed, and I may say with the Psalmist, "In my distress I called upon the Lord, and cried to my God," who, in infinite goodness, looked upon my affliction, and in my private retirement sent the Comforter for my relief, for which I humbly bless his holy name.

The sense I had of the state of the churches

brought a weight of distress upon me. The gold to me appeared dim, and the fine gold changed, and though this is the case too generally, yet the sense of it in these parts hath in a particular manner borne heavy upon me. It appeared to me that through the prevailing of the spirit of this world the minds of many were brought to an inward desolation, and instead of the spirit of meekness, gentleness, and heavenly wisdom, which are the necessary companions of the true sheep of Christ, a spirit of fierceness and the love of dominion too generally prevailed. From small beginnings in error great buildings by degrees are raised, and from one age to another are more and more strengthened by the general concurrence of the people; and as men obtain reputation by their profession of the truth, their virtues are mentioned as arguments in favor of general error; and those of less note, to justify themselves, say, such and such good men did the like. By what other steps could the people of Judah arise to that height in wickedness as to give just ground for the Prophet Isaiah to declare, in the name of the Lord, "that none calleth for justice, nor any pleadeth for truth" (Isa. lix. 4), or for the Almighty to call upon the great city of Jerusalem just before the Babylonish captivity, "If ye can find a man, if there be any who executeth judgment, that seeketh the truth, and I will pardon it"? (Jer. v. 1.)

The prospect of a way being open to the same degeneracy, in some parts of this newly settled land of America, in respect to our conduct towards the negroes, hath deeply bowed my mind in this journey, and though briefly to relate how these people are treated is no agreeable work, yet, after often reading over the notes I made as I travelled, I find my mind engaged to preserve them. Many of the white people in those provinces take little or no care of negro marriages; and when negroes marry after their own way, some make so little account of those marriages that with views of outward interest they often part men from their wives by selling them far asunder, which is common when estates are sold by executors at vendue. Many whose labor is heavy being followed at their business in the field by a man with a whip, hired for that purpose, have in common little else allowed but one peck of Indian corn and some salt, for one week, with a few potatoes; the potatoes they commonly raise by their labor on the first day of the week. The correction ensuing on their disobedience to overseers, or slothfulness in business, is often very severe, and sometimes desperate.

Men and women have many times scarcely clothes sufficient to hide their nakedness, and boys and girls ten and twelve years old are often quite naked amongst their master's children. Some of our Society, and some of the society called New-lights, use some endeavors to instruct those they have in reading; but in common this is not only neglected, but disapproved. These are the people by whose labor the other inhabitants are in a great measure supported, and many of them in the luxuries of life. These are the people who have made no agreement to serve us, and who have not forfeited their liberty that we know of. These are the souls for whom Christ died, and for our conduct towards them we must answer before Him who is no respecter of persons. They who know the only true God, and Jesus Christ whom he hath sent, and are thus acquainted with the merciful, benevolent, gospel spirit, will therein perceive that the indignation of God is kindled against oppression and cruelty, and in beholding the great distress of so numerous a people will find cause for mourning.

From my lodgings I went to Burleigh Meeting, where I felt my mind drawn in a quiet, resigned state. After long silence I felt an engagement to stand up, and through the powerful operation of Divine love we were favored with an edifying meeting. The next meeting we had was at Black-Water, and from thence went to the Yearly Meeting at the Western Branch. When business began, some queries were introduced by some of their members for consideration, and, if approved, they were to be answered hereafter by their respective Monthly Meetings. They were the Pennsylvania queries, which had been examined by a committee of Virginia Yearly Meeting appointed the last year, who made some alterations in them, one of which alterations was made in favor of a custom which troubled me. The query was, "Are there any concerned in the importation of negroes, or in buying them after imported?" which was thus altered, "Are there any concerned in the importation of negroes, or buying them to trade in?" As one query admitted with unanimity was, "Are any concerned in buying or vending goods unlawfully imported, or prize goods?" I found my mind engaged to say that as we profess the truth, and were there assembled to support the testimony of it, it was necessary for us to dwell deep and act in that wisdom which is pure, or otherwise we could not prosper. I then mentioned their alteration, and referring to the last-mentioned query, added, that as purchasing any merchandise taken by the sword was always allowed to be inconsistent with our principles, so negroes being captives of war, or taken by stealth, it was inconsistent with our testimony to buy them; and their being our fellow-creatures, and sold as slaves, added greatly to the iniquity. Friends appeared attentive to what was said; some expressed a care and concern about their negroes; none made any objection, by way of reply to what I said, but the query was admitted as they had altered it.

As some of their members have heretofore traded in negroes, as in other merchandise, this query being admitted will be one step further than they have hitherto gone, and I did not see it my duty to press for an alteration, but felt easy to leave it all to Him who alone is able to turn the hearts of the mighty, and make way for the spreading of truth on the earth, by means agreeable to his infinite wisdom.

In regard to those they already had, I felt my mind engaged to labor with them, and said that as we believe the Scriptures were given forth by holy men, as they were moved by the Holy Ghost, and many of us know by experience that they are often helpful and comfortable, and believe ourselves bound in duty to teach our children to read them; I believed that if we were divested of all selfish views, the same good spirit that gave them forth would engage us to teach the negroes to read, that they might have the benefit of them. Some present manifested a concern to take more care in the education of their negroes.

Twenty-ninth fifth month. — At the house where I lodged was a meeting of ministers and elders. I found an engagement to speak freely and plainly to them concerning their slaves; mentioning how they as the first rank in the society, whose conduct in that case was much noticed by others, were under the stronger obligations to look carefully to themselves. Expressing how needful it was for them in that situation to be thoroughly divested of all selfish views; that, living in the pure truth, and acting conscientiously towards those people in their education and otherwise, they might be instrumental in helping forward a work so exceedingly necessary, and so much neglected amongst them. At the twelfth hour the meeting of worship began, which was a solid meeting.

The next day, about the tenth hour, Friends met to finish their business, and then the meeting for worship ensued, which to me was a laborious time; but through the goodness of the Lord, truth, I believed, gained some ground, and it was a strengthening opportunity to the honest-hearted.

About this time I wrote an epistle to Friends in the back settlements of North Carolina, as follows:—

To Friends at their Monthly Meeting at New Garden and Cane Creek, in North Carolina:—

Dear Friends,—It having pleased the Lord to draw me forth on a visit to some parts of Virginia and Carolina, you have often been in my mind; and though my way is not clear to come in person to visit you, yet I feel it in my heart to communicate a few things, as they arise in the love of truth. First, my dear friends, dwell in humility; and take heed that no views of outward gain get too deep hold of you, that so your eyes being single to the Lord, you may be preserved in the way of safety. Where people let loose their minds after the love of outward things, and are more engaged in pursuing the profits and seeking the friendships of this world than to be inwardly acquainted with the way of true peace, they walk in a vain shadow, while the true comfort of life is wanting. Their examples are often hurtful to others; and their treasures thus collected do many times prove dangerous snares to their children.

But where people are sincerely devoted to follow Christ, and dwell under the influence of his Holy Spirit, their stability and firmness, through a Divine blessing, is at times like dew on the tender plants round about them, and the weightiness of their spirits secretly works on the minds of others. In this condition, through the spreading influence of Divine love, they feel a care over the flock, and way is opened for maintaining good order in the Society. And though we may meet with opposition from another spirit, yet, as there is a dwelling in meekness, feeling our spirits subject, and moving only in the gentle, peaceable wisdom, the inward reward of quietness will be greater than all our difficulties. Where the pure life is kept to, and meetings of discipline are held in the authority of it, we find by experience that they are comfortable, and tend to the health of the body.

While I write, the youth come fresh in my way. Dear young people, choose God for your portion; love his truth, and be not ashamed of it; choose for your company such as serve him in uprightness; and shun as most dangerous the conversation of those whose lives are of an ill savor; for by frequenting such company some hopeful young people have come to great loss, and been drawn from less evils to greater, to their utter ruin. In the bloom of youth no ornament is so lovely as that of virtue, nor any enjoyments equal to those which we partake of in fully resigning ourselves to the Divine will. These enjoyments add sweetness to all other comforts, and give true satisfaction in company and conversation, where people are mutually acquainted with it; and as your minds are thus seasoned with the truth, you will find strength to abide steadfast to the testimony of it, and be prepared for services in the church.

And now, dear friends and brethren, as you are improving a wilderness, and may be numbered amongst the first planters in one part of a province, I beseech you, in the love of Jesus Christ, wisely to consider the force of your examples, and think how much your successors may be thereby affected. It is a help in a country, yea, and a great favor and blessing, when customs first settled are agreeable to sound wisdom; but when they are otherwise the effect of them is grievous; and children feel themselves encompassed with difficulties prepared for them by their predecessors.

As moderate care and exercise, under the direction of true wisdom, are useful both to mind and body, so by these means in general the real wants of life are easily supplied, our gracious Father having so proportioned one to the other that keeping in the medium we may pass on quietly. Where slaves are purchased to do our labor numerous difficulties attend it. To rational creatures bondage is uneasy, and frequently occasions sourness and discontent in them; which affects the family and such as claim the mastery over them. Thus people and their children are many times encompassed with vexations, which arise from their applying to wrong methods to get a living.

I have been informed that there is a large number of Friends in your parts who have no slaves; and in tender and most affectionate love I beseech you to keep clear from purchasing any. Look, my dear friends, to Divine Providence, and follow in simplicity that exercise of body, that plainness and frugality, which true wisdom leads to; so may you be preserved from those dangers which attend such as are aiming at outward ease and greatness.

Treasures, though small, attained on a true principle of virtue, are sweet; and while we walk in the light of the Lord there is true comfort and satisfaction in the possession; neither the murmurs of an oppressed people, nor a throbbing, uneasy conscience, nor anxious thoughts about the events of things, hinder the enjoyment of them.

When we look towards the end of life, and think on the division of our substance among our successors, if we know that it was collected in the fear of the Lord, in honesty, in equity, and in uprightness of heart before him, we may consider it as his gift to us, and, with a single eye to his blessing, bestow it on those we leave behind us. Such is the happiness of the plain ways of true virtue. "The work of righteousness shall be peace; and the effect of righteousness, quietness and assurance forever." (Isa. xxxii. 17.)

Dwell here, my dear friends; and then in remote and solitary deserts you may find true peace and satisfaction. If the Lord be our God, in truth and reality, there is safety for us; for he is a stronghold in the day of trouble, and knoweth them that trust in him.

ISLE OF WIGHT COUNTY, in Virginia,
20th of the 5th month, 1757.

From the Yearly Meeting in Virginia I went to Carolina, and on the 1st of sixth month was at Wells Monthly Meeting, where the spring of the gospel ministry was opened, and the love of Jesus Christ experienced among us; to his name be the praise.

Here my brother joined with some Friends from New Garden who were going homeward; and I went next to Simons Creek Monthly Meeting, where I was silent during the meeting for worship. When business came on, my mind was exercised concerning the poor slaves, but I did not feel my way clear to speak. In this condition I was bowed in spirit before the Lord, and with tears and inward supplication besought him so to open my understanding that I might know his will concerning me; and, at length, my mind was settled in silence. Near the end of their business a member of their meeting expressed a concern that had some time lain upon him, on account of Friends so much neglecting their duty in the education of their slaves, and proposed having meetings sometimes appointed for them on a week-day, to be attended only by some Friends to be named in their Monthly Meetings. Many present appeared to unite with the proposal. One said he had often wondered that they, being our fellow-creatures, and capable of religious understanding, had been so exceedingly neglected; another expressed the like concern, and appeared zealous that in future it might be more closely considered. At length a minute was made, and the further consideration of it referred to their next Monthly Meeting. The Friend who made this proposal hath negroes; he told me that he was at New Garden, about two hundred and fifty miles from home, and came back alone; that in this solitary journey this exercise, in regard to the education of their negroes, was from time to time renewed in his mind. A Friend of some note in Virginia, who hath slaves, told me that he being far from home on a lonesome journey had many serious thoughts about them; and his mind was so impressed therewith that he believed he saw a time coming when Divine Providence would alter the circumstance of these people, respecting their condition as slaves.

From hence I went to a meeting at Newbegun Creek, and sat a considerable time in much weakness; then I felt truth open the way to speak a little in much plainness and simplicity, till at length, through the increase of Divine love amongst us, we had a seasoning opportunity. This was also the case at the head of Little River, where we had a crowded meeting on a first-day. I went thence to the Old Neck, where I was led into a careful searching out of the secret workings of the mystery of iniquity, which, under a cover of religion, exalts itself against that pure spirit which leads in the way of meekness and self-denial. Pineywoods was the last meeting I was at in Carolina; it was large, and my heart being deeply engaged, I was drawn forth into a fervent labor amongst them.

When I was at Newbegun Creek a Friend was

there who labored for his living, having no negroes, and who had been a minister many years. He came to me the next day, and as we rode together, he signified that he wanted to talk with me concerning a difficulty he had been under, which he related nearly as follows. That as moneys had of late years been raised by a tax to carry on the wars, he had a scruple in his mind in regard to paying it, and chose rather to suffer distraint of his goods; but as he was the only person who refused it in those parts, and knew not that any one else was in the like circumstances, he signified that it had been a heavy trial to him, especially as some of his brethren had been uneasy with his conduct in that case. He added, that from a sympathy he felt with me yesterday in meeting, he found freedom thus to open the matter in the way of querying concerning Friends in our parts; I told him the state of Friends amongst us as well as I was able, and also that I had for some time been under the like scruple. I believed him to be one who was concerned to walk uprightly before the Lord, and esteemed it my duty to preserve this note concerning him, Samuel Newby.

From hence I went back into Virginia, and had a meeting near James Cowpland's; it was a time of inward suffering, but through the goodness of the Lord I was made content; at another meeting, through the renewings of pure love, we had a very comfortable season.

Travelling up and down of late, I have had renewed evidences that to be faithful to the Lord, and content with his will concerning me, is a most necessary and useful lesson for me to be learning; looking less at the effects of my labor than at the pure motion and reality of the concern, as it arises from heavenly love. In the Lord Jehovah is everlasting strength; and as the mind, by humble resignation, is united to Him, and we utter words from an inward knowledge that they arise from the heavenly spring, though our way may be difficult, and it may require close attention to keep in it, and though the manner in which we may be led may tend to our own abasement; yet, if we continue in patience and meekness, heavenly peace will be the reward of our labors.

I attended Curles Meeting, which, though small, was reviving to the honest-hearted. Afterwards I went to Black Creek and Caroline Meetings, from whence, accompanied by William Standley before mentioned, I rode to Goose Creek, being much through the woods, and about one hundred miles. We lodged the first night at a public-house; the second in the woods; and the next day we reached a Friend's house at Goose Creek. In the woods we were under some disadvantage, having no fire-works nor bells for our horses, but we stopped a little before night and let them feed on the wild grass, which was plentiful, in the mean time cutting with our knives a store against night. We then secured our horses, and gathering some bushes under an oak we lay down; but the mosquitoes being numerous and the ground damp I slept but little. Thus lying in the wilderness, and looking at the stars, I was led to contemplate on the condition of our first parents when they were sent forth from the garden; how the Almighty, though they had been disobedient, continued to be a father to them, and showed them what tended to their felicity as intelligent creatures, and was acceptable to him. To provide things relative to our outward living, in the way of true wisdom, is good, and the gift of improving in things useful is a good gift, and comes from the Father of Lights. Many have had this gift; and from age to age there have been improvements of this kind made in the world. But some, not keeping to the pure gift, have in the creaturely cunning and self-exaltation sought out many inventions. As the first motive to these inventions of men, as distinct from that uprightness in which man was created, was evil, so the effects have been and are evil. It is, therefore, as necessary for us at this day constantly to attend on the heavenly gift, to be qualified to use rightly the good things in this life amidst great improvements, as it was for our first parents when they were without any improvements, without any friend or father but God only.

I was at a meeting at Goose Creek, and next at a Monthly Meeting at Fairfax, where, through the gracious dealing of the Almighty with us, his power prevailed over many hearts. From thence I went to Monoquacy and Pipe Creek in Maryland; at both places I had cause humbly to adore Him who had supported me through many exercises, and by whose help I was enabled to reach the true witness in the hearts of others. There were some hopeful young people in those parts. I had meetings afterwards at John Everit's, in Monalen, and at Huntingdon, and I was made humbly thankful to the Lord, who opened my heart amongst the people in these new settlements, so that it was a time of encouragement to the honest-minded.

At Monalen a Friend gave me some account of a religious society among the Dutch, called Mennonists, and amongst other things related a passage in substance as follows: One of the Mennonists having acquaintance with a man of another society at a considerable distance, and being with his wagon on business near the house of his said acquaintance, and night coming on, he had thoughts of putting up with him, but passing by his fields, and observing the distressed appearance of his slaves, he kindled a fire in the woods hard by, and lay there that night. His said acquaintance hearing where he lodged, and afterward meeting the Mennonist, told him of it, adding he should have been heartily welcome at his house, and from their acquaintance in former time wondered at his conduct in that case. The Mennonist replied, "Ever since I lodged by thy field I have wanted an opportunity to speak with thee. I had intended to come to thy house for entertainment, but seeing thy slaves at their work, and observing the manner of their dress, I had no liking to come to partake with thee." He then admonished him to use them with more humanity, and added, "As I lay by the fire that night, I thought that as I was a man of substance thou wouldst have received me freely; but if I had been as poor as one of thy slaves, and had no power to help myself, I should have received from thy hand no kinder usage than they."

In this journey I was out about two months, and travelled about eleven hundred and fifty miles. I returned home under an humbling sense of the gracious dealings of the Lord with me, in preserving me through many trials and afflictions.

CHAPTER V.

1757, 1758.

Considerations on the Payment of a Tax laid for Carrying on the War against the Indians. — Meetings of the Committee of the Yearly Meeting at Philadelphia. — Some Notes on Thomas à Kempis and John Huss. — The present Circumstances of Friends in Pennsylvania and New Jersey very Different from those of our Predecessors. — The Drafting of the Militia in New Jersey to serve in the Army, with some Observations on the State of the Members of our Society at that time. — Visit to Friends in Pennsylvania, accompanied by Benjamin Jones. — Proceedings at the Monthly, Quarterly, and Yearly Meetings in Philadelphia, respecting those who keep Slaves.

A FEW years past, money being made current in our province for carrying on wars, and to be called in again by taxes laid on the inhabitants, my mind was often affected with the thoughts of paying such taxes; and I believe it right for me to preserve a memorandum concerning it. I was told that Friends in England frequently paid taxes, when the money was applied to such purposes. I had conversation with several noted Friends on the subject, who all favored the payment of such taxes; some of them I preferred before myself, and this made me easier for a time; yet there was in the depth of my mind a scruple which I never could get over; and at certain times I was greatly distressed on that account.

I believed that there were some upright-hearted men who paid such taxes, yet could not see that their example was a sufficient reason for me to do so, while I believe that the spirit of truth required of me, as an individual, to suffer patiently the distress of goods, rather than pay actively.

To refuse the active payment of a tax which our Society generally paid was exceedingly disagreeable; but to do a thing contrary to my conscience appeared yet more dreadful. When this exercise came upon me, I knew of none under the like difficulty; and in my distress I besought the Lord to enable me to give up all, that so I might follow him wheresoever he was pleased to lead me. Under this exercise I went to our Yearly Meeting at Philadelphia in the year 1755; at which a committee was appointed of some from each Quarterly Meeting, to correspond with the meeting for sufferings in London; and another to visit our Monthly and Quarterly Meetings. After their appointment, before the last adjournment of the meeting, it was agreed that these two committees should meet together in Friends' school-house in the city, to consider some things in which the cause of truth was concerned. They accordingly had a weighty conference in the fear of the Lord; at which time I perceived there were many Friends under a scruple like that before mentioned.*

As scrupling to pay a tax on account of the

* Christians refused to pay taxes to support heathen temples. See Cave's Primitive Christianity, Part III. p. 327.

application hath seldom been heard of heretofore, even amongst men of integrity, who have steadily borne their testimony against outward wars in their time, I may therefore note some things which have occurred to my mind, as I have been inwardly exercised on that account. From the steady opposition which faithful Friends in early times made to wrong things then approved, they were hated and persecuted by men living in the spirit of this world, and, suffering with firmness, they were made a blessing to the church, and the work prospered. It equally concerns men in every age to take heed to their own spirits; and in comparing their situation with ours, to me it appears that there was less danger of their being infected with the spirit of this world, in paying such taxes, than is the case with us now. They had little or no share in civil government, and many of them declared that they were, through the power of God, separated from the spirit in which wars were, and being afflicted by the rulers on account of their testimony, there was less likelihood of their uniting in spirit with them in things inconsistent with the purity of truth. We, from the first settlement of this land, have known little or no troubles of that sort. The profession of our predecessors was for a time accounted reproachful, but at length their uprightness being understood by the rulers, and their innocent sufferings moving them, our way of worship was tolerated, and many of our members in these colonies became active in civil government. Being thus tried with favor and prosperity, this world appeared inviting; our minds have been turned to the improvement of our country, to merchandise and the sciences, amongst which are many things useful, if followed in pure wisdom; but in our present condition I believe it will not be denied that a carnal mind is gaining upon us. Some of our members, who are officers in civil government, are, in one case or other, called upon in their respective stations to assist in things relative to the wars; but being in doubt whether to act or to crave to be excused from their office, if they see their brethren united in the payment of a tax to carry on the said wars, may think their case not much different, and so might quench the tender movings of the Holy Spirit in their minds. Thus, by small degrees, we might approach so near to fighting that the distinction would be little else than the name of a peaceable people.

It requires great self-denial and resignation of ourselves to God, to attain that state wherein we can freely cease from fighting when wrongfully invaded, if, by our fighting, there were a probability of overcoming the invaders. Whoever rightly attains to it does in some degree feel that spirit in which our Redeemer gave his life for us; and through Divine goodness many of our predecessors, and many now living, have learned this blessed lesson; but many others, having their religion chiefly by education, and not being enough acquainted with that cross which crucifies to the world, do manifest a temper distinguishable from that of an entire trust in God. In calmly considering these things, it hath not appeared strange to me that an exercise hath now fallen upon some, which, with respect to the outward means, is different from what was known to many of those who went before us.

Some time after the Yearly Meeting, the said committees met at Philadelphia, and, by adjournments, continued sitting several days. The calamities of war were now increasing; the frontier inhabitants of Pennsylvania were frequently surprised; some were slain, and many taken captive by the Indians; and while these committees sat, the corpse of one so slain was brought in a wagon, and taken through the streets of the city in his bloody garments, to alarm the people and rouse them to war.

Friends thus met were not all of one mind in relation to the tax, which, to those who scrupled it, made the way more difficult. To refuse an active payment at such a time might be construed into an act of disloyalty, and appeared likely to displease the rulers, not only here but in England; still there was a scruple so fixed on the minds of many Friends that nothing moved it. It was a conference the most weighty that ever I was at, and the hearts of many were bowed in reverence before the Most High. Some Friends of the said committees who appeared easy to pay the tax, after several adjournments, withdrew; others of them continued till the last. At length an epistle of tender love and caution to Friends in Pennsylvania was drawn up, and being read several times and corrected, was signed by such as were free to sign it, and afterward sent to the Monthly and Quarterly Meetings.

Ninth of eighth month, 1757.—Orders came at night to the military officers in our county (Burlington), directing them to draft the militia, and prepare a number of men to go off as soldiers, to the relief of the English at Fort William Henry, in New York government; a few days after which, there was a general review of the militia at Mount Holly, and a number of men were chosen and sent off under some officers. Shortly after, there came orders to draft three times as many, who were to hold themselves in readiness to march when fresh orders came. On the 17th there was a meeting of the military officers at Mount Holly, who agreed on draft; orders were sent to the men so chosen to meet their respective captains at set times and places, those in our township to meet at Mount Holly, amongst whom were a considerable number of our Society. My mind being affected herewith, I had fresh opportunity to see and consider the advantage of living in the real substance of religion, where practice doth harmonize with principle. Amongst the officers are men of understanding, who have some regard to sincerity where they see it; and when such in the execution of their office have men to deal with whom they believe to be upright-hearted, it is a painful task to put them to trouble on account of scruples of conscience, and they will be likely to avoid it as much as easily may be. But where men profess to be so meek and heavenly-minded, and to have their trust so firmly settled in God that they cannot join in wars, and yet by their spirit and conduct in common life manifest a contrary disposition, their difficulties are great at such a time.

When officers who are anxiously endeavoring to get troops to answer the demands of their superiors see men who are insincere pretend scruple of conscience in hopes of being excused from a dangerous employment, it is likely they will be roughly handled. In this time of commotion some of our young men left these parts and tarried abroad till it was over; some came, and proposed to go as soldiers; others appeared to have a real tender scruple in their minds against joining in wars, and were much humbled under the apprehension of a trial so near. I had conversation with several of them to my satisfaction. When the captain came to town, some of the last-mentioned went and told him in substance as follows: That they could not bear arms for conscience' sake; nor could they hire any to go in their places, being resigned as to the event. At length the captain acquainted them all that they might return home for the present, but he required them to provide themselves as soldiers, and be in readiness to march when called upon. This was such a time as I had not seen before; and yet I may say, with thankfulness to the Lord, that I believed the trial was intended for our good; and I was favored with resignation to him. The French army having taken the fort they were besieging, destroyed it and went away; the company of men who were first drafted, after some days' march, had orders to return home, and those on the second draft were no more called upon on that occasion.

Fourth of fourth month, 1758. — Orders came to some officers in Mount Holly to prepare quarters for a short time for about one hundred soldiers. An officer and two other men, all inhabitants of our town, came to my house. The officer told me that he came to desire me to provide lodging and entertainment for two soldiers, and that six shillings a week per man would be allowed as pay for it. The case being new and unexpected I made no answer suddenly, but sat a time silent, my mind being inward. I was fully convinced that the proceedings in wars are inconsistent with the purity of the Christian religion; and to be hired to entertain men, who were then under pay as soldiers, was a difficulty with me. I expected they had legal authority for what they did; and after a short time I said to the officer, if the men are sent here for entertainment I believe I shall not refuse to admit them into my house, but the nature of the case is such that I expect I cannot keep them on hire; one of the men intimated that he thought I might do it consistently with my religious principles. To which I made no reply, believing silence at that time best for me. Though they spake of two, there came only one, who tarried at my house about two weeks, and behaved himself civilly. When the officer came to pay me, I told him I could not take pay, having admitted him into my house in a passive obedience to authority. I was on horseback when he spake to me, and as I turned from him, he said he was obliged to me; to which I said nothing; but, thinking on the expression, I grew uneasy; and afterwards, being near where he lived, I went and told him on what grounds I refused taking pay for keeping the soldier.

I have been informed that Thomas à Kempis lived and died in the profession of the Roman Catholic religion; and, in reading his writings, I have believed him to be a man of a true Christian spirit, as fully so as many who died martyrs because they could not join with some superstitions in that church. All true Christians are of the same spirit, but their gifts are diverse, Jesus Christ appointing to each one his peculiar office, agreeably to his infinite wisdom.

John Huss contended against the errors which had crept into the church, in opposition to the Council of Constance, which the historian reports to have consisted of some thousand persons. He modestly vindicated the cause which he believed was right; and though his language and conduct towards his judges appear to have been respectful, yet he never could be moved from the principles settled in his mind. To use his own words: "This

I most humbly require and desire of you all, even for his sake who is the God of us all, that I be not compelled to the thing which my conscience doth repugn or strive against." And again, in his answer to the Emperor: "I refuse nothing, most noble Emperor, whatsoever the council shall decree or determine upon me, only this one thing I except, that I do not offend God and my conscience."* At length, rather than act contrary to that which he believed the Lord required of him, he chose to suffer death by fire. Thomas à Kempis, without disputing against the articles then generally agreed to, appears to have labored, by a pious example as well as by preaching and writing, to promote virtue and the inward spiritual religion; and I believe they were both sincere-hearted followers of Christ. True charity is an excellent virtue; and sincerely to labor for their good, whose belief in all points doth not agree with ours, is a happy state.

Near the beginning of the year 1758, I went one evening, in company with a friend, to visit a sick person; and before our return we were told of a woman living near, who had for several days been disconsolate, occasioned by a dream, wherein death, and the judgments of the Almighty after death, were represented to her mind in a moving manner. Her sadness on that account being worn off, the friend with whom I was in company went to see her, and had some religious conversation with her and her husband. With this visit they were somewhat af-

* Fox's Acts and Monuments, p. 233.

fected, and the man, with many tears, expressed his satisfaction. In a short time after the poor man, being on the river in a storm of wind, was with one more drowned.

Eighth month, 1758.—Having had drawings in my mind to be at the Quarterly Meeting in Chester County, and at some meetings in the county of Philadelphia, I went first to said Quarterly Meeting, which was large. Several weighty matters came under consideration and debate, and the Lord was pleased to qualify some of his servants with strength and firmness to bear the burden of the day. Though I said but little, my mind was deeply exercised; and, under a sense of God's love, in the anointing and fitting of some young men for his work, I was comforted, and my heart was tendered before him. From hence I went to the Youth's Meeting at Darby, where my beloved friend and brother Benjamin Jones met me by an appointment before I left home, to join in the visit. We were at Radnor, Merion, Richland, North Wales, Plymouth, and Abington meetings, and had cause to bow in reverence before the Lord, our gracious God, by whose help way was opened for us from day to day. I was out about two weeks, and rode about two hundred miles.

The Monthly Meeting of Philadelphia having been under a concern on account of some Friends who this summer (1758) had bought negro slaves, proposed to their Quarterly Meeting to have the minute reconsidered in the Yearly Meeting, which was made last on that subject, and the said Quarterly Meeting appointed a committee to consider it, and to report to their next. This committee having met once and adjourned, and I, going to Philadelphia to meet a committee of the Yearly Meeting, was in town the evening on which the Quarterly Meeting's committee met the second time, and finding an inclination to sit with them, I, with some others, was admitted, and Friends had a weighty conference on the subject. Soon after their next Quarterly Meeting I heard that the case was coming to our Yearly Meeting. This brought a weighty exercise upon me, and under a sense of my own infirmities, and the great danger I felt of turning aside from perfect purity, my mind was often drawn to retire alone, and put up my prayers to the Lord that he would be graciously pleased to strengthen me ; that setting aside all views of self-interest and the friendship of this world, I might stand fully resigned to his holy will.

In this Yearly Meeting several weighty matters were considered, and toward the last that in relation to dealing with persons who purchase slaves. During the several sittings of the said meeting, my mind was frequently covered with inward prayer, and I could say with David, "that tears were my meat day and night." The case of slave-keeping lay heavy upon me, nor did I find any engagement to speak directly to any other matter before the meeting. Now when this case was opened several faithful Friends spake weightily thereto, with which

I was comforted; and feeling a concern to cast in my mite, I said in substance as follows: —

"In the difficulties attending us in this life nothing is more precious than the mind of truth inwardly manifested; and it is my earnest desire that in this weighty matter we may be so truly humbled as to be favored with a clear understanding of the mind of truth, and follow it; this would be of more advantage to the Society than any medium not in the clearness of Divine wisdom. The case is difficult to some who have slaves, but if such set aside all self-interest, and come to be weaned from the desire of getting estates, or even from holding them together, when truth requires the contrary, I believe way will so open that they will know how to steer through those difficulties."

Many Friends appeared to be deeply bowed under the weight of the work, and manifested much firmness in their love to the cause of truth and universal righteousness on the earth. And though none did openly justify the practice of slave-keeping in general, yet some appeared concerned lest the meeting should go into such measures as might give uneasiness to many brethren, alleging that if Friends patiently continued under the exercise the Lord in his time might open a way for the deliverance of these people. Finding an engagement to speak, I said, "My mind is often led to consider the purity of the Divine Being, and the justice of his judgments; and herein my soul is covered with awfulness. I cannot omit to hint of some cases where people have not been treated with the purity of justice, and the event hath been lamentable. Many slaves on this continent are oppressed, and their cries have reached the ears of the Most High. Such are the purity and certainty of his judgments, that he cannot be partial in our favor. In infinite love and goodness he hath opened our understanding from one time to another concerning our duty towards this people, and it is not a time for delay. Should we now be sensible of what he requires of us, and through a respect to the private interest of some persons, or through a regard to some friendships which do not stand on an immutable foundation, neglect to do our duty in firmness and constancy, still waiting for some extraordinary means to bring about their deliverance, God may by terrible things in righteousness answer us in this matter."

Many faithful brethren labored with great firmness, and the love of truth in a good degree prevailed. Several who had negroes expressed their desire that a rule might be made to deal with such Friends as offenders who bought slaves in future. To this it was answered that the root of this evil would never be effectually struck at until a thorough search was made in the circumstances of such Friends as kept negroes, with respect to the righteousness of their motives in keeping them, that impartial justice might be administered throughout. Several Friends expressed their desire that a visit might be made to such Friends as kept slaves, and many others said that they believed liberty was the negro's right; to which, at length, no opposition was publicly made. A minute was made more full on that subject than any heretofore; and the names of several Friends entered who were free to join in a visit to such as kept slaves.

CHAPTER VI.

1758, 1759.

Visit to the Quarterly Meetings in Chester County. — Joins Daniel Stanton and John Scarborough in a Visit to such as kept Slaves there. — Some Observations on the Conduct which those should maintain who speak in Meetings for Discipline. — More Visits to such as kept Slaves, and to Friends near Salem. — Account of the Yearly Meeting in the Year 1759, and of the increasing Concern in Divers Provinces to Labor against Buying and Keeping Slaves. — The Yearly Meeting Epistle. — Thoughts on the Small-Pox spreading, and on Inoculation.

ELEVENTH of eleventh month, 1758. — This day I set out for Concord; the Quarterly Meeting heretofore held there was now, by reason of a great increase of members, divided into two by the agreement of Friends at our last Yearly Meeting. Here I met with our beloved friends Samuel Spavold and Mary Kirby from England, and with Joseph White from Buck's County; the latter had taken leave of his family in order to go on a religious visit to Friends in England, and, through Divine goodness, we were favored with a strengthening opportunity together.

After this meeting I joined with my friends, Daniel Stanton and John Scarborough, in visiting Friends who had slaves. At night we had a family meeting at William Trimble's, many young people being there; and it was a precious, reviving opportunity. Next morning we had a comfortable sitting with a sick neighbor, and thence to the burial of the corpse of a Friend at Uwchland Meeting, at which were many people, and it was a time of Divine favor, after which we visited some who had slaves. In the evening we had a family meeting at a Friend's house, where the channel of the gospel love was opened, and my mind was comforted after a hard day's labor. The next day we were at Goshen Monthly Meeting, and on the 18th attended the Quarterly Meeting at London Grove, it being first held at that place. Here we met again with all the before-mentioned Friends, and had some edifying meetings. Near the conclusion of the meeting for business, Friends were incited to constancy in supporting the testimony of truth, and reminded of the necessity which the disciples of Christ are under to attend principally to his business as he is pleased to open it to us, and to be particularly careful to have our minds redeemed from the love of wealth, and our outward affairs in as little room as may be, that no temporal concerns may entangle our affections or hinder us from diligently following the dictates of truth in laboring to promote the pure spirit of meekness and heavenly-mindedness amongst the children of men in these days of calamity and distress, wherein God is visiting our land with his just judgments.

Each of these Quarterly Meetings was large and sat near eight hours. I had occasion to consider that it is a weighty thing to speak much in large meetings for business, for except our minds are rightly prepared, and we clearly understand the case we speak to, instead of forwarding, we hinder business, and make more labor for those on whom the burden of the work is laid. If selfish views or a partial spirit have any room in our minds, we are unfit for the Lord's work; if we have a clear prospect of the business, and proper weight on our minds to speak, we should avoid useless apologies and repetitions. Where people are gathered from far, and adjourning a meeting of business is attended with great difficulty, it behoves all to be cautious how they detain a meeting, especially when they have sat six or seven hours, and have a great distance to ride home. After this meeting I rode home.

In the beginning of the twelfth month I joined, in company with my friends John Sykes and Daniel Stanton, in visiting such as had slaves. Some whose hearts were rightly exercised about them appeared to be glad of our visit, but in some places our way was more difficult. I often saw the necessity of keeping down to that root from whence our concern proceeded, and have cause, in reverent thankfulness, humbly to bow down before the Lord, who was near to me, and preserved my mind in calmness under some sharp conflicts, and begat a spirit of sympathy and tenderness in me towards some who were grievously entangled by the spirit of this world.

First month, 1759. — Having found my mind

drawn to visit some of the more active members in our Society at Philadelphia, who had slaves, I met my friend John Churchman there by agreement, and we continued about a week in the city. We visited some that were sick, and some widows and their families, and the other part of our time was mostly employed in visiting such as had slaves. It was a time of deep exercise, but looking often to the Lord for his assistance, he in unspeakable kindness favored us with the influence of that spirit which crucifies to the greatness and splendor of this world, and enabling us to go through some heavy labors, in which we found peace.

Twenty-fourth of third month, 1759.—After attending our general Spring Meeting at Philadelphia I again joined with John Churchman on a visit to some who had slaves in Philadelphia, and with thankfulness to our Heavenly Father I may say that Divine love and a true sympathizing tenderness of heart prevailed at times in this service.

Having at times perceived a shyness in some Friends of considerable note towards me, I found an engagement in gospel love to pay a visit to one of them; and as I dwelt under the exercise, I felt a resignedness in my mind to go and tell him privately that I had a desire to have an opportunity with him alone; to this proposal he readily agreed, and then, in the fear of the Lord, things relating to that shyness were searched to the bottom, and we had a large conference, which, I believe was of use to both of us, and I am thankful that way was opened for it.

Fourteenth of sixth month. — Having felt drawings in my mind to visit Friends about Salem, and having the approbation of our Monthly Meeting, I attended their Quarterly Meeting, and was out seven days, and attended seven meetings; in some of them I was chiefly silent; in others, through the baptizing power of truth, my heart was enlarged in heavenly love, and I found a near fellowship with the brethren and sisters, in the manifold trials attending their Christian progress through this world.

Seventh month. — I have found an increasing concern on my mind to visit some active members in our Society who have slaves, and having no opportunity of the company of such as were named in the minutes of the Yearly Meeting, I went alone to their houses, and, in the fear of the Lord, acquainted them with the exercise I was under; and thus, sometimes by a few words, I found myself discharged from a heavy burden. After this, our friend John Churchman coming into our province with a view to be at some meetings, and to join again in the visit to those who had slaves, I bore him company in the said visit to some active members, and found inward satisfaction.

At our Yearly Meeting this year, we had some weighty seasons, in which the power of truth was largely extended, to the strengthening of the honest-minded. As the epistles which were to be sent to the Yearly Meetings on this continent were read, I observed that in most of them, both this year and the last, it was recommended to Friends to labor against buying and keeping slaves, and in some of them the subject was closely treated upon. As this practice hath long been a heavy exercise to me, and I have often waded through mortifying labors on that account, and at times in some meetings have been almost alone therein, I was humbly bowed in thankfulness in observing the increasing concern in our religious society, and seeing how the Lord was raising up and qualifying servants for his work, not only in this respect, but for promoting the cause of truth in general.

This meeting continued near a week. For several days, in the fore part of it, my mind was drawn into a deep inward stillness, and being at times covered with the spirit of supplication. my heart was secretly poured out before the Lord. Near the conclusion of the meeting for business, way opened in the pure flowings of Divine love for me to express what lay upon me, which, as it then arose in my mind, was first to show how deep answers to deep in the hearts of the sincere and upright; though, in their different growths, they may not all have attained to the same clearness in some points relating to our testimony. And I was then led to mention the integrity and constancy of many martyrs who gave their lives for the testimony of Jesus, and yet, in some points, they held doctrines distinguishable from some which we hold, that, in all ages, where people were faithful to the light and understanding which the Most High afforded them, they found acceptance with Him, and though there may be different ways of thinking amongst us in some particulars, yet, if we mutually keep to that spirit and power which crucifies to the world, which teaches us to be content with things really needful, and to avoid all superfluities, and give up our hearts to fear and serve the Lord, true unity may still be preserved amongst us; that if those who were at times under sufferings on account of some scruples of conscience kept low and humble, and in their conduct in life manifested a spirit of true charity, it would be more likely to reach the witness in others, and be of more service in the church, than if their sufferings were attended with a contrary spirit and conduct. In this exercise I was drawn into a sympathizing tenderness with the sheep of Christ, however distinguished one from another in this world, and the like disposition appeared to spread over others in the meeting. Great is the goodness of the Lord towards his poor creatures.

An epistle went forth from this Yearly Meeting which I think good to give a place in this Journal. It is as follows.

From the Yearly Meeting held at Philadelphia, for Pennsylvania and New Jersey, from the twenty-second day of the ninth month to the twenty-eighth of the same, inclusive, 1759.

TO THE QUARTERLY AND MONTHLY MEETINGS OF FRIENDS BELONGING TO THE SAID YEARLY MEETING.

DEARLY BELOVED FRIENDS AND BRETHREN, — In an awful sense of the wisdom and goodness of the

Lord our God, whose tender mercies have been continued to us in this land, we affectionately salute you, with sincere and fervent desires that we may reverently regard the dispensations of his providence, and improve under them.

The empires and kingdoms of the earth are subject to his almighty power. He is the God of the spirits of all flesh, and deals with his people agreeable to that wisdom, the depth whereof is to us unsearchable. We in these provinces may say, He hath, as a gracious and tender parent, dealt bountifully with us, even from the days of our fathers. It was he who strengthened them to labor through the difficulties attending the improvement of a wilderness, and made way for them in the hearts of the natives, so that by them they were comforted in times of want and distress. It was by the gracious influences of his Holy Spirit that they were disposed to work righteousness, and walk uprightly towards each other, and towards the natives; in life and conversation to manifest the excellency of the principles and doctrines of the Christian religion whereby they retain their esteem and friendship. Whilst they were laboring for the necessaries of life, many of them were fervently engaged to promote piety and virtue in the earth, and to educate their children in the fear of the Lord.

If we carefully consider the peaceable measures pursued in the first settlement of the land, and that freedom from the desolations of wars which for a long time we enjoyed, we shall find ourselves under strong obligations to the Almighty, who, when the earth is so generally polluted with wickedness, gives us a being in a part so signally favored with tranquillity and plenty, and in which the glad tidings of the gospel of Christ are so freely published that we may justly say with the Psalmist, "What shall we render unto the Lord for all his benefits?"

Our own real good, and the good of our posterity, in some measure depends on the part we act, and it nearly concerns us to try our foundations impartially. Such are the different rewards of the just and unjust in a future state, that to attend diligently to the dictates of the spirit of Christ, to devote ourselves to his service, and to engage fervently in his cause, during our short stay in this world, is a choice well becoming a free, intelligent creature. We shall thus clearly see and consider that the dealings of God with mankind, in a national capacity, as recorded in Holy Writ, do sufficiently evidence the truth of that saying, "It is righteousness which exalteth a nation"; and though he doth not at all times suddenly execute his judgments on a sinful people in this life, yet we see in many instances that when "men follow lying vanities they forsake their own mercies"; and as a proud, selfish spirit prevails and spreads among a people, so partial judgment, oppression, discord, envy, and confusions increase, and provinces and kingdoms are made to drink the cup of adversity as a reward of their own doings. Thus the inspired prophet, reasoning with the degenerated Jews, saith, "Thine own wickedness shall correct thee, and thy backsliding shall reprove thee; know, therefore, that it is an evil thing and bitter that thou hast forsaken the Lord thy God, and that my fear is not in thee, saith the Lord God of Hosts." (Jeremiah ii. 19.)

The God of our fathers, who hath bestowed on us many benefits, furnished a table for us in the wilderness, and made the deserts and solitary places to rejoice. He doth now mercifully call upon us to serve him more faithfully. We may truly say with the Prophet, "It is his voice which crieth to the city, and men of wisdom see his name. They regard the rod, and Him who hath appointed it." People who look chiefly at things outward too little consider the original cause of the present troubles; but they who fear the Lord, and think often upon his name, see and feel that a wrong spirit is spreading amongst the inhabitants of our country; that the hearts of many are waxed fat, and their ears dull of hearing; that the Most High, in his visitations to us, instead of calling, lifteth up his voice and crieth: he crieth to our country, and his voice waxeth louder and louder. In former wars between the English and other nations, since the settlement of our provinces, the calamities attending them have fallen chiefly on other places, but now of late they have reached to our borders; many of our fellow-subjects have suffered on and near our frontiers, some have been slain in battle, some killed in their houses, and some in their fields, some wounded and left in great misery, and others separated from their wives and little children, who have been carried captives among the Indians. We have seen men and women who have been witnesses of these scenes of sorrow, and, being reduced to want, have come to our houses asking relief. It is not long since many young men in one of these provinces were drafted, in order to be taken as soldiers; some were at that time in great distress, and had occasion to consider that their lives had been too little conformable to the purity and spirituality of that religion which we profess, and found themselves too little acquainted with that inward humility, in which true fortitude to endure hardness for the truth's sake is experienced. Many parents were concerned for their children, and in that time of trial were led to consider that their care to get outward treasure for them had been greater than their care for their settlement in that religion which crucifieth to the world, and enableth to bear a clear testimony to the peaceable government of the Messiah. These troubles are removed, and for a time we are released from them.

Let us not forget that "The Most High hath his way in the deep, in clouds, and in thick darkness"; that it is his voice which crieth to the city and to the country, and O that these loud and awakening cries may have a proper effect upon us, that heavier chastisement may not become necessary! For though things, as to the outward, may for a short time afford a pleasing prospect, yet, while a selfish spirit, that is not subject to the cross of Christ, continueth to spread and prevail, there can be no long continuance in outward peace and tranquillity. If we desire an inheritance incorruptible, and to be at rest in that state of peace and happiness which ever continues; if we desire in this life to dwell under the favor and protection of that Almighty Being whose habitation is in holiness, whose ways are all equal, and whose anger is now kindled because of our backslidings, — let us then awfully regard these beginnings of his sore judgments, and with abasement and humiliation turn to him whom we have offended.

Contending with one equal in strength is an uneasy exercise; but if the Lord is become our enemy, if we persist in contending with him who is omnipotent, our overthrow will be unavoidable.

Do we feel an affectionate regard to posterity? and are we employed to promote their happiness? Do our minds, in things outward, look beyond our own dissolution? and are we contriving for the prosperity of our children after us? Let us then, like wise builders, lay the foundation deep, and by our constant uniform regard to an inward piety and virtue let them see that we really value it. Let us labor in the fear of the Lord, that their innocent minds, while young and tender, may be preserved from corruptions; that as they advance in age they may rightly understand their true interest, may consider the uncertainty of temporal things, and, above all, have their hope and confidence firmly settled in the blessing of that Almighty Being who inhabits eternity and preserves and supports the world.

In all our cares about worldly treasures, let us steadily bear in mind that riches possessed by children who do not truly serve God are likely to prove snares that may more grievously entangle them in that spirit of selfishness and exaltation which stands in opposition to real peace and happiness, and renders those who submit to the influence of it enemies to the cross of Christ.

To keep a watchful eye towards real objects of charity, to visit the poor in their lonesome dwelling-places, to comfort those who, through the dispensations of Divine Providence, are in strait and painful circumstances in this life, and steadily to endeavor to honor God with our substance, from a real sense of the love of Christ influencing our minds, is more likely to bring a blessing to our children, and will afford more satisfaction to a Christian favored with plenty, than an earnest desire to collect much wealth to leave behind us; for, "here we have no continuing city"; may we therefore diligently "seek one that is to come, whose builder and maker is God."

"Finally, brethren, whatsoever things are true, whatsoever things are just, whatsoever things are pure, whatsoever things are lovely, whatsoever things are of good report, if there be any virtue, if there be any praise, think on these things, and do them, and the God of peace shall be with you."

(Signed by appointment, and on behalf of said meeting.)

Twenty-eighth eleventh month. — This day I attended the Quarterly Meeting in Bucks County. In the meeting of ministers and elders my heart was enlarged in the love of Jesus Christ, and the favor of the Most High was extended to us in that and the ensuing meeting.

I had conversation at my lodging with my beloved friend Samuel Eastburn, who expressed a concern to join in a visit to some Friends in that county who had negroes, and as I had felt a drawing in my mind to the said work, I came home and put things in order. On 11th of twelfth month I went over the river, and on the next day was at Buckingham Meeting, where, through the descendings of heavenly dew, my mind was comforted and drawn into a near unity with the flock of Jesus Christ.

Entering upon this business appeared weighty, and before I left home my mind was often sad, under which exercise I felt at times the Holy Spirit which helps our infirmities, and through which my prayers were at times put up to God in private that he would be pleased to purge me from all selfishness, that I might be strengthened to discharge my duty faithfully, how hard soever to the natural part. We proceeded on the visit in a weighty frame of spirit, and went to the houses of the most active members who had negroes throughout the county. Through the goodness of the Lord my mind was preserved in resignation in times of trial, and though the work was hard to nature, yet through the strength of that love which is stronger than death, tenderness of heart was often felt amongst us in our visits, and we parted from several families with greater satisfaction than we expected.

We visited Joseph White's family, he being in England; we had also a family-sitting at the house of an elder who bore us company, and were at Makefield on a first day: at all which times my heart was truly thankful to the Lord who was graciously pleased to renew his loving-kindness to us, his poor servants, uniting us together in his work.

In the winter of this year, the small-pox being in our town, and many being inoculated, of whom a few died, some things were opened in my mind, which I wrote as follows:—

The more fully our lives are conformable to the will of God, the better it is for us; I have looked on the small-pox as a messenger from the Almighty, to be an assistant in the cause of virtue, and to incite us to consider whether we employ our time only in such things as are consistent with perfect wisdom and goodness. Building houses suitable to dwell in, for ourselves and our creatures; preparing clothing suitable for the climate and season, and food convenient, are all duties incumbent on us. And under these general heads are many branches of business in which we may venture health and life, as necessity may require.

This disease being in a house, and my business

calling me to go near it, incites me to consider whether this is a real indispensable duty; whether it is not in conformity to some custom which would be better laid aside, or, whether it does not proceed from too eager a pursuit after some outward treasure. If the business before me springs not from a clear understanding and a regard to that use of things which perfect wisdom approves, to be brought to a sense of it and stopped in my pursuit is a kindness, for when I proceed to business without some evidence of duty, I have found by experience that it tends to weakness.

If I am so situated that there appears no probability of missing the infection, it tends to make me think whether my manner of life in things outward has nothing in it which may unfit my body to receive this messenger in a way the most favorable to me. Do I use food and drink in no other sort and in no other degree than was designed by Him who gave these creatures for our sustenance? Do I never abuse my body by inordinate labor, striving to accomplish some end which I have unwisely proposed? Do I use action enough in some useful employ, or do I sit too much idle while some persons who labor to support me have too great a share of it? If in any of these things I am deficient, to be incited to consider it is a favor to me. Employment is necessary in social life, and this infection, which often proves mortal, incites me to think whether these social acts of mine are real duties. If I go on a visit to the widows and fatherless, do I go purely on a principle of charity, free from any selfish views? If I go to a religious meeting it puts me on thinking whether I go in sincerity and in a clear sense of duty, or whether it is not partly in conformity to custom, or partly from a sensible delight which my animal spirits feel in the company of other people, and whether to support my reputation as a religious man has no share in it.

Do affairs relating to civil society call me near this infection? If I go, it is at the hazard of my health and life, and it becomes me to think seriously whether love to truth and righteousness is the motive of my attending; whether the manner of proceeding is altogether equitable, or whether aught of narrowness, party interest, respect to outward dignities, names, or distinctions among men, do not stain the beauty of those assemblies, and render it doubtful; in point of duty, whether a disciple of Christ ought to attend as a member united to the body or not. Whenever there are blemishes which for a series of time remain such, that which is a means of stirring us up to look attentively on these blemishes, and to labor according to our capacities, to have health and soundness restored in our country, we may justly account a kindness from our gracious Father, who appointed that means.

The care of a wise and good man for his only son is inferior to the regard of the great Parent of the universe for his creatures. He hath the command of all the powers and operations in nature, and "doth not afflict willingly, nor grieve the children of men." Chastisement is intended for instruction, and instruction being received by gentle chastisement, greater calamities are prevented. By an earthquake hundreds of houses are sometimes shaken down in a few minutes, multitudes of people perish suddenly, and many more, being crushed and bruised in the ruins of the buildings, pine away and die in great misery.

By the breaking in of enraged merciless armies, flourishing countries have been laid waste great numbers of people have perished in a short time, and many more have been pressed with poverty and grief. By the pestilence, people have died so fast in a city, that, through fear, grief, and confusion, those in health have found great difficulty in burying the dead, even without coffins. By famine, great numbers of people in some places have been brought to the utmost distress, and have pined away for want of the necessaries of life. Thus, when the kind invitations and gentle chastisements of a gracious God have not been attended to, his sore judgments have at times been poured out upon people.

While some rules approved in civil society and conformable to human policy, so called, are distinguishable from the purity of truth and righteousness, — while many professing the truth are declining from that ardent love and heavenly-mindedness which was amongst the primitive followers of Jesus Christ, it is time for us to attend diligently to the intent of every chastisement, and to consider the most deep and inward design of them.

The Most High doth not often speak with an outward voice to our outward ears, but if we humbly meditate on his perfections, consider that he is perfect wisdom and goodness, and that to afflict his creatures to no purpose would be utterly averse to his nature, we shall hear and understand his language both in his gentle and more heavy chastisements, and shall take heed that we do not, in the wisdom of this world, endeavor to escape his hand by means too powerful for us.

Had he endowed men with understanding to prevent this disease (the small-pox) by means which had never proved hurtful nor mortal, such a discovery might be considered as the period of chastisement by this distemper, where that knowledge extended.* But as life and health are his gifts, and are not to be disposed of in our own wills, to take upon us by inoculation when in health a disorder of which some die, requires great clearness of knowledge that it is our duty to do so.

* Whatever may be thought of these scruples of John Woolman in regard to inoculation, his objections can scarcely be considered valid against vaccination, which, since his time, has so greatly mitigated the disease. He almost seems to have anticipated some such preventive.

CHAPTER VII.

1760.

Visit, in Company with Samuel Eastburn, to Long Island, Rhode Island, Boston, etc. — Remarks on the Slave-Trade at Newport; also on Lotteries. — Some Observations on the Island of Nantucket.

FOURTH month, 1760. — Having for some time past felt a sympathy in my mind with Friends eastward, I opened my concern in our Monthly Meeting, and, obtaining a certificate, set forward on the 17th of this month, in company with my beloved friend Samuel Eastburn. We had meetings at Woodbridge, Rahway, and Plainfield, and were at their Monthly Meeting of ministers and elders in Rahway. We labored under some discouragement, but through the invisible power of truth our visit was made reviving to the lowly-minded, with whom I felt a near unity of spirit, being much reduced in my mind. We passed on and visited most of the meetings on Long Island. It was my concern from day to day to say neither more nor less than what the spirit of truth opened in me, being jealous over myself lest I should say anything to make my testimony look agreeable to that mind in people which is not in pure obedience to the cross of Christ.

The spring of the ministry was often low, and

through the subjecting power of truth we were kept low with it; from place to place they whose hearts were truly concerned for the cause of Christ appeared to be comforted in our labors, and though it was in general a time of abasement of the creature, yet through his goodness who is a helper of the poor we had some truly edifying seasons both in meetings and in families where we tarried; sometimes we found strength to labor earnestly with the unfaithful, especially with those whose station in families or in the Society was such that their example had a powerful tendency to open the way for others to go aside from the purity and soundness of the blessed truth.

At Jericho, on Long Island, I wrote home as follows: —

24th of the fourth month, 1760.

DEARLY BELOVED WIFE!

We are favored with health; have been at sundry meetings in East Jersey and on this island. My mind hath been much in an inward, watchful frame since I left thee, greatly desiring that our proceedings may be singly in the will of our Heavenly Father.

As the present appearance of things is not joyous, I have been much shut up from outward cheerfulness, remembering that promise, "Then shalt thou delight thyself in the Lord"; as this from day to day has been revived in my memory, I have considered that his internal presence in our minds is a delight of all others the most pure, and that the honest-hearted not only delight in this, but in the effect of it upon them. He regards the helpless and distressed, and reveals his love to his children under affliction, who delight in beholding his benevolence, and in feeling Divine charity moving in them. Of this I may speak a little, for though since I left you I have often an engaging love and affection towards thee and my daughter, and friends about home, and going out at this time, when sickness is so great amongst you, is a trial upon me; yet I often remember there are many widows and fatherless, many who have poor tutors, many who have evil examples before them, and many whose minds are in captivity; for whose sake my heart is at times moved with compassion, so that I feel my mind resigned to leave you for a season, to exercise that gift which the Lord hath bestowed on me, which though small compared with some, yet in this I rejoice, that I feel love unfeigned towards my fellow-creatures. I recommend you to the Almighty, who I trust, cares for you, and under a sense of his heavenly love remain,

Thy loving husband,

J. W.

We crossed from the east end of Long Island to New London, about thirty miles, in a large open boat; while we were out, the wind rising high, the waves several times beat over us, so that to me it appeared dangerous, but my mind was at that time turned to Him who made and governs the deep, and my life was resigned to him; as he was mercifully pleased to preserve us I had fresh occasion to consider every day as a day lent to me, and felt a renewed engagement to devote my time, and all I had, to him who gave it.

We had five meetings in Narraganset, and went thence to Newport on Rhode Island. Our gracious Father preserved us in an humble dependence on him through deep exercises that were mortifying to the creaturely will. In several families in the country where we lodged, I felt an engagement on my mind to have a conference with them in private, concerning their slaves; and through Divine aid I was favored to give up thereto. Though in this concern I differ from many whose service in travelling is, I believe, greater than mine, yet I do not think hardly of them for omitting it; I do not repine at having so unpleasant a task assigned me, but look with awfulness to him who appoints to his servants their respective employments, and is good to all who serve him sincerely.

We got to Newport in the evening, and on the next day visited two sick persons, with whom we had comfortable sittings, and in the afternoon attended the burial of a Friend. The next day we were at meetings at Newport, in the forenoon and afternoon; the spring of the ministry was opened, and strength was given to declare the Word of Life to the people.

The day following we went on our journey, but

the great number of slaves in these parts, and the continuance of that trade from thence to Guinea, made a deep impression on me, and my cries were often put up to my Heavenly Father in secret, that he would enable me to discharge my duty faithfully in such way as he might be pleased to point out to me.

We took Swansea, Freetown, and Taunton in our way to Boston, where also we had a meeting; our exercise was deep, and the love of truth prevailed, for which I bless the Lord. We went eastward about eighty miles beyond Boston, taking meetings, and were in a good degree preserved in an humble dependence on that arm which drew us out; and though we had some hard labor with the disobedient, by laying things home and close to such as were stout against the truth, yet through the goodness of God we had at times to partake of heavenly comfort with those who were meek, and were often favored to part with Friends in the nearness of true gospel fellowship. We returned to Boston and had another comfortable opportunity with Friends there, and thence rode back a day's journey eastward of Boston. Our guide being a heavy man, and the weather hot, my companion and I expressed our freedom to go on without him, to which he consented, and we respectfully took our leave of him; this we did as believing the journey would have been hard to him and his horse.

In visiting the meetings in those parts we were

measurably baptized into a feeling of the state of the Society, and in bowedness of spirit went to the Yearly Meeting at Newport, where we met with John Storer from England, Elizabeth Shipley, Ann Gaunt, Hannah Foster, and Mercy Redman, from our parts, all ministers of the gospel, of whose company I was glad. Understanding that a large number of slaves had been imported from Africa into that town, and were then on sale by a member of our Society, my appetite failed, and I grew outwardly weak, and had a feeling of the condition of Habakkuk, as thus expressed, "When I heard, my belly trembled, my lips quivered, I trembled in myself, that I might rest in the day of trouble." I had many cogitations, and was sorely distressed. I was desirous that Friends might petition the Legislature to use their endeavors to discourage the future importation of slaves, for I saw that this trade was a great evil, and tended to multiply troubles, and to bring distresses on the people for whose welfare my heart was deeply concerned. But I perceived several difficulties in regard to petitioning, and such was the exercise of my mind that I thought of endeavoring to get an opportunity to speak a few words in the House of Assembly, then sitting in town.

This exercise came upon me in the afternoon on the second day of the Yearly Meeting, and on going to bed I got no sleep till my mind was wholly resigned thereto. In the morning I inquired of a Friend how long the Assembly was likely to continue sitting, who told me it was expected to be prorogued that day or the next As I was desirous to attend the business of the meeting, and perceived the Assembly was likely to separate before the business was over, after considerable exercise, humbly seeking to the Lord for instruction, my mind settled to attend on the business of the meeting; on the last day of which I had prepared a short essay of a petition to be presented to the Legislature, if way opened. And being informed that there were some appointed by that Yearly Meeting to speak with those in authority on cases relating to the Society, I opened my mind to several of them, and showed them the essay I had made, and afterwards I opened the case in the meeting for business, in substance as follows:—

"I have been under a concern for some time on account of the great number of slaves which are imported into this colony. I am aware that it is a tender point to speak to, but apprehend I am not clear in the sight of Heaven without doing so. I have prepared an essay of a petition to be presented to the Legislature, if way open; and what I have to propose to this meeting is that some Friends may be named to withdraw and look over it, and report whether they believe it suitable to be read in the meeting. If they should think well of reading it, it will remain for the meeting to consider whether to take any further notice of it, as a meeting, or not." After a short conference some Friends went out, and, looking over it, expressed their willingness to have it read, which being done, many expressed their unity with the proposal, and some signified that to have the subjects of the petition enlarged upon, and signed out of meeting by such as were free, would be more suitable than to do it there. Though I expected at first that if it was done it would be in that way, yet such was the exercise of my mind that to move it in the hearing of Friends when assembled appeared to me as a duty, for my heart yearned towards the inhabitants of these parts, believing that by this trade there had been an increase of inquietude amongst them, and way had been made for the spreading of a spirit opposite to that meekness and humility which is a sure resting-place for the soul; and that the continuance of this trade would not only render their healing more difficult, but would increase their malady.

Having proceeded thus far, I felt easy to leave the essay amongst Friends, for them to proceed in it as they believed best. And now an exercise revived in my mind in relation to lotteries, which were common in those parts. I had mentioned the subject in a former sitting of this meeting, when arguments were used in favor of Friends being held excused who were only concerned in such lotteries as were agreeable to law. And now, on moving it again, it was opposed as before; but the hearts of some solid Friends appeared to be united to discourage the practice amongst their members, and the matter was zealously handled by some on both sides. In this debate it appeared very clear to me that the spirit of lotteries was a spirit of selfishness, which tended to confuse and darken the understanding, and that pleading for it in our meetings, which were set apart for the Lord's work, was not right. In the heat of zeal, I made reply to what an ancient Friend said, and when I sat down I saw that my words were not enough seasoned with charity. After this I spoke no more on the subject. At length a minute was made, a copy of which was to be sent to their several Quarterly Meetings, inciting Friends to labor to discourage the practice amongst all professing with us.

Some time after this minute was made I remained uneasy with the manner of my speaking to the ancient Friend, and could not see my way clear to conceal my uneasiness, though I was concerned that I might say nothing to weaken the cause in which I had labored. After some close exercise and hearty repentance for not having attended closely to the safe guide, I stood up, and, reciting the passage, acquainted Friends that though I durst not go from what I had said as to the matter, yet I was uneasy with the manner of my speaking, believing milder language would have been better. As this was uttered in some degree of creaturely abasement after a warm debate, it appeared to have a good savor amongst us.

The Yearly Meeting being now over, there yet remained on my mind a secret though heavy exercise, in regard to some leading active members about Newport, who were in the practice of keeping slaves. This I mentioned to two ancient Friends who came out of the country, and proposed to them, if way opened, to have some conversation with those members. One of them and I, having consulted one of the most noted elders who had slaves, he, in a respectful manner, encouraged me to proceed to clear myself of what lay upon me. Near the beginning of the Yearly Meeting, I had had a private conference with this said elder and his wife, concerning their slaves, so that the way seemed clear to me to advise with him about the manner of proceeding. I told him I was free to have a conference with them all together in a private house; or if he thought they would take it unkind to be asked to come together, and to be spoken with in the hearing of one another, I was free to spend some time amongst them, and to visit them all in their own houses. He expressed his liking to the first proposal, not doubting their willingness to come together; and, as I proposed a visit to only ministers, elders, and overseers, he named some others whom he desired might also be present. A careful messenger being wanted to acquaint them in a proper manner, he offered to go to all their houses, to open the matter to them, — and did so. About the eighth hour the next morning we met in the meeting-house chamber, the last-mentioned country Friend, my companion, and John Storer being with us. After a short time of retirement,

I acquainted them with the steps I had taken in procuring that meeting, and opened the concern I was under, and we then proceeded to a free conference upon the subject. My exercise was heavy, and I was deeply bowed in spirit before the Lord, who was pleased to favor with the seasoning virtue of truth, which wrought a tenderness amongst us; and the subject was mutually handled in a calm and peaceable spirit. At length, feeling my mind released from the burden which I had been under, I took my leave of them in a good degree of satisfaction; and by the tenderness they manifested in regard to the practice, and the concern several of them expressed in relation to the manner of disposing of their negroes after their decease, I believed that a good exercise was spreading amongst them; and I am humbly thankful to God, who supported my mind and preserved me in a good degree of resignation through these trials.

Thou who sometimes travellest in the work of the ministry, and art made very welcome by thy friends, seest many tokens of their satisfaction in having thee for their guest. It is good for thee to dwell deep, that thou mayest feel and understand the spirits of people. If we believe truth points towards a conference on some subjects in a private way, it is needful for us to take heed that their kindness, their freedom, and affability do not hinder us from the Lord's work. I have experienced that, in the midst of kindness and smooth conduct, to speak close and home to them who entertain us, on points that relate to outward interest, is hard labor. Sometimes, when I have felt truth lead towards it, I have found myself disqualified by a superficial friendship; and as the sense thereof hath abased me, and my cries have been to the Lord, so I have been humbled and made content to appear weak, or as a fool for his sake; and thus a door hath been opened to enter upon it. To attempt to do the Lord's work in our own way, and to speak of that which is the burden of the Word, in a way easy to the natural part, doth not reach the bottom of the disorder. To see the failings of our friends, and think hard of them, without opening that which we ought to open, and still carry a face of friendship, tends to undermine the foundation of true unity. The office of a minister of Christ is weighty. And they who now go forth as watchmen have need to be steadily on their guard against the snares of prosperity and an outside friendship.

After the Yearly Meeting we were at meetings at Newtown, Cushnet, Long Plain, Rochester, and Dartmouth. From thence we sailed for Nantucket, in company with Ann Gaunt, Mercy Redman, and several other Friends. The wind being slack we only reached Tarpawling Cove the first day; where, going on shore, we found room in a public-house, and beds for a few of us, — the rest slept on the floor. We went on board again about break of day, and though the wind was small, we were favored to come within about four miles of Nantucket; and then about ten of us got into our boat and rowed to the harbor before dark; a large boat went off and brought in the rest of the passengers about midnight. The next day but one was their Yearly Meeting, which held four days, the last of which was their Monthly Meeting for business. We had a laborious time amongst them; our minds were closely exercised, and I believe it was a time of great searching of heart. The longer I was on the Island the more I became sensible that there was a considerable number of valuable Friends there, though an evil spirit, tending to strife, had been at work amongst them. I was cautious of making any visits except as my mind was particularly drawn to them; and in that way we had some sittings in Friends' houses, where the heavenly wing was at times spread over us, to our mutual comfort. My beloved companion had very acceptable service on this island.

When meeting was over we all agreed to sail the next day if the weather was suitable and we were well; and being called up the latter part of the night, about fifty of us went on board a vessel; but, the wind changing, the seamen thought best to stay in the harbor till it altered, so we returned on shore. Feeling clear as to any further visits, I spent my time in my chamber, chiefly alone; and after some hours, my heart being filled with the spirit of supplication, my prayers and tears were poured out before my Heavenly Father for his help and instruction in the manifold difficulties which attended me in life. While I was waiting upon the Lord, there came a messenger from the women Friends who lodged at another house, desiring to confer with us about appointing a meeting, which to me appeared weighty, as we had been at so many before; but after a short conference, and advising with some elderly Friends, a meeting was appointed, in which the Friend who first moved it, and who had been much shut up before, was largely opened in the love of the gospel. The next morning about break of day going again on board the vessel, we reached Falmouth on the Main before night, where our horses being brought, we proceeded towards Sandwich Quarterly Meeting.

Being two days in going to Nantucket, and having been there once before, I observed many shoals in their bay, which make sailing more dangerous, especially in stormy nights; also, that a great shoal, which encloses their harbor, prevents the entrance of sloops except when the tide is up. Waiting without for the rising of the tide is sometimes hazardous in storms, and by waiting within they sometimes miss a fair wind. I took notice that there was on that small island a great number of inhabitants, and the soil not very fertile, the timber being so gone that for vessels, fences, and firewood, they depend chiefly on buying from the Main, for the cost whereof, with most of their other expenses, they depend principally upon the whale fishery. I considered that as towns grew larger, and lands near navigable waters were more cleared, it would require more labor to get timber and wood. I understood that the whales, being much hunted and sometimes wounded and not killed, grow more shy and difficult to come at. I considered that the formation of the earth, the seas, the islands, bays, and rivers, the motions of the winds, and great waters, which cause bars and shoals in particular places, were all the works of Him who is perfect wisdom and goodness; and as people attend to his heavenly instruction, and put their trust in him, he provides for them in all parts where he gives them a being; and as in this visit to these people I felt a strong desire for their firm establishment on the sure foundation, besides what was said more publicly, I was concerned to speak with the women Friends in their Monthly Meeting of business, many being present, and in the fresh spring of pure love to open before them the advantage, both inwardly and outwardly, of attending singly to the pure guidance of the Holy Spirit, and therein to educate their children in true humility and the disuse of all superfluities. I reminded them of the difficulties their husbands and sons were frequently exposed to at sea, and that the more plain and simple their way of living was the less need there would be of running great hazards to support them. I also encouraged the young women to continue their neat, decent way of attending themselves on the affairs of the house; showing, as the way opened, that where people were truly humble, used themselves to business, and were content with a plain way of life, they had ever had more true peace and calmness of mind than they who, aspiring to greatness and outward show, have grasped hard for an income to support themselves therein. And as I observed they had few or no slaves, I had to encourage them to be content without them, making mention of the numerous troubles and vexations which frequently attended the minds of people who depend on slaves to do their labor.

We attended the Quarterly Meeting at Sandwich, in company with Ann Gaunt and Mercy Redman, which was preceded by a Monthly Meeting, and in the whole held three days. We were in various ways exercised amongst them, in gospel love, according to the several gifts bestowed on us, and were at times overshadowed with the virtue of truth, to the comfort of the sincere and stirring up of the negligent. Here we parted with Ann and Mercy, and went to Rhode Island, taking one meeting in our way, which was a satisfactory time. Reaching Newport the evening before their Quarterly Meeting, we attended it, and after that had a meeting with our young people, separated from those of other societies. We went through much labor in this town; and now, in taking leave of it, though I felt close inward exercise to the last, I found inward peace, and was in some degree comforted in a belief that a good number remain in that place who retain a sense of truth, and that there are some young people attentive to the voice of the Heavenly Shepherd. The last meeting, in which Friends from the several parts of the quarter came together, was a select meeting, and through the renewed manifestation of the Father's love the hearts of the sincere were united together.

The poverty of spirit and inward weakness, with which I was much tried the fore part of this journey, has of late appeared to me a dispensation of kindness. Appointing meetings never appeared more weighty to me, and I was led into a deep search, whether in all things my mind was resigned to the will of God ; often querying with myself what should be the cause of such inward poverty, and greatly desiring that no secret reserve in my heart might hinder my access to the Divine fountain. In these humbling times I was made watchful, and excited to attend to the secret movings of the heavenly principle in my mind, which prepared the way to some duties, that, in more easy and prosperous times as to the outward, I believe I should have been in danger of omitting.

From Newport we went to Greenwich, Shanticut, and Warwick, and were helped to labor amongst Friends in the love of our gracious Redeemer. Afterwards, accompanied by our friend John Casey from Newport, we rode through Connecticut to Oblong, visited the meetings in those parts, and thence proceeded to the Quarterly Meeting at Ryewoods. Through the gracious extendings of Divine help, we had some seasoning opportunities in those places. We also visited Friends at New York and Flushing, and thence to Rahway Here our roads parting, I took leave of my beloved companion and true yokemate Samuel Eastburn, and reached home the 10th of eighth month, where I found my family well. For the favors and protection of the Lord, both inward and outward, extended to me in this journey, my heart is humbled in grateful acknowledgments, and I find renewed desires to dwell and walk in resignedness before him.

CHAPTER VIII.

1761, 1762.

Visits Pennsylvania, Shrewsbury, and Squan. — Publishes the Second Part of his Considerations on keeping Negroes. — The Grounds of his appearing in some Respects singular in his Dress. — Visit to the Families of Friends of Ancocas and Mount Holly Meetings. — Visits to the Indians at Wehaloosing on the River Susquehanna.

HAVING felt my mind drawn towards a visit to a few meetings in Pennsylvania, I was very desirous to be rightly instructed as to the time of setting off. On the 10th of fifth month, 1761, being the first day of the week, I went to Haddonfield Meeting, concluding to seek for heavenly instruction, and come home, or go on, as I might then believe best for me, and there through the springing up of pure love I felt encouragement, and so crossed the river. In this visit I was at two quarterly and three monthly meetings, and in the love of truth I felt my way open to labor with some noted Friends who kept negroes. As I was favored to keep to the root, and endeavor to discharge what I believed was required of me, I found inward peace therein, from time to time, and thankfulness of heart to the Lord, who was graciously pleased to be a guide to me.

Eighth month, 1761. — Having felt drawings in

my mind to visit Friends in and about Shrewsbury, I went there, and was at their Monthly Meeting, and their first-day meeting; I had also a meeting at Squan, and another at Squanquam, and, as way opened, had conversation with some noted Friends concerning their slaves. I returned home in a thankful sense of the goodness of the Lord.

From the concern I felt growing in me for some years, I wrote part the second of a work entitled "Considerations on keeping Negroes," which was printed this year, 1762. When the overseers of the press had done with it, they offered to get a number printed, to be paid for out of the Yearly Meeting's stock, to be given away; but I being most easy to publish it at my own expense, and offering my reasons, they appeared satisfied.

This stock is the contribution of the members of our religious society in general, among whom are some who keep negroes, and, being inclined to continue them in slavery, are not likely to be satisfied with such books being spread among a people, especially at their own expense, many of whose slaves are taught to read, and such, receiving them as a gift, often conceal them. But as they who make a purchase generally buy that which they have a mind for, I believed it best to sell them, expecting by that means they would more generally be read with attention. Advertisements were signed by order of the overseers of the press, and directed to be read in the Monthly Meetings of business within our own Yearly Meeting, informing where the books were, and that the price was no more than the cost of printing and binding them. Many were taken off in our parts; some I sent to Virginia, some to New York, some to my acquaintance at Newport, and some I kept, intending to give part of them away, where there appeared a prospect of service.

In my youth I was used to hard labor, and though I was middling healthy, yet my nature was not fitted to endure so much as many others. Being often weary, I was prepared to sympathize with those whose circumstances in life, as free men, required constant labor to answer the demands of their creditors, as well as with others under oppression. In the uneasiness of body which I have many times felt by too much labor, not as a forced but a voluntary oppression, I have often been excited to think on the original cause of that oppression which is imposed on many in the world. The latter part of the time wherein I labored on our plantation, my heart, through the fresh visitations of heavenly love, being often tender, and my leisure time being frequently spent in reading the life and doctrines of our blessed Redeemer, the account of the sufferings of martyrs, and the history of the first rise of our Society, a belief was gradually settled in my mind, that if such as had great estates generally lived in that humility and plainness which belong to a Christian life, and laid much easier rents and interests on their lands and moneys, and thus led the way to a right use of things, so great a number of people might be employed in things useful, that labor both for men and other creatures would need to be no more than an agreeable employ, and divers branches of business, which serve chiefly to please the natural inclinations of our minds, and which at present seem necessary to circulate that wealth which some gather, might, in this way of pure wisdom, be discontinued. As I have thus considered these things, a query at times hath arisen: Do I, in all my proceedings, keep to that use of things which is agreeable to universal righteousness? And then there hath some degree of sadness at times come over me, because I accustomed myself to some things which have occasioned more labor than I believe Divine wisdom intended for us.

From my early acquaintance with truth I have often felt an inward distress, occasioned by the striving of a spirit in me against the operation of the heavenly principle; and in this state I have been affected with a sense of my own wretchedness, and in a mourning condition have felt earnest longings for that Divine help which brings the soul into true liberty. Sometimes, on retiring into private places, the spirit of supplication hath been given me, and under a heavenly covering I have asked my gracious Father to give me a heart in all things resigned to the direction of his wisdom; in uttering language like this, the thought of my wearing hats and garments dyed with a dye hurtful to them, has made lasting impression on me.

In visiting people of note in the Society who had

slaves, and laboring with them in brotherly love on that account, I have seen, and the sight has affected me, that a conformity to some customs distinguishable from pure wisdom has entangled many, and that the desire of gain to support these customs has greatly opposed the work of truth. Sometimes when the prospect of the work before me has been such that in bowedness of spirit I have been drawn into retired places, and have besought the Lord with tears that he would take me wholly under his direction, and show me the way in which I ought to walk, it hath revived with strength of conviction that if I would be his faithful servant I must in all things attend to his wisdom, and be teachable, and so cease from all customs contrary thereto, however used among religious people.

As he is the perfection of power, of wisdom, and of goodness, so I believe he hath provided that so much labor shall be necessary for men's support in this world as would, being rightly divided, be a suitable employment of their time; and that we cannot go into superfluities, or grasp after wealth in a way contrary to his wisdom, without having connection with some degree of oppression, and with that spirit which leads to self-exaltation and strife, and which frequently brings calamities on countries by parties contending about their claims.

Being thus fully convinced, and feeling an increasing desire to live in the spirit of peace, I have often been sorrowfully affected with thinking on the unquiet spirit in which wars are generally carried on, and with the miseries of many of my fellow-creatures engaged therein; some suddenly destroyed; some wounded, and after much pain remaining cripples; some deprived of all their outward substance and reduced to want; and some carried into captivity. Thinking often on these things, the use of hats and garments dyed with a dye hurtful to them, and wearing more clothes in summer than are useful, grew more uneasy to me, believing them to be customs which have not their foundation in pure wisdom. The apprehension of being singular from my beloved friends was a strait upon me, and thus I continued in the use of some things contrary to my judgment.

On the 31st of fifth month, 1761, I was taken ill of a fever, and after it had continued near a week I was in great distress of body. One day there was a cry raised in me that I might understand the cause of my affliction, and improve under it, and my conformity to some customs which I believed were not right was brought to my remembrance. In the continuance of this exercise I felt all the powers in me yield themselves up into the hands of Him who gave me being, and was made thankful that he had taken hold of me by his chastisements. Feeling the necessity of further purifying, there was now no desire in me for health until the design of my correction was answered. Thus I lay in abasement and brokenness of spirit, and as I felt a sinking down into a calm resignation, so I felt, as in an instant, an inward healing in my nature; and from that time forward I grew better.

Though my mind was thus settled in relation to hurtful dyes, I felt easy to wear my garments heretofore made, and continued to do so about nine months. Then I thought of getting a hat the natural color of the fur, but the apprehension of being looked upon as one affecting singularity felt uneasy to me. Here I had occasion to consider that things, though small in themselves, being clearly enjoined by Divine authority, become great things to us; and I trusted that the Lord would support me in the trials that might attend singularity, so long as singularity was only for his sake. On this account I was under close exercise of mind in the time of our General Spring Meeting, 1762, greatly desiring to be rightly directed; when, being deeply bowed in spirit before the Lord, I was made willing to submit to what I apprehended was required of me, and when I returned home got a hat of the natural color of the fur.

In attending meetings this singularity was a trial to me, and more especially at this time, as white hats were used by some who were fond of following the changeable modes of dress, and as some Friends who knew not from what motives I wore it grew shy of me, I felt my way for a time shut up in the exercise of the ministry. In this condition, my mind being turned toward my Heavenly Father with fervent cries that I might be preserved to walk before him in the meekness of wisdom, my heart was often tender in meetings, and I felt an inward consolation which to me was very precious under these difficulties.

I had several dyed garments fit for use which I believed it best to wear till I had occasion for new ones. Some Friends were apprehensive that my wearing such a hat savored of an affected singularity; those who spoke with me in a friendly way I generally informed, in a few words, that I believed my wearing it was not in my own will. I had at times been sensible that a superficial friendship had been dangerous to me; and many Friends being now uneasy with me, I had an inclination to acquaint some with the manner of my being led into these things; yet upon a deeper thought I was for a time most easy to omit it, believing the present dispensation was profitable, and trusting that if I kept my place the Lord in his own time would open the hearts of Friends towards me. I have since had cause to admire his goodness and loving-kindness in leading about and instructing me, and in opening and enlarging my heart in some of our meetings.

In the eleventh month this year, feeling an engagement of mind to visit some families in Mansfield, I joined my beloved friend Benjamin Jones, and we spent a few days together in that service. In the second month, 1763, I joined, in company with Elizabeth Smith and Mary Noble, in a visit to the families of Friends at Ancocas. In both these visits, through the baptizing power of truth, the sincere laborers were often comforted, and the hearts of Friends opened to receive us. In the fourth month following, I accompanied some Friends in a visit to the families of Friends in Mount Holly; during this visit my mind was often drawn into an inward awfulness, wherein strong desires were raised for the everlasting welfare of my fellow-creatures, and through the kindness of our Heavenly Father our hearts were at times enlarged, and Friends were invited, in the flowings of Divine love, to attend to that which would settle them on the sure foundation.

Having for many years felt love in my heart towards the natives of this land who dwell far back in the wilderness, whose ancestors were formerly the owners and possessors of the land where we dwell, and who for a small consideration assigned their inheritance to us, and being at Philadelphia in the 8th month, 1761, on a visit to some Friends who had slaves, I fell in company with some of those natives who lived on the east branch of the river Susquehanna, at an Indian town called Wehaloosing, two hundred miles from Philadelphia. In conversation with them by an interpreter, as also by observations on their countenances and conduct, I believed some of them were measurably acquainted with that Divine power which subjects the rough and froward will of the creature. At times I felt inward drawings towards a visit to that place, which I mentioned to none except my dear wife until it came to some ripeness. In the winter of 1762 I laid my prospects before my friends at our Monthly and Quarterly, and afterwards at our General Spring Meeting; and having the unity of Friends, and being thoughtful about an Indian pilot, there came a man and three women from a little beyond that town to Philadelphia on business. Being informed thereof by letter, I met them in town in the 5th month, 1763; and after some conversation, finding they were sober people, I, with the concurrence of Friends in that place, agreed to join them as companions in their return, and we appointed to meet at Samuel Foulk's, at Richland, in Bucks County, on the 7th of sixth month. Now, as this visit felt weighty, and was performed at a time when travelling appeared perilous, so the dispensations of Divine Providence in preparing my mind for it have been memorable, and I believe it good for me to give some account thereof.

After I had given up to go, the thoughts of the journey were often attended with unusual sadness; at which times my heart was frequently turned to the Lord with inward breathings for his heavenly support, that I might not fail to follow him wheresoever he might lead me. Being at our youth's meeting at Chesterfield, about a week before the time I expected to set off, I was there led to speak on that prayer of our Redeemer to the Father: "I pray not that thou shouldest take them out of the world, but that thou shouldest keep them from the evil." And in attending to the pure openings of truth, I had to mention what he elsewhere said to his Father: "I know that thou hearest me at all times"; so, as some of his followers kept their places, and as his prayer was granted, it followed necessarily that they were kept from evil; and as some of those met with great hardships and afflictions in this world, and at last suffered death by cruel men, so it appears that whatsoever befalls men while they live in pure obedience to God certainly works for their good, and may not be considered an evil as it relates to them. As I spake on this subject my heart was much tendered, and great awfulness came over me. On the first day of the week, being at our own afternoon meeting, and my heart being enlarged in love, I was led to speak on the care and protection of the Lord over his people, and to make mention of that passage where a band of Syrians, who were endeavoring to take captive the prophet, were disappointed; and how the Psalmist said, "The angel of the Lord encampeth round about them that fear him." Thus, in true love and tenderness, I parted from Friends, expecting the next morning to proceed on my journey. Being weary I went early to bed. After I had been asleep a short time I was awoke by a man calling at my door, and inviting me to meet some Friends at a public-house in our town, who came from Philadelphia so late that Friends were generally gone to bed. These Friends informed me that an express had arrived the last morning from Pittsburg, and brought news that the Indians had taken a fort from the English westward, and had slain and scalped some English people near the said Pittsburg, and in divers places. Some elderly Friends in Philadelphia, knowing the time of my intending to set off, had conferred together, and thought good to inform me of these things before I left home, that I might consider them and proceed as I believed best. Going to bed again, I told not my wife till morning. My heart was turned to the Lord for his heavenly instruction; and it was an humbling time to me. When I told my dear wife, she appeared to be deeply concerned about it; but in a few hours' time my mind became settled in a belief that it was my duty to proceed on my journey, and she bore it with a good degree of resignation. In this conflict of spirit there were great searchings of heart and strong cries to the Lord, that no motion might in the least degree be attended to but that of the pure spirit of truth.

The subjects before mentioned, on which I had so lately spoken in public, were now fresh before me, and I was brought inwardly to commit myself to the Lord, to be disposed of as he saw best. I took leave of my family and neighbors in much bowedness of spirit, and went to our Monthly Meeting at Burlington. After taking leave of Friends there, I crossed the river, accompanied by my friends Israel and John Pemberton; and parting the next morning with Israel, John bore me company to Samuel Foulk's, where I met the before-mentioned Indians; and we were glad to see each other. Here my friend Benjamin Parvin met me, and proposed joining me as a companion, — we had before exchanged some letters on the subject,—and now I had a sharp trial on his account; for, as the journey appeared perilous, I thought if he went chiefly to bear me company, and we should be taken captive, my having been the means of drawing him into these difficulties would add to my own afflictions; so I told him my mind freely, and let him know that I was resigned to go alone; but after all, if he really believed it to be his duty to go on, I believed his company would be very comfortable to me. It was, indeed, a time of deep exercise, and Benjamin appeared to be so fastened to the visit that be could not be easy to leave me; so we went on, accompanied by our friends John Pemberton and William Lightfoot of Pikeland. We lodged at Bethlehem, and there parting with John, William and we went forward on the 9th of the sixth month, and got lodging on the floor of a house, about five miles from Fort Allen. Here we parted with William, and at this place we met with an Indian trader lately come from Wyoming. In conversation with him, I perceived that many white people often sell rum to the Indians, which I believe is a great evil. In the first place, they are thereby deprived of the use of reason, and, their spirits being violently agitated, quarrels often arise which end in mischief, and the bitterness and resentment occasioned hereby are frequently of long continuance. Again, their skins and furs, gotten through much fatigue and hard travels in hunting, with which they intended to buy clothing, they often sell at a low rate for more rum, when they become intoxicated; and afterward, when they suffer for want of the necessaries of life, are angry with those who, for the sake of gain, took advantage of their weakness. Their chiefs have often complained of this in their treaties with the English. Where cunning people pass counterfeits and impose on others that which is good for nothing, it is considered as wickedness; but for the sake of gain to sell that which we know does people harm, and which often works their ruin, manifests a hardened and corrupt heart, and is an evil which demands the care of all true lovers of virtue to suppress. While my mind this evening was thus employed, I also remembered that the people on the frontiers, among whom this evil is too common, are often poor; and that they venture to the outside of a colony in order to live more independently of the wealthy, who often set high rents on their land. I was renewedly confirmed in a belief, that if all our inhabitants lived according to sound wisdom, laboring to promote universal love and righteousness, and ceased from every inordinate desire after wealth, and from all customs which are tinctured with luxury, the way would be easy for our inhabitants, though they might be much more numerous than at present, to live comfortably on honest employments, without the temptation they are so often under of being drawn into schemes to make settlements on lands which have not been purchased of the Indians, or of applying to that wicked practice of selling rum to them.

Tenth of sixth month. — We set out early this morning and crossed the western branch of Delaware, called the Great Lehie, near Fort Allen. The water being high, we went over in a canoe. Here we met an Indian, had friendly conversation with him, and gave him some biscuit; and he, having killed a deer, gave some of it to the Indians with us. After travelling some miles, we met several Indian men and women with a cow and horse, and some household goods, who were lately come from their dwelling at Wyoming, and were going to settle at another place. We made them some small presents, and, as some of them understood English, I told them my motive for coming into their country, with which they appeared satisfied. One of our guides talking awhile with an ancient woman concerning us, the poor old woman came to my companion and me and took her leave of us with an appearance of sincere affection. We pitched our tent near the banks of the same river, having labored hard in crossing some of those mountains called the Blue Ridge. The roughness of the stones and the cavities between them, with the steepness of the hills, made it appear dangerous. But we were preserved in safety, through the kindness of Him whose works in these mountainous deserts appeared awful, and towards whom my heart was turned during this day's travel.

Near our tent, on the sides of large trees peeled for that purpose, were various representations of men going to and returning from the wars, and of some being killed in battle. This was a path heretofore used by warriors, and as I walked about viewing those Indian histories, which were painted mostly in red or black, and thinking on the innumerable afflictions which the proud, fierce spirit produceth in the world, also on the toils and fatigues of warriors in travelling over mountains and deserts; on their miseries and distresses when far from home and wounded by their enemies; of their bruises and great weariness in chasing one another over the rocks and mountains; of the restless, unquiet state of mind of those who live in this spirit, and of the hatred which mutually grows up in the minds of their children, — the desire to cherish the spirit of love and peace among these people arose very fresh in me. This was the first night that we lodged in the woods, and being wet with travelling in the rain, as were also our blankets, the ground, our tent, and the bushes under which we purposed to lay, all looked discouraging; but I believed that it was the Lord who had thus far brought me forward, and that he would dispose of me as he saw good, and so I felt easy. We kindled a fire, with our tent open to it, then laid some bushes next the ground, and put our blankets upon them for our bed, and, lying down, got some sleep. In the morning, feeling a little unwell, I went into the river; the water was cold, but soon after I felt fresh and well. About eight o'clock we set forward and crossed a high mountain supposed to be upward of four miles over, the north side being the steepest. About noon we were overtaken by one of the Moravian brethren going to Wehaloosing, and an Indian man with him who could talk English; and we being together while our horses ate grass had some friendly conversation; but they, travelling faster than we, soon left us. This Moravian, I understood, had this spring spent some time at Wehaloosing, and was invited by some of the Indians to come again.

Twelfth of sixth month being the first of the week and a rainy day, we continued in our tent, and I was led to think on the nature of the exercise which hath attended me. Love was the first motion, and thence a concern arose to spend some time with the Indians, that I might feel and understand their life and the spirit they live in, if haply I might receive some instruction from them, or they might be in any degree helped forward by my following the leadings of truth among them; and as it pleased the Lord to make way for my going at a time when the troubles of war were increasing, and when, by reason of much wet weather, travelling was more difficult than usual at that season, I looked upon it as a more favorable opportunity to season my mind, and to bring me into a nearer sympathy with them. As mine eye was to the great Father of Mercies, humbly desiring to learn his will concerning me, I was made quiet and content.

Our guide's horse strayed, though hoppled, in the night, and after searching some time for him his footsteps were discovered in the path going back, whereupon my kind companion went off in the rain, and after about seven hours returned with him. Here we lodged again, tying up our horses before we went to bed, and loosing them to feed about break of day.

Thirteenth of sixth month. — The sun appearing, we set forward, and as I rode over the barren hills my meditations were on the alterations in the circumstances of the natives of this land since the coming in of the English. The lands near the sea are conveniently situated for fishing; the lands near the rivers, where the tides flow, and some above, are in many places fertile, and not mountainous, while the changing of the tides makes passing up and down easy with any kind of traffic. The natives have in some places, for trifling considerations, sold their inheritance so favorably situated, and in other places have been driven back by superior force; their way of clothing themselves is also altered from what it was, and they being far removed from us have to pass over mountains, swamps, and barren deserts, so that travelling is very troublesome in bringing their skins and furs to trade with us. By the extension of English settlements, and partly by the increase of English hunters, the wild beasts on which the natives chiefly depend for subsistence are not so plentiful as they were, and people too often, for the sake of gain, induce them to waste their skins and furs in purchasing a liquor which tends to the ruin of them and their families.

My own will and desires were now very much broken, and my heart was with much earnestness turned to the Lord, to whom alone I looked for help in the dangers before me. I had a prospect of the English along the coast for upwards of nine hundred miles, where I travelled, and their favorable situation and the difficulties attending the natives as well as the negroes in many places were open before me. A weighty and heavenly care came over my mind, and love filled my heart towards all mankind, in which I felt a strong engagement that we might be obedient to the Lord while in tender mercy he is yet calling to us, and that we might so attend to pure universal righteousness as to give no just cause of offence to the gentiles, who do not profess Christianity, whether they be the blacks from Africa, or the native inhabitants of this continent. Here I was led into a close and laborious inquiry whether I, as an individual, kept clear from all things which tended to stir up or were connected with wars, either in this land or in Africa; my heart was deeply concerned that in future I might in all things keep steadily to the pure truth, and live and walk in the plainness and simplicity of a sincere follower of Christ. In this lonely journey I did greatly bewail the spreading of a wrong spirit, believing that the prosperous, convenient situation of the English would require a constant attention in us to Divine love and wisdom, in order to their being guided and supported in a way answerable to the will of that good, gracious, and Almighty Being, who hath an equal regard to all mankind. And here luxury and covetousness, with the numerous oppressions and other evils attending them, appeared very afflicting to me, and I felt in that which is immutable that the seeds of great calamity and desolation are sown and growing fast on this continent. Nor have I words sufficient to set forth the longing I then felt, that we who are placed along the coast, and have tasted the love and goodness of God, might arise in the strength thereof, and like faithful messengers labor to check the growth of these seeds, that they may not ripen to the ruin of our posterity.

On reaching the Indian settlement at Wyoming, we were told that an Indian runner had been at that place a day or two before us, and brought news of the Indians having taken an English fort westward, and destroyed the people, and that they were endeavoring to take another; also that another Indian runner came there about the middle of the previous night from a town about ten miles from Wehaloosing, and brought the news that some Indian warriors from distant parts came to that town with two English scalps, and told the people that it was war with the English.

Our guides took us to the house of a very ancient man. Soon after we had put in our baggage there came a man from another Indian house some distance off. Perceiving there was a man near the door I went out; the man had a tomahawk wrapped under his match-coat out of sight. As

I approached him he took it in his hand; I went forward, and, speaking to him in a friendly way, perceived he understood some English. My companion joining me, we had some talk with him concerning the nature of our visit in these parts; he then went into the house with us, and, talking with our guides, soon appeared friendly, sat down and smoked his pipe. Though taking his hatchet in his hand at the instant I drew near to him had a disagreeable appearance, I believe he had no other intent than to be in readiness in case any violence were offered to him.

On hearing the news brought by these Indian runners, and being told by the Indians where we lodged, that the Indians about Wyoming expected in a few days to move to some larger towns, I thought, to all outward appearance, it would be dangerous travelling at this time. After a hard day's journey I was brought into a painful exercise at night, in which I had to trace back and view the steps I had taken from my first moving in the visit; and though I had to bewail some weakness which at times had attended me, yet I could not find that I had ever given way to wilful disobedience. Believing I had, under a sense of duty, come thus far, I was now earnest in spirit, beseeching the Lord to show me what I ought to do. In this great distress I grew jealous of myself, lest the desire of reputation as a man firmly settled to persevere through dangers, or the fear of disgrace from my returning without performing the visit, might have some place in me. Full of these thoughts, I lay great part of the night, while my beloved companion slept by me, till the Lord, my gracious Father, who saw the conflicts of my soul, was pleased to give quietness. Then I was again strengthened to commit my life, and all things relating thereto, into his heavenly hands, and got a little sleep towards day.

Fourteenth of sixth month. — We sought out and visited all the Indians hereabouts that we could meet with, in number about twenty. They were chiefly in one place, about a mile from where we lodged. I expressed to them the care I had on my mind for their good, and told them that true love had made me willing thus to leave my family to come and see the Indians and speak with them in their houses. Some of them appeared kind and friendly. After taking leave of them, we went up the river Susquehanna about three miles, to the house of an Indian called Jacob January. He had killed his hog, and the women were making store of bread and preparing to move up the river. Here our pilots had left their canoe when they came down in the spring, and lying dry it had become leaky. This detained us some hours, so that we had a good deal of friendly conversation with the family; and, eating dinner with them, we made them some small presents. Then putting our baggage into the canoe, some of them pushed slowly up the stream, and the rest of us rode our horses. We swam them over a creek called Lahawahamunk, and pitched our tent above it in the evening. In a sense of God's goodness in helping me in my distress, sustaining me under trials, and inclining my heart to trust in him, I lay down in an humble, bowed frame of mind, and had a comfortable night's lodging.

Fifteenth of sixth month. — We proceeded forward till the afternoon, when, a storm appearing, we met our canoe at an appointed place and stayed all night, the rain continuing so heavy that it beat through our tent and wet both us and our baggage. The next day we found abundance of trees blown down by the storm yesterday, and had occasion reverently to consider the kind dealings of the Lord, who provided a safe place for us in a valley while this storm continued. We were much hindered by the trees which had fallen across our path, and in some swamps our way was so stopped that we got through with extreme difficulty. I had this day often to consider myself as a sojourner in this world. A belief in the all-sufficiency of God to support his people in their pilgrimage felt comfortable to me, and I was industriously employed to get to a state of perfect resignation.

We seldom saw our canoe but at appointed places, by reason of the path going off from the river. This afternoon Job Chilaway, an Indian from Wehaloosing, who talks good English and is acquainted with several people in and about Philadelphia, met our people on the river. Understanding where we expected to lodge, he pushed back about six miles, and came to us after night;

and in a while our own canoe arrived, it being hard work pushing up the stream. Job told us that an Indian came in haste to their town yesterday and told them that three warriors from a distance lodged in a town above Wehaloosing a few nights past, and that these three men were going against the English at Juniata. Job was going down the river to the province-store at Shamokin. Though I was so far favored with health as to continue travelling, yet, through the various difficulties in our journey, and the different way of living from which I had been used to, I grew sick. The news of these warriors being on their march so near us, and not knowing whether we might not fall in with them, was a fresh trial of my faith; and though, through the strength of Divine love, I had several times been enabled to commit myself to the Divine disposal, I still found the want of a renewal of my strength, that I might be able to persevere therein; and my cries for help were put up to the Lord, who, in great mercy, gave me a resigned heart, in which I found quietness.

Parting from Job Chilaway on the 17th, we went on and reached Wehaloosing about the middle of the afternoon. The first Indian that we saw was a woman of a modest countenance, with a Bible, who spake first to our guide, and then with an harmonious voice expressed her gladness at seeing us, having before heard of our coming. By the direction of our guide we sat down on a log while he went to the town to tell the people we were come

My companion and I, sitting thus together in a deep inward stillness, the poor woman came and sat near us; and, great awfulness coming over us, we rejoiced in a sense of God's love manifested to our poor souls. After a while we heard a conch-shell blow several times, and then came John Curtis and another Indian man, who kindly invited us into a house near the town, where we found about sixty people sitting in silence. After sitting with them a short time I stood up, and in some tenderness of spirit acquainted them, in a few short sentences, with the nature of my visit, and that a concern for their good had made me willing to come thus far to see them; which some of them understanding interpreted to the others, and there appeared gladness among them. I then showed them my certificate, which was explained to them; and the Moravian who overtook us on the way, being now here, bade me welcome. But the Indians knowing that this Moravian and I were of different religious societies, and as some of their people had encouraged him to come and stay awhile with them, they were, I believe, concerned that there might be no jarring or discord in their meetings; and having, I suppose, conferred together, they acquainted me that the people, at my request, would at any time come together and hold meetings. They also told me that they expected the Moravian would speak in their settled meetings, which are commonly held in the morning and near evening. So finding liberty in my heart to speak to the Moravian, I told him of the care I felt on my mind for the good of these people, and my belief that no ill effects would follow if I sometimes spake in their meetings when love engaged me thereto, without calling them together at times when they did not meet of course. He expressed his good-will towards my speaking at any time all that I found in my heart to say.

On the evening of the 18th I was at their meeting, where pure gospel love was felt, to the tendering of some of our hearts. The interpreters endeavored to acquaint the people with what I said, in short sentences, but found some difficulty, as none of them were quite perfect in the English and Delaware tongues, so they helped one another, and we labored along, Divine love attending. Afterwards, feeling my mind covered with the spirit of prayer, I told the interpreters that I found it in my heart to pray to God, and believed, if I prayed aright, he would hear me; and I expressed my willingness for them to omit interpreting; so our meeting ended with a degree of Divine Love. Before the people went out, I observed Papunehang (the man who had been zealous in laboring for a reformation in that town, being then very tender) speaking to one of the interpreters, and I was afterwards told that he said in substance as follows: "I love to feel where words come from."

Nineteenth of sixth month and first of the week. — This morning the Indian who came with the Moravian, being also a member of that society, prayed in the meeting, and then the Moravian spake a short time to the people. In the afternoon, my heart being filled with a heavenly care for their good, I spake to them awhile by interpreters; but none of them being perfect in the work, and I feeling the current of love run strong, told the interpreters that I believed some of the people would understand me, and so I proceeded without them; and I believe the Holy Ghost wrought on some hearts to edification where all the words were not understood. I looked upon it as a time of Divine favor, and my heart was tendered and truly thankful before the Lord. After I sat down, one of the interpreters seemed spirited to give the Indians the substance of what I said.

Before our first meeting this morning, I was led to meditate on the manifold difficulties of these Indians who, by the permission of the Six Nations, dwell in these parts. A near sympathy with them was raised in me, and, my heart being enlarged in the love of Christ, I thought that the affectionate care of a good man for his only brother in affliction does not exceed what I then felt for that people. I came to this place through much trouble; and though through the mercies of God I believed that if I died in the journey it would be well with me, yet the thoughts of falling into the hands of Indian warriors were, in times of weakness, afflicting to me; and being of a tender constitution of body, the thoughts of captivity among them were also grievous; supposing that as they were strong and hardy they might demand service of me beyond what I could well bear. But the Lord alone was my keeper, and I believed that if I went into captivity it would be for some good end. Thus, from time to time, my mind was centred in resignation, in which I always found quietness. And this day, though I had the same dangerous wilderness between me and home, I was inwardly joyful that the Lord had strengthened me to come on this visit, and had manifested a fatherly care over me in my poor lowly condition, when, in mine own eyes, I appeared inferior to many among the Indians.

When the last-mentioned meeting was ended, it being night, Papunehang went to bed; and hearing him speak with an harmonious voice, I suppose for a minute or two, I asked the interpreter, who told me that he was expressing his thankfulness to God for the favors he had received that day, and prayed that he would continue to favor him with the same, which he had experienced in that meeting. Though Papunehang had before agreed to receive the Moravian and join with them, he still appeared kind and loving to us.

I was at two meetings on the 20th, and silent in them. The following morning, in meeting, my heart was enlarged in pure love among them, and in short plain sentences I expressed several things that rested upon me, which one of the interpreters gave the people pretty readily. The meeting ended in supplication, and I had cause humbly to acknowledge the loving-kindness of the Lord towards us; and then I believed that a door remained open for the faithful disciples of Jesus Christ to labor among these people. And now, feeling my mind at liberty to return, I took my leave of them in general at the conclusion of what I said in meeting, and we then prepared to go homeward. But some of their most active men told us that when we were ready to move the people would choose to come and shake hands with us. Those who usually came to meeting did so; and from a secret draught in my mind I went among some who did not usually go to meeting, and took my leave of them also. The Moravian and his Indian interpreter appeared respectful to us at parting. This town, Wehaloosing, stands on the bank of the Susquehanna, and consists, I believe, of about forty houses, mostly compact together, some about thirty feet long and eighteen wide, — some bigger, some less. They are built mostly of split plank, one end being set in the ground, and the other pinned to a plate on which rafters are laid, and then covered with bark. I understand a great flood last winter overflowed the greater part of the ground where the town stands, and some were now about moving their houses to higher ground.

We expected only two Indians to be of our company, but when we were ready to go we found many of them were going to Bethlehem with skins and furs, and chose to go in company with us. So they loaded two canoes in which they desired us to go, telling us that the waters were so raised with the rains that the horses should be taken by such as were better acquainted with the fording-places. We, therefore, with several Indians, went in the canoes, and others went on horses, there being seven besides ours. We met with the horsemen once on the way by appointment, and at night we lodged a little below a branch called Tankhannah, and some of the young men, going out a little before dusk with their guns, brought in a deer.

Through diligence we reached Wyoming before night, the 22d, and understood that the Indians were mostly gone from this place. We went up a small creek into the woods with our canoes, and, pitching our tent, carried out our baggage, and before dark our horses came to us. Next morning, the horses being loaded and our baggage prepared, we set forward, being in all fourteen, and with diligent travelling were favored to get near half-way to Fort Allen. The land on this road from Wyoming to our frontier being mostly poor, and good grass being scarce, the Indians chose a piece of low ground to lodge on, as the best for grazing. I had sweat much in travelling, and, being weary, slept soundly. In the night I perceived that I had taken cold, of which I was favored soon to get better.

Twenty-fourth of sixth month. — This day we passed Fort Allen and lodged near it in the woods. We forded the westerly branch of the Delaware three times, which was a shorter way than going over the top of the Blue Mountains called the Second Ridge. In the second time of fording where the river cuts through the mountain, the waters being rapid and pretty deep, my companion's mare, being a tall, tractable animal, was sundry times driven back through the river, being laden with the burdens of some small horses which were thought unable to come through with their loads. The troubles westward, and the difficulty for Indians to pass through our frontier, was, I apprehend, one reason why so many came, expecting that our being in company would prevent the outside inhabitants being surprised. We reached Bethlehem on the 25th, taking care to keep foremost, and to acquaint people on and near the road who these Indians were. This we found very needful, for the frontier inhabitants were often alarmed at the report of the English being killed by Indians westward. Among our company were some whom I did not remember to have seen at meeting, and some of these at first were very reserved; but we being several days together, and behaving in a friendly manner towards them, and making them suitable return for the services they did us, they became more free and sociable.

Twenty-sixth of sixth month. — Having carefully endeavored to settle all affairs with the Indians relative to our journey, we took leave of them, and I thought they generally parted from us affectionately. We went forward to Richland and had a very comfortable meeting among our friends, it being the first day of the week. Here I parted with my kind friend and companion Benjamin Parvin, and, accompanied by my friend Samuel Foulk, we rode to John Cadwallader's, from whence I reached home the next day, and found my family tolerably well. They and my friends appeared glad to see me return from a journey which they apprehended would be dangerous; but my mind, while I was out, had been so employed in striving for perfect resignation, and had so often been confirmed in a belief, that, whatever the Lord might be pleased to allot for me, it would work for good, that I was careful lest I should admit any degree of selfishness in being glad overmuch, and labored to improve by those trials in such a manner as my gracious Father and Protector designed. Between the English settlements and Wehaloosing we had only a narrow path, which in many places is much grown up with bushes, and interrupted by abundance of trees lying across it. These, together with the mountain swamps and rough stones, make it a difficult road to travel, and the more so because rattlesnakes abound here, of which we killed four. People who have never been in such places have but an imperfect idea of them; and I was not only taught patience, but also made thankful to God, who thus led about and instructed me, that I might have a quick and lively feeling of the afflictions of my fellow-creatures, whose situation in life is difficult.

CHAPTER IX.

1763 - 1769.

Religious Conversation with a Company met to see the Tricks of a Juggler. — Account of John Smith's Advice and of the Proceedings of a Committee at the Yearly Meeting in 1764. — Contemplations on the Nature of True Wisdom. — Visit to the Families of Friends at Mount Holly, Mansfield, and Burlington, and to the Meetings on the Sea-Coast from Cape May towards Squan. — Some Account of Joseph Nichols and his Followers. — On the different State of the First Settlers in Pennsylvania who depended on their own Labor, compared with those of the Southern Provinces who kept Negroes. — Visit to the Northern Parts of New Jersey and the Western Parts of Maryland and Pennsylvania; also to the Families of Friends at Mount Holly and several Parts of Maryland. — Further Considerations on keeping Slaves, and his Concern for having been a Party to the Sale of One. — Thoughts on Friends exercising Offices in Civil Government.

THE latter part of the summer, 1763, there came a man to Mount Holly who had previously published a printed advertisement that at a certain public-house he would show many wonderful operations, which were therein enumerated. At the appointed time he did, by sleight of hand, per form sundry things which appeared strange to the spectators. Understanding that the show was to be repeated the next night, and that the people were to meet about sunset, I felt an exercise on that account. So I went to the public-house in the evening, and told the man of the house that I had an inclination to spend a part of the evening there; with which he signified that he was content. Then, sitting down by the door, I spoke to the people in the fear of the Lord, as they came together, concerning this show, and labored to convince them that their thus assembling to see these sleight-of-hand tricks, and bestowing their money to support men who, in that capacity, were of no use to the world, was contrary to the nature of the Christian religion. One of the company endeavored to show by arguments the reasonableness of their proceedings herein; but after considering some texts of Scripture and calmly debating the matter he gave up the point. After spending about an hour among them, and feeling my mind easy, I departed.

Twenty-fifth of ninth month, 1764.—At our Yearly Meeting at Philadelphia this day, John Smith, of Marlborough, aged upwards of eighty years, a faithful minister, though not eloquent, stood up in our meeting of ministers and elders, and, appearing to be under a great exercise of spirit, informed Friends in substance as follows: "That he had been a member of our Society upwards of sixty years, and he well remembered, that, in those early times, Friends were a plain, lowly-minded people, and that there was much tenderness and contrition in their meetings. That, at twenty years from that time, the Society increasing in wealth and in some degree conforming to the fashions of the world, true humility was less apparent, and their meetings in general were not so lively and edifying. That at the end of forty years many of them were grown very rich, and many of the Society made a specious appearance in the world; that wearing fine costly garments, and using silver and other watches, became customary with them, their sons, and their daughters. These marks of outward wealth and greatness appeared on some in our meetings of ministers and elders; and, as such things became more prevalent, so the powerful overshadowings of the Holy Ghost were less manifest in the Society. That there had been a continued increase of such ways of life, even until the present time; and that the weakness which hath now overspread the Society and the barrenness manifest among us is matter of much sorrow." He then mentioned the uncertainty of his attending these meetings in future, expecting his dissolution was near; and, having tenderly expressed his concern for us, signified that he had seen in the true light that the Lord would bring back his people from these things, into which they were thus degenerated, but that his faithful servants must go through great and heavy exercises.

Twentieth of ninth month. — The committee appointed by the Yearly Meeting to visit the Quarterly and Monthly Meetings gave an account in writing of their proceedings in that service. They signified that in the course of the visit they had been apprehensive that some persons holding offices in government inconsistent with our principles, and others who kept slaves, remaining active members in our meetings for discipline, had been one means of weakness prevailing in some places. After this report was read, an exercise revived in my mind which had attended me for several years, and inward cries to the Lord were raised in me that the fear of man might not prevent me from doing what he required of me, and, standing up, I spoke in substance as follows: "I have felt a tenderness in my mind towards persons in two circumstances mentioned in that report; namely, towards such active members as keep slaves and such as hold offices in civil government; and I have desired that Friends, in all their conduct, may be kindly affectioned one towards another. Many Friends who keep slaves are under some exercise on that account; and at times think about trying them with freedom, but find many things in their way. The way of living and the annual expenses of some of them are such that it seems impracticable for them to set their slaves free without changing their own way of life. It has been my lot to be often abroad; and I have observed in some places, at Quarterly and Yearly Meetings, and at some houses where travelling Friends and their horses are often entertained, that the yearly expense of individuals therein is very considerable. And Friends in some places crowding much on persons in these circumstances for entertainment hath rested as a burden on my mind for some years past. I now express it in the fear of the Lord, greatly desiring that Friends here present may duly consider it."

In the fall of this year, having hired a man to work, I perceived in conversation with him that he had been a soldier in the late war on this continent; and he informed me in the evening, in a narrative of his captivity among the Indians, that he saw two of his fellow-captives tortured to death in a very cruel manner. This relation affected me with sadness, under which I went to bed; and the next morning, soon after I awoke, a fresh and living sense of Divine love overspread my mind, in which I had a renewed prospect of the nature of that wisdom from above which leads to a right use of all gifts, both spiritual and temporal, and gives content therein. Under a feeling thereof, I wrote as follows: —

"Hath He who gave me a being attended with many wants unknown to brute creatures given me a capacity superior to theirs, and shown me that a moderate application to business is suitable to my present condition; and that this, attended with his blessing, may supply all my outward wants while they remain within the bounds he hath fixed, and while no imaginary wants proceeding from an evil spirit have any place in me? Attend then, O my soul! to this pure wisdom as thy sure conductor through the manifold dangers of this world.

"Doth pride lead to vanity? Doth vanity form imaginary wants? Do these wants prompt men to exert their power in requiring more from others than they would be willing to perform themselves, were the same required of them? Do those proceedings beget hard thoughts? Do hard thoughts, when ripe, become malice? Does malice, when ripe, become revengeful, and in the end inflict terrible pains on our fellow-creatures and spread desolations in the world?

"Do mankind, walking in uprightness, delight in each other's happiness? And do those who are capable of this attainment, by giving way to an evil spirit, employ their skill and strength to afflict and destroy one another? Remember then, O my soul! the quietude of those in whom Christ governs, and in all thy proceedings feel after it.

"Doth he condescend to bless thee with his presence? To move and influence thee to action? To dwell and to walk in thee? Remember then thy station as a being sacred to God. Accept of the strength freely offered to thee, and take heed that no weakness in conforming to unwise, expensive, and hard-hearted customs, gendering to discord and strife, be given way to. Doth he claim my body as his temple, and graciously require that I may be sacred to him? O that I may prize this favor, and that my whole life may be conformable to this character! Remember, O my soul! that the Prince of Peace is thy Lord; that he communicates his unmixed wisdom to his family, that they, living in perfect simplicity, may give no just cause of offence to any creature, but that they may walk as He walked!"

Having felt an openness in my heart towards visiting families in our own meeting, and especially in the town of Mount Holly, the place of my abode, I mentioned it at our Monthly Meeting in the fore part of the winter of 1764, which being agreed to, and several Friends of our meeting being united in the exercise, we proceeded therein; and through Divine favor we were helped in the work, so that it appeared to me as a fresh reviving of godly care among Friends. The latter part of the same winter I joined my friend William Jones in a visit to Friends' families in Mansfield, in which labor I had cause to admire the goodness of the Lord toward us.

My mind being drawn towards Friends along the sea-coast from Cape May to near Squan, and also to visit some people in those parts, among whom there is no settled worship, I joined with my beloved friend Benjamin Jones in a visit to them, having Friends' unity therein. We set off the 24th of tenth month, 1765, and had a prosperous and very satisfactory journey, feeling at times, through the goodness of the Heavenly Shepherd, the gospel to flow freely towards a poor people scattered in these places. Soon after our return I joined my friends John Sleeper and Elizabeth Smith in a visit to Friends' families at Burlington, there being at this time about fifty families of our Society in that city; and we had cause humbly to adore our Heavenly Father, who baptized us into a feeling of the state of the people, and strengthened us to labor in true gospel love among them.

Having had a concern at times for several years

to pay a religious visit to Friends on the Eastern Shore of Maryland, and to travel on foot among them, that by so travelling I might have a more lively feeling of the condition of the oppressed slaves, set an example of lowliness before the eyes of their masters, and be more out of the way of temptation to unprofitable converse; and the time drawing near in which I believed it my duty to lay my concern before our Monthly Meeting, I perceived, in conversation with my beloved friend John Sleeper, that he also was under a similar concern to travel on foot in the form of a servant among them, as he expressed it. This he told me before he knew aught of my exercise. Being thus drawn the same way, we laid our exercise and the nature of it before Friends; and, obtaining certificates, we set off the 6th of fifth month, 1766, and were at meetings with Friends at Wilmington, Duck Creek, Little Creek, and Motherkill. My heart was often tendered under the Divine influence, and enlarged in love towards the people among whom we travelled.

From Motherkill we crossed the country about thirty-five miles to Tuckahoe, in Maryland, and had a meeting there, and also at Marshy Creek. At the last three meetings there were a considerable number of the followers of one Joseph Nichols, a preacher, who, I understand, is not in outward fellowship with any religious society, but professeth nearly the same principles as those of our Society, and often travels up and down, appointing meetings which many people attend. I heard of some who had been irreligious people that were now his followers, and were become sober, well-behaved men and women. Some irregularities, I hear, have been among the people at several of his meetings; but from what I have perceived I believe the man and some of his followers are honestly disposed, but that skilful fathers are wanting among them.

We then went to Choptank and Third Haven, and thence to Queen Anne's. The weather for some days past having been hot and dry, and we having travelled pretty steadily and having had hard labor in meetings, I grew weakly, at which I was for a time discouraged; but looking over our journey and considering how the Lord had supported our minds and bodies, so that we had gone forward much faster than I expected before we came out, I saw that I had been in danger of too strongly desiring to get quickly through the journey, and that the bodily weakness now attending me was a kindness; and then, in contrition of spirit, I became very thankful to my gracious Father for this manifestation of his love, and in humble submission to his will my trust in him was renewed.

In this part of our journey I had many thoughts on the different circumstances of Friends who inhabit Pennsylvania and Jersey from those who dwell in Maryland, Virginia, and Carolina. Pennsylvania and New Jersey were settled by Friends who were convinced of our principles in England in times of suffering; these, coming over, bought lands of the natives, and applied to husbandry in a peaceable way, and many of their children were taught to labor for their living. Few of these, I believe, settled in any of the southern provinces; but by the faithful labors of travelling Friends in early times there was considerable convincement among the inhabitants of these parts. I also remembered having read of the warlike disposition of many of the first settlers in those provinces, and of their numerous engagements with the natives in which much blood was shed even in the infancy of the colonies. Some of the people inhabiting those places, being grounded in customs contrary to the pure truth, were affected with the powerful preaching of the Word of Life and joined in fellowship with our Society, and in so doing they had a great work to go through. In the history of the reformation from Popery it is observable that the progress was gradual from age to age. The uprightness of the first reformers in attending to the light and understanding given to them opened the way for sincere-hearted people to proceed further afterwards; and thus each one truly fearing God and laboring in the works of righteousness appointed for him in his day findeth acceptance with Him. Through the darkness of the times and the corruption of manners and customs, some upright men may have had little more for their day's work than to attend to the righteous principle in their minds as it related to their own conduct in life without pointing out to others the whole extent of that into which the same principle would lead succeeding ages. Thus, for instance, among an imperious, warlike people, supported by oppressed slaves, some of these masters, I suppose, are awakened to feel and to see their error, and through sincere repentance cease from oppression and become like fathers to their servants, showing by their example a pattern of humility in living, and moderation in governing, for the instruction and admonition of their oppressing neighbors; these, without carrying the reformation further, have, I believe, found acceptance with the Lord. Such was the beginning; and those who succeeded them, and who faithfully attended to the nature and spirit of the reformation, have seen the necessity of proceeding forward, and have not only to instruct others by their own example in governing well, but have also to use means to prevent their successors from having so much power to oppress others.

Here I was renewedly confirmed in my mind that the Lord (whose tender mercies are over all his works, and whose ear is open to the cries and groans of the oppressed) is graciously moving in the hearts of people to draw them off from the desire of wealth and to bring them into such an humble, lowly way of living that they may see their way clearly to repair to the standard of true righteousness, and may not only break the yoke of oppression, but may know him to be their strength and support in times of outward affliction.

We crossed Chester River, had a meeting there, and also at Cecil and Sassafras. My bodily weakness, joined with a heavy exercise of mind, was to me an humbling dispensation, and I had a very lively feeling of the state of the oppressed; yet I often thought that what I suffered was little compared with the sufferings of the blessed Jesus and many of his faithful followers; and I may say with thankfulness that I was made content. From Sassafras we went pretty directly home, where we found our families well. For several weeks after our return I had often to look over our journey; and though to me it appeared as a small service, and that some faithful messengers will yet have more bitter cups to drink in those southern provinces for Christ's sake than we have had, yet I found peace in that I had been helped to walk in sincerity according to the understanding and strength given to me.

Thirteenth of eleventh month.—With the unity of Friends at our monthly meeting, and in company with my beloved friend Benjamin Jones, I set out on a visit to Friends in the upper part of this province, having had drawings of love in my heart that way for a considerable time. We travelled as far as Hardwick, and I had inward peace in my labors of love among them. Through the humbling dispensations of Divine Providence my mind hath been further brought into a feeling of the difficulties of Friends and their servants southwestward; and being often engaged in spirit on their account I believed it my duty to walk into some parts of the western shore of Maryland on a religious visit. Having obtained a certificate from Friends of our

Monthly Meeting, I took leave of my family under the heart-tendering operation of truth, and on the 20th of fourth month, 1767, rode to the ferry opposite to Philadelphia, and thence walked to William Horne's, at Derby, the same evening. Next day I pursued my journey alone and reached Concord Week-Day Meeting.

Discouragements and a weight of distress had at times attended me in this lonesome walk, but through these afflictions I was mercifully preserved. Sitting down with Friends, my mind was turned towards the Lord to wait for his holy leadings; and in infinite love he was pleased to soften my heart into humble contrition, and renewedly to strengthen me to go forward, so that to me it was a time of heavenly refreshment in a silent meeting. The next day I came to New Garden Week-Day Meeting, in which I sat in bowedness of spirit, and being baptized into a feeling of the state of some present, the Lord gave us a heart-tendering season; to his name be the praise. Passing on, I was at Nottingham Monthly Meeting, and at a meeting at Little Britain on first-day; in the afternoon several Friends came to the house where I lodged and we had a little afternoon meeting, and through the humbling power of truth I had to admire the loving-kindness of the Lord manifested to us.

Twenty-sixth of fourth month.—I crossed the Susquehanna, and coming among people in outward ease and greatness, supported chiefly on the labor of slaves, my heart was much affected, and in awful retiredness my mind was gathered inward to the Lord, humbly desiring that in true resignation I might receive instruction from him respecting my duty among this people. Though travelling on foot was wearisome to my body, yet it was agreeable to the state of my mind. Being weakly, I was covered with sorrow and heaviness on account of the prevailing spirit of this world by which customs grievous and oppressive are introduced on the one hand, and pride and wantonness on the other.

In this lonely walk and state of abasement and humiliation, the condition of the church in these parts was opened before me, and I may truly say with the Prophet, "I was bowed down at the hearing of it; I was dismayed at the seeing of it." Under this exercise I attended the Quarterly Meeting at Gunpowder, and in bowedness of spirit I had to express with much plainness my feelings respecting Friends living in fulness on the labors of the poor oppressed negroes; and that promise of the Most High was now revived, "I will gather all nations and tongues, and they shall come and see my glory." Here the sufferings of Christ and his tasting death for every man, and the travels, sufferings, and martyrdom of the Apostles and primitive Christians in laboring for the conversion of the Gentiles, were livingly revived in me, and according to the measure of strength afforded I labored in some tenderness of spirit, being deeply affected among them. The difference between the present treatment which these gentiles, the negroes, receive at our hands, and the labors of the primitive Christians for the conversion of the Gentiles, were pressed home, and the power of truth came over us, under a feeling of which my mind was united to a tender-hearted people in these parts. The meeting concluded in a sense of God's goodness towards his humble, dependent children.

The next day was a general meeting for worship, much crowded, in which I was deeply engaged in inward cries to the Lord for help, that I might stand wholly resigned, and move only as he might be pleased to lead me. I was mercifully helped to labor honestly and fervently among them, in which I found inward peace, and the sincere were comforted. From this place I turned towards Pipe Creek and the Red Lands, and had several meetings among Friends in those parts. My heart was often tenderly affected under a sense of the Lord's goodness in sanctifying my troubles and exercises, turning them to my comfort, and I believe to the benefit of many others, for I may say with thankfulness that in this visit it appeared like a tendering visitation in most places.

I passed on to the Western Quarterly Meeting in Pennsylvania. During the several days of this meeting I was mercifully preserved in an inward feeling after the mind of truth, and my public labors tended to my humiliation, with which I was content. After the Quarterly Meeting for worship ended, I felt drawings to go to the women's meeting for business, which was very full; here the humility of Jesus Christ as a pattern for us to walk by was livingly opened before me, and in treating on it my heart was enlarged, and it was a baptizing time. I was afterwards at meetings at Concord, Middletown, Providence, and Haddonfield, whence I returned home and found my family well. A sense of the Lord's merciful preservation in this my journey excites reverent thankfulness to him.

Second of ninth month, 1767.—With the unity of Friends, I set off on a visit to Friends in the upper part of Berks and Philadelphia counties; was at eleven meetings in about two weeks, and have renewed cause to bow in reverence before the Lord, who, by the powerful extendings of his humbling goodness, opened my way among Friends, and I trust made the meetings profitable to us. The following winter I joined some Friends in a family visit to some part of our meeting, in which exercise the pure influence of Divine love made our visits reviving.

Fifth of fifth month, 1768.—I left home under the humbling hand of the Lord, with a certificate to visit some meetings in Maryland, and to proceed without a horse seemed clearest to me. I was at the Quarterly Meetings at Philadelphia and Concord, whence I proceeded to Chester River, and, crossing the bay, was at the Yearly Meeting at West River; I then returned to Chester River, and, taking a few meetings in my way, proceeded home. It was a journey of much inward waiting, and as my eye was to the Lord, way was several times opened to my humbling admiration when things appeared very difficult. On my return I felt a very comfortable relief of mind, having through Divine help labored in much plainness, both with Friends selected and in the more public meetings, so that I trust the pure witness in many minds was reached.

Eleventh of sixth month, 1769. — There have been sundry cases of late years within the limits of our Monthly Meeting, respecting the exercising of pure righteousness towards the negroes, in which I have lived under a labor of heart that equity might be steadily preserved. On this account I have had some close exercises among Friends, in which, I may thankfully say, I find peace. And as my meditations have been on universal love, my own conduct in time past became of late very grievous to me. As persons setting negroes free in our province are bound by law to maintain them in case they have need of relief, some in the time of my youth who scrupled to keep slaves for term of life were wont to detain their young negroes in their service without wages till they were thirty years of age. With this custom I so far agreed that being joined with another Friend in executing the will of a deceased Friend, I once sold a negro lad till he might attain the age of thirty years, and applied the money to the use of the estate.

With abasement of heart I may now say that sometimes as I have sat in a meeting with my heart exercised towards that awful Being who respecteth not persons nor colors, and have thought upon this lad, I have felt that all was not clear in my mind respecting him; and as I have attended to this exercise and fervently sought the Lord, it hath appeared to me that I should make some restitution; but in what way I saw not till lately, when being under some concern that I might be resigned to go on a visit to some part of the West Indies, and under close engagement of spirit seeking to the Lord for counsel herein, the aforesaid transaction came heavily upon me, and my mind for a time was covered with darkness and sorrow. Under this sore affliction my heart was softened to receive instruction, and I now first perceived that as I had been one of the two executors who had sold this lad for nine years longer than is common for our own children to serve, so I should now offer part of my substance to redeem the last half of the nine years; but as the time was not yet come, I executed a bond, binding myself and my executors to pay to the man to whom he was sold what to candid men might appear equitable for the last four and a half years of his time, in case the said youth should be living, and in a condition likely to provide comfortably for himself.

Ninth of tenth month. — My heart hath often been deeply afflicted under a feeling that the standard of pure righteousness is not lifted up to the people by us, as a society, in that clearness which it might have been, had we been as faithful as we ought to be to the teachings of Christ. And as my mind hath been inward to the Lord, the purity of Christ's government hath been made clear to my understanding, and I have believed, in the opening of universal love, that where a people who are convinced of the truth of the inward teachings of Christ are active in putting laws in execution which are not consistent with pure wisdom, it hath a necessary tendency to bring dimness over their minds. My heart having been thus exercised for several years with a tender sympathy towards my fellow-members, I have within a few months past expressed my concern on this subject in several meetings for discipline.

CHAPTER X.

1769, 1770.

Bodily Indisposition. — Exercise of his Mind for the Good of the People in the West Indies. — Communicates to Friends his Concern to visit some of those Islands. — Preparations to embark. — Considerations on the Trade to the West Indies. — Release from his Concern and return Home. —Religious Engagements. — Sickness, and Exercise of his Mind therein.

TWELFTH of third month, 1769. — Having for some years past dieted myself on account of illness and weakness of body, and not having ability to travel by land as heretofore, I was at times favored to look with awfulness towards the Lord, before whom are all my ways, who alone hath the power of life and death, and to feel thankfulness raised in me for this his fatherly chastisement, believing that if I was truly humbled under it all would work for good. While under this bodily weakness, my mind was at times exercised for my fellow-creatures in the West Indies, and I grew jealous over myself lest the disagreeableness of the prospect should hinder me from obediently attending thereto; for, though I knew not that the Lord required me to go there, yet I believed that resignation was now called for in that respect. Feeling a danger of not being wholly devoted to him, I was frequently engaged to watch unto prayer that I might be preserved; and upwards of a year having passed, as I one day walked in a solitary wood, my mind being covered with awfulness, cries were raised in me to my merciful Father, that he would graciously keep me in faithfulness; and it then settled on my mind, as a duty, to open my condition to Friends at our Monthly Meeting, which I did soon after, as follows:—

"An exercise hath attended me for some time past, and of late hath been more weighty upon me, which is, that I believe it is required of me to be resigned to go on a visit to some parts of the West Indies." In the Quarterly and General Spring Meetings I found no clearness to express anything further than that I believed resignation herein was required of me. Having obtained certificates from all the said meetings, I felt like a sojourner at my outward habitation, and kept free from worldly encumbrances, and I was often bowed in spirit before the Lord, with inward breathings to him that I might be rightly directed. I may here note that the circumstance before related of my having, when young, joined with another executor in selling a negro lad till he might attain the age of thirty years, was now the cause of much sorrow to me; and, after having settled matters relating to this youth, I provided a sea-store and bed, and things for the voyage. Hearing of a vessel likely to sail from Philadelphia for Barbadoes, I spake with one of the owners at Burlington, and soon after went to Philadelphia on purpose to speak to him again.

He told me there was a Friend in town who was part owner of the said vessel. I felt no inclination to speak with the latter, but returned home. Awhile after I took leave of my family, and, going to Philadelphia, had some weighty conversation with the first-mentioned owner, and showed him a writing, as follows :—

"On the 25th of eleventh month, 1769, as an exercise with respect to a visit to Barbadoes hath been weighty on my mind, I may express some of the trials which have attended me, under which I have at times rejoiced that I have felt my own self-will subjected.

"Some years ago I retailed rum, sugar, and molasses, the fruits of the labor of slaves, but had not then much concern about them save only that the rum might be used in moderation; nor was this concern so weightily attended to as I now believe it ought to have been. Having of late years been further informed respecting the oppressions too generally exercised in these islands, and thinking often on the dangers there are in connections of interest and fellowship with the works of darkness (Eph. v. 11), I have felt an increasing concern to be wholly given up to the leadings of the Holy Spirit, and it hath seemed right that my small gain from this branch of trade should be applied in promoting righteousness on the earth. This was the first motion towards a visit to Barbadoes. I believed also that part of my outward substance should be applied in paying my passage, if I went, and providing things in a lowly way for my subsistence; but when the time drew near in which I believed it required of me to be in readiness, a difficulty arose which hath been a continual trial for some months past, under which I have, with abasement of mind from day to day, sought the Lord for instruction, having often had a feeling of the condition of one formerly, who bewailed himself because the Lord hid his face from him. During these exercises my heart hath often been contrite, and I have had a tender feeling of the temptations of my fellow-creatures, laboring under expensive customs not agreeable to the simplicity that 'there is in Christ' (2 Cor. ii. 3), and sometimes in the renewings of gospel love I have been helped to minister to others.

"That which hath so closely engaged my mind, in seeking to the Lord for instruction, is, whether, after the full information I have had of the oppression which the slaves lie under who raise the West India produce, which I have gained by reading a caution and warning to Great Britain and her colonies, written by Anthony Benezet, it is right for me to take passage in a vessel employed in the West India trade.

"To trade freely with oppressors without laboring to dissuade them from such unkind treatment, and to seek for gain by such traffic, tends, I believe, to make them more easy respecting their conduct than they would be if the cause of universal righteousness was humbly and firmly attended to by those in general with whom they have commerce; and that complaint of the Lord by his prophet, "They have strengthened the hands of the wicked," hath very often revived in my mind. I may here add some circumstances which occurred to me before I had any prospect of a visit there. David longed for some water in a well beyond an army of Philistines who were at war with Israel, and some of his men, to please him, ventured their lives in passing through this army, and brought that water.

"It doth not appear that the Israelites were then scarce of water, but rather that David gave way to delicacy of taste; and having reflected on the danger to which these men had been exposed, he considered this water as their blood, and his heart smote him that he could not drink it, but he poured it out to the Lord. The oppression of the slaves which I have seen in several journeys southward on this continent, and the report of their treatment in the West Indies, have deeply affected me, and a care to live in the spirit of peace and minister no just cause of offence to my fellow-creatures having from time to time livingly revived in my mind, I have for some years past declined to gratify my palate with those sugars.

"I do not censure my brethren in these things, but I believe the Father of Mercies, to whom all mankind by creation are equally related, hath heard the groans of this oppressed people, and that he is preparing some to have a tender feeling of their condition. Trading in or the frequent use of any produce known to be raised by the labor of those who are under such lamentable oppression hath appeared to be a subject which may hereafter require the more serious consideration of the humble followers of Christ, the Prince of Peace.

"After long and mournful exercise I am now free to mention how things have opened in my mind, with desires that if it may please the Lord further to open his will to any of his children in this matter they may faithfully follow him in such further manifestation.

"The number of those who decline the use of West India produce, on account of the hard usage of the slaves who raise it, appears small, even among people truly pious; and the labors in Christian love on that subject of those who do are not very extensive. Were the trade from this continent to the West Indies to be stopped at once, I believe many there would suffer for want of bread. Did we on this continent and the inhabitants of the West Indies generally dwell in pure righteousness, I believe a small trade between us might be right. Under these considerations, when the thoughts of wholly declining the use of trading-vessels and of trying to hire a vessel to go under ballast have arisen in my mind, I have believed that the labors in gospel love hitherto bestowed in the cause of universal righteousness have not reached that height. If the trade to the West Indies were no more than was consistent with pure wisdom, I believe the passage-money would for good reasons be higher than it is now; and therefore, under deep exercise of mind, I have believed that I should not take advantage of this great trade and small passage-money, but, as a testimony in favor of less trading, should pay more than is common for others to pay if I go at this time."

The first-mentioned owner, having read the paper, went with me to the other owner, who also read over the paper, and we had some solid conversation, under which I felt myself bowed in reverence before the Most High. At length one of them asked me if I would go and see the vessel. But not having clearness in my mind to go, I went to my lodging and retired in private under great exercise of mind; and my tears were poured out before the Lord with inward cries that he would graciously help me under these trials. I believe my mind was resigned, but I did not feel clearness to proceed; and my own weakness and the necessity of Divine instruction were impressed upon me.

I was for a time as one who knew not what to do and was tossed as in a tempest; under which affliction the doctrine of Christ, "Take no thought for the morrow," arose livingly before me, and I was favored to get into a good degree of stillness. Having been near two days in town, I believed my obedience to my Heavenly Father consisted in returning homeward; I therefore went over among Friends on the Jersey shore and tarried till the morning on which the vessel was appointed to sail.

As I lay in bed the latter part of that night my mind was comforted, and I felt what I esteemed a fresh confirmation that it was the Lord's will that I should pass through some further exercises near home; so I went thither, and still felt like a sojourner with my family. In the fresh spring of pure love I had some labors in a private way among Friends on a subject relating to truth's testimony, under which I had frequently been exercised in heart for some years. I remember, as I walked on the road under this exercise, that passage in Ezekiel came fresh upon me, "Whithersoever their faces were turned thither they went." And I was graciously helped to discharge my duty in the fear and dread of the Almighty.

In the course of a few weeks it pleased the Lord to visit me with a pleurisy; and after I had lain a few days and felt the disorder very grievous, I was thoughtful how it might end. I had of late, through various exercises, been much weaned from the pleasant things of this life; and I now thought if it were the Lord's will to put an end to my labors and graciously to receive me into the arms of his mercy, death would be acceptable to me; but if it were his will further to refine me under affliction, and to make me in any degree useful in his church, I desired not to die. I may with thankfulness say that in this case I felt resignedness wrought in me and had no inclination to send for a doctor, believing, if it were the Lord's will through outward means to raise me up, some sympathizing Friends would be sent to minister to me; which accordingly was the case. But though I was carefully attended, yet the disorder was at times so heavy that I had no expectation of recovery. One night in particular my bodily distress was great; my feet grew cold, and the cold increased up my legs towards my body; at that time I had no inclination to ask my nurse to apply anything warm to my feet, expecting my end was near. After I had lain near ten hours in this condition, I closed my eyes, thinking whether I might now be delivered out of the body; but in these awful moments my mind was livingly opened to behold the church; and strong engagements were begotten in me for the everlasting well-being of my fellow-creatures. I felt in the spring of pure love that I might remain some time longer in the body, to fill up according to my measure that which remains of the afflictions of Christ, and to labor for the good of the church; after which I requested my nurse to apply warmth to my feet, and I revived. The next night, feeling a weighty exercise of spirit and having a solid friend sitting up with me, I requested him to write what I said, which he did as follows: —

"Fourth day of the first month, 1770, about five in the morning. — I have seen in the Light of the Lord that the day is approaching when the man that is most wise in human policy shall be the greatest fool; and the arm that is mighty to support injustice shall be broken to pieces; the enemies of righteousness shall make a terrible rattle, and shall mightily torment one another; for He that is omnipotent is rising up to judgment, and will plead the cause of the oppressed; and He commanded me to open the vision." *

Near a week after this, feeling my mind livingly opened, I sent for a neighbor, who, at my request, wrote as follows:—

"The place of prayer is a precious habitation; for I now saw that the prayers of the saints were precious incense; and a trumpet was given to me that I might sound forth this language; that the children might hear it and be invited together to this precious habitation, where the prayers of the saints, as sweet incense, arise before the throne of God and the Lamb. I saw this habitation to be safe,—to be inwardly quiet when there were great stirrings and commotions in the world.

"Prayer, at this day, in pure resignation, is a precious place: the trumpet is sounded; the call goes forth to the church that she gather to the place of pure inward prayer; and her habitation is safe."

* The reader, who may be disposed to regard this as the language of distempered imagination, may perhaps find a truer explanation of it in the late civil conflict by which "the arm mighty to support injustice" has been "broken in pieces," and in which it may be said the Lord did "rise up to judgment and plead the cause of the oppressed."

CHAPTER XI.

1772.

Embarks at Chester, with Samuel Emlen, in a Ship bound for London. — Exercise of Mind respecting the Hardships of the Sailors. — Considerations on the Dangers of training Youth to a Seafaring Life. — Thoughts during a Storm at Sea. — Arrival in London.

HAVING been some time under a religious concern to prepare for crossing the seas, in order to visit Friends in the northern parts of England, and more particularly in Yorkshire, after consideration I thought it expedient to inform Friends of it at our Monthly Meeting at Burlington, who, having unity with me therein, gave me a certificate. I afterwards communicated the same to our Quarterly Meeting, and they likewise certified their concurrence. Some time after, at the General Spring Meeting of ministers and elders, I thought it my duty to acquaint them with the religious exercise which attended my mind; and they likewise signified their unity therewith by a certificate, dated the 24th of third month, 1772, directed to Friends in Great Britain.

In the fourth month following I thought the time was come for me to make some inquiry for a suitable conveyance; and as my concern was principally towards the northern parts of England, it seemed most proper to go in a vessel bound to Liverpool or Whitehaven. While I was at Philadelphia deliberating on this subject I was informed that my beloved friend Samuel Emlen, junior, intended to go to London, and had taken a passage for himself in the cabin of the ship called the Mary and Elizabeth, of which James Sparks was master, and John Head, of the city of Philadelphia, one of the owners; and feeling a draught in my mind towards the steerage of the same ship, I went first and opened to Samuel the feeling I had concerning it.

My beloved friend wept when I spake to him, and appeared glad that I had thoughts of going in the vessel with him, though my prospect was toward the steerage; and he offering to go with me, we went on board, first into the cabin, — a commodious room, — and then into the steerage, where we sat down on a chest, the sailors being busy about us. The owner of the ship also came and sat down with us. My mind was turned towards Christ, the Heavenly Counsellor, and feeling at this time my own will subjected, my heart was contrite before him. A motion was made by the owner to go and sit in the cabin, as a place more retired; but I felt easy to leave the ship, and, making no agreement as to a passage in her, told the owner if I took a passage in the ship I believed it would be in the steerage; but did not say much as to my exercise in that case.

After I went to my lodgings, and the case was a little known in town, a Friend laid before me the great inconvenience attending a passage in the steerage, which for a time appeared very discouraging to me.

I soon after went to bed, and my mind was under a deep exercise before the Lord, whose helping hand was manifested to me as I slept that night, and his love strengthened my heart. In the morning I went with two Friends on board the vessel again, and after a short time spent therein, I went with Samuel Emlen to the house of the owner, to whom, in the hearing of Samuel only, I opened my exercise in relation to a scruple I felt with regard to a passage in the cabin, in substance as follows:—

"That on the outside of that part of the ship where the cabin was I observed sundry sorts of carved work and imagery; that in the cabin I observed some superfluity of workmanship of several sorts; and that according to the ways of men's reckoning, the sum of money to be paid for a passage in that apartment has some relation to the expense of furnishing it to please the minds of such as give way to a conformity to this world; and that in this, as in other cases, the moneys received from the passengers are calculated to defray the cost of these superfluities, as well as the other expenses of their passage. I therefore felt a scruple with regard to paying my money to be applied to such purposes."

As my mind was now opened, I told the owner that I had, at several times, in my travels, seen great oppressions on this continent, at which my heart had been much affected and brought into a feeling of the state of the sufferers; and having many times been engaged in the fear and love of God to labor with those under whom the oppressed have been borne down and afflicted, I have often perceived that with a view to get riches and to provide estates for children, that they may live conformably to the customs and honors of this world, many are entangled in the spirit of oppression, and the exercise of my soul had been such that I could not find peace in joining in anything which I saw was against that wisdom which is pure.

After this I agreed for a passage in the steerage; and hearing that Joseph White had desired to see me, I went to his house, and next day home, where I tarried two nights. Early the next morning I parted with my family under a sense of the humbling hand of God upon me, and, going to Philadelphia, had an opportunity with several of my beloved friends, who appeared to be concerned for me on account of the unpleasant situation of that part of the vessel in which I was likely to lodge. In these opportunities my mind, through the mercies of the Lord, was kept low in an inward waiting for his help; and Friends having expressed their desire that I might have a more convenient place than the steerage, did not urge it, but appeared disposed to leave me to the Lord.

Having stayed two nights at Philadelphia, I went the next day to Derby Monthly Meeting, where through the strength of Divine love my heart was enlarged towards the youth there present, under which I was helped to labor in some tenderness of spirit. I lodged at William Horn's and afterwards went to Chester, where I met with Samuel Emlen, and we went on board 1st of fifth month, 1772. As I sat alone on the deck I felt a satisfactory evidence that my proceedings were not in my own will, but under the power of the cross of Christ.

Seventh of fifth month. — We have had rough weather mostly since I came on board, and the passengers, James Reynolds, John Till Adams, Sarah Logan and her hired maid, and John Bispham, all sea-sick at times; from which sickness, through the tender mercies of my Heavenly Father, I have been preserved, my afflictions now being of another kind. There appeared an openness in the minds of the master of the ship and in the cabin passengers towards me. We are often together on the deck, and sometimes in the cabin. My mind, through the merciful help of the Lord, hath been preserved in a good degree watchful and quiet, for which I have great cause to be thankful.

As my lodging in the steerage, now near a week, hath afforded me sundry opportunities of seeing, hearing, and feeling with respect to the life and spirit of many poor sailors, an exercise of soul hath attended me in regard to placing out children and youth where they may be likely to be exampled and instructed in the pure fear of the Lord.

Being much among the seamen I have, from a motion of love, taken sundry opportunities with one of them at a time, and have in free conversation labored to turn their minds towards the fear of the Lord. This day we had a meeting in the cabin, where my heart was contrite under a feeling of Divine love.

I believe a communication with different parts of the world by sea is at times consistent with the will of our Heavenly Father, and to educate some youth in the practice of sailing, I believe may be right; but how lamentable is the present corruption of the world! How impure are the channels through which trade is conducted! How great is the danger to which poor lads are exposed when placed on shipboard to learn the art of sailing! Five lads training up for the seas were on board this ship. Two of them were brought up in our Society, and the other, by name James Naylor, is a member, to whose father James Naylor, mentioned in Sewel's history, appears to have been uncle. I often feel a tenderness of heart towards these poor lads, and at times look at them as though they were my children according to the flesh.

O that all may take heed and beware of covetousness! O that all may learn of Christ, who was meek and lowly of heart. Then in faithfully following him he will teach us to be content with food and raiment without respect to the customs or honors of this world. Men thus redeemed will feel a tender concern for their fellow-creatures, and a desire that those in the lowest stations may be assisted and encouraged, and where owners of ships attain to the perfect law of liberty and are doers of the Word, these will be blessed in their deeds.

A ship at sea commonly sails all night, and the seamen take their watches four hours at a time. Rising to work in the night, it is not commonly pleasant in any case, but in dark rainy nights it is very disagreeable, even though each man were furnished with all conveniences. If, after having been on deck several hours in the night, they come down into the steerage soaking wet, and are so closely stowed that proper convenience for change of garments is not easily come at, but for want of proper room their wet garments are thrown in heaps, and sometimes, through much crowding, are trodden under foot in going to their lodgings and getting out of them, and it is difficult at times for each to find his own. Here are trials for the poor sailors.

Now, as I have been with them in my lodge, my heart hath often yearned for them, and tender desires have been raised in me that all owners and masters of vessels may dwell in the love of God and therein act uprightly, and by seeking less for gain and looking carefully to their ways they may earnestly labor to remove all cause of provocation from the poor seamen, so that they may neither fret nor use excess of strong drink; for, indeed, the poor creatures, in the wet and cold, seem to apply at times to strong drink to supply the want of other convenience. Great reformation is wanting in the world, and the necessity of it among those who do business on great waters hath at this time been abundantly opened before me.

Eighth of fifth month. — This morning the clouds gathered, the wind blew strong from the southeast, and before noon so increased that sailing appeared dangerous. The seamen then bound up some of their sails and took down others, and the storm increasing they put the dead-lights, so called, into the cabin windows and lighted a lamp as at night. The wind now blew vehemently, and the sea wrought to that degree that an awful seriousness prevailed in the cabin, in which I spent, I believe, about seventeen hours, for the cabin passengers had given me frequent invitations, and I thought the poor wet toiling seamen had need of all the room in the crowded steerage. They now ceased from sailing and put the vessel in the posture called lying to.

My mind during this tempest, through the gracious assistance of the Lord, was preserved in a good degree of resignation; and at times I expressed a few words in his love to my shipmates in regard to the all-sufficiency of Him who formed the great deep, and whose care is so extensive that a sparrow falls not without his notice; and thus in a tender frame of mind I spoke to them of the necessity of our yielding in true obedience to the instructions of our Heavenly Father, who sometimes through adversities intendeth our refinement.

About eleven at night I went out on the deck. The sea wrought exceedingly, and the high, foaming waves round about had in some sort the appearance of fire, but did not give much if any light. The sailor at the helm said he lately saw a corposant at the head of the mast. I observed that the master of the ship ordered the carpenter to keep on the deck; and, though he said little, I apprehended his care was that the carpenter with his axe might be in readiness in case of any extremity. Soon after this the vehemency of the wind abated, and before morning they again put the ship under sail.

Tenth of fifth month. — It being the first day of the week and fine weather, we had a meeting in the cabin, at which most of the seamen were present; this meeting was to me a strengthening time. 13th. — As I continue to lodge in the steerage I feel an openness this morning to express something further of the state of my mind in respect to poor lads bound apprentice to learn the art of sailing. As I believe sailing is of use in the world, a labor of soul attends me that the pure counsel of truth may be humbly waited for in this case by all concerned in the business of the seas. A pious father whose mind is exercised for the everlasting welfare of his child may not with a peaceable mind place him out to an employment among a people whose common course of life is manifestly corrupt and profane. Great is the present defect among seafaring men in regard to virtue and piety; and, by reason of an abundant traffic and many ships being used for war, so many people are employed on the sea that the subject of placing lads to this employment appears very weighty.

When I remember the saying of the Most High through his prophet, "This people have I formed for myself; they shall show forth my praise," and think of placing children among such to learn the practice of sailing, the consistency of it with a pious education seems to me like that mentioned by the prophet, "There is no answer from God."

Profane examples are very corrupting and very forcible. And as my mind day after day and night after night hath been affected with a sympathizing tenderness towards poor children who are put to the employment of sailors, I have sometimes had weighty conversation with the sailors in the steerage, who were mostly respectful to me and became more so the longer I was with them. They mostly appeared to take kindly what I said to them; but their minds were so deeply impressed with the almost universal depravity among sailors that the poor creatures in their answers to me have revived in my remembrance that of the degenerate Jews a little before the captivity, as repeated by Jeremiah the prophet, "There is no hope."

Now under this exercise a sense of the desire of outward gain prevailing among us felt grievous; and a strong call to the professed followers of Christ was raised in me that all may take heed lest, through loving this present world, they be found in a continued neglect of duty with respect to a faithful labor for reformation.

To silence every motion proceeding from the love of money and humbly to wait upon God to know his will concerning us have appeared necessary. He alone is able to strengthen us to dig deep, to remove all which lies between us and the safe foundation, and so to direct us in our outward employments that pure universal love may shine forth in our proceedings. Desires arising from the spirit of truth are pure desires; and when a mind divinely opened towards a young generation is made sensible of corrupting examples powerfully working and extensively spreading among them, how moving is the prospect! In a world of dangers and difficulties, like a desolate, thorny wilderness, how precious, how comfortable, how safe, are the leadings of Christ the good Shepherd, who said, "I know my sheep, and am known of mine"!

Sixteenth of sixth month. — Wind for several days past often high, what the sailors call squally, with a rough sea and frequent rains. This last night has been a very trying one to the poor seamen, the water the most part of the night running over the main-deck, and sometimes breaking waves came on the quarter-deck. The latter part of the night, as I lay in bed, my mind was humbled under the power of Divine love; and resignedness to the great Creator of the earth and the seas was renewedly wrought in me, and his fatherly care over his children felt precious to my soul. I was now desirous to embrace every opportunity of being inwardly acquainted with the hardships and difficulties of my fellow-creatures, and to labor in his love for the spreading of pure righteousness on the earth. Opportunities were frequent of hearing conversation among the sailors respecting the voyages to Africa and the manner of bringing the deeply oppressed slaves into our islands. They are frequently brought on board the vessels in chains and fetters, with hearts loaded with grief under the apprehension of miserable slavery; so that my mind was frequently engaged to meditate on these things.

Seventeenth of fifth month and first of the week. — We had a meeting in the cabin, to which the seamen generally came. My spirit was contrite before the Lord, whose love at this time affected my heart. In the afternoon I felt a tender sympathy of soul with my poor wife and family left behind, in which state my heart was enlarged in desires that they may walk in that humble obedience wherein the everlasting Father may be their guide and support through all their difficulties in this world; and a sense of that gracious assistance, through which my mind hath been strengthened to take up the cross and leave them to travel in the love of truth, hath begotten thankfulness in my heart to our great Helper.

Twenty-fourth of fifth month. — A clear, pleasant morning. As I sat on deck I felt a reviving in my nature, which had been weakened through much rainy weather and high winds and being shut up in a close, unhealthy air. Several nights of late I have felt my breathing difficult; and a little after the rising of the second watch, which is about midnight, I have got up and stood near an hour with my face near the hatchway, to get the fresh air at the small vacancy under the hatch door, which is commonly shut down, partly to keep out rain and sometimes to keep the breaking waves from dashing into the steerage. I may with thankfulness to the Father of Mercies acknowledge that in my present weak state my mind hath been supported to bear this affliction with patience; and I have looked at the present dispensation as a kindness from the great Father of mankind, who, in this my floating pilgrimage, is in some degree bringing me to feel what many thousands of my fellow-creatures often suffer in a greater degree.

My appetite failing, the trial hath been the heavier; and I have felt tender breathings in my soul after God, the fountain of comfort, whose inward help hath supplied at times the want of outward convenience; and strong desires have attended me that his family, who are acquainted with the movings of his Holy Spirit, may be so redeemed from the love of money and from that spirit in which men seek honor one of another, that in all business, by sea or land, they may constantly keep in view the coming of his kingdom on earth as it is in Heaven, and, by faithfully following this safe guide, may show forth examples tending to lead out of that under which the creation groans. This day we had a meeting in the cabin, in which I was favored in some degree to experience the fulfilling of that saying of the prophet, "The Lord hath been a strength to the poor, a strength to the needy in their distress"; for which my heart is bowed in thankfulness before him.

Twenty-eighth fifth month. — Wet weather of late and small winds, inclining to calms. Our seamen cast a lead, I suppose about one hundred fathoms, but found no bottom. Foggy weather this morning. Through the kindness of the great Preserver of men my mind remains quiet; and a degree of exercise from day to day attends me, that the pure peaceable government of Christ may spread and prevail among mankind.

The leading of a young generation in that pure way in which the wisdom of this world hath no place, where parents and tutors, humbly waiting for the heavenly Counsellor, may example them in the truth as it is in Jesus, hath for several days been the exercise of my mind. O, how safe, how quiet, is that state where the soul stands in pure obedience to the voice of Christ and a watchful care is maintained not to follow the voice of the stranger! Here Christ is felt to be our Shepherd, and under his leading people are brought to a stability; and where he doth not lead forward, we are bound in the bonds of pure love to stand still and wait upon him.

In the love of money and in the wisdom of this world, business is proposed, then the urgency of affairs push forward, and the mind cannot in this state discern the good and perfect will of God concerning us. The love of God is manifested in graciously calling us to come out of that which stands in confusion; but if we bow not in the name of Jesus, if we give not up those prospects of gain which in the wisdom of this world are open before us, but say in our hearts, "I must needs go on; and in going on I hope to keep as near the purity of truth as the business before me will admit of," the mind remains entangled and the shining of the light of life into the soul is obstructed.

Surely the Lord calls to mourning and deep humiliation that in his fear we may be instructed and led safely through the great difficulties and perplexities in this present age. In an entire subjection of our wills the Lord graciously opens a way for his people, where all their wants are bounded by his wisdom; and here we experience the substance of what Moses the prophet figured out in the water of separation as a purification from sin.

Esau is mentioned as a child red all over like a hairy garment. In Esau is represented the natural will of man. In preparing the water of separation a red heifer without blemish, on which there had been no yoke, was to be slain and her blood sprinkled by the priest seven times towards the tabernacle of the congregation; then her skin, her flesh, and all pertaining to her, was to be burnt without the camp, and of her ashes the water was prepared. Thus, the crucifying of the old man, or natural will, is represented; and hence comes a separation from that carnal mind which is death. "He who toucheth the dead body of a man and purifieth not himself with the water of separation, defileth the tabernacle of the Lord; he is unclean." (Num. xix. 13.)

If any through the love of gain engage in business wherein they dwell as among the tombs and touch the bodies of those who are dead should through the infinite love of God feel the power of the cross of Christ to crucify them to the world, and therein learn humbly to follow the divine Leader, here is the judgment of this world, here the prince of this world is cast out. The water of separation is felt; and though we have been among the slain, and through the desire of gain have touched the dead body of a man, yet in the purifying love of Christ we are washed in the water of separation; we are brought off from that business, from that gain and from that fellowship which is not agreeable to his holy will. I have felt a renewed confirmation in the time of this voyage, that the Lord, in his infinite love, is calling to his visited children so to give up all outward possessions and means of getting treasures, that his Holy Spirit may have free course in their hearts and direct them in all their proceedings. To feel the substance pointed at in this figure man must know death as to his own will.

"No man can see God and live." This was spoken by the Almighty to Moses the prophet and opened by our blessed Redeemer. As death comes on our own wills, and a new life is formed in us the heart is purified and prepared to understand clearly, "Blessed are the pure in heart, for they shall see God." In purity of heart the mind is divinely opened to behold the nature of universal righteousness, or the righteousness of the kingdom of God. "No man hath seen the Father save he that is of God, he hath seen the Father."

The natural mind is active about the things of this life, and in this natural activity business is proposed and a will is formed in us to go forward in it. And so long as this natural will remains unsubjected, so long there remains an obstruction to the clearness of Divine light operating in us; but when we love God with all our heart and with all our strength, in this love we love our neighbor as ourselves; and a tenderness of heart is felt towards all people for whom Christ died, even those who, as to outward circumstances, may be to us as the Jews were to the Samaritans. "Who is my neighbor?" See this question answered by our Saviour, Luke x. 30. In this love we can say that Jesus is the Lord; and in this reformation in our souls, manifested in a full reformation of our lives, wherein all things are new, and all things are of God (2 Cor. v. 18), the desire of gain is subjected.

When employment is honestly followed in the light of truth, and people become diligent in business, "fervent in spirit, serving the Lord" (Rom. xii. 11), the meaning of the name is opened to us: "This is the name by which he shall be called, THE LORD OUR RIGHTEOUSNESS." (Jer.

xxiii. 6.) O, how precious is this name! it is like ointment poured out. The chaste virgins are in love with the Redeemer; and for promoting his peaceable kingdom in the world are content to endure hardness like good soldiers; and are so separated in spirit from the desire of riches, that in their employments they become extensively careful to give no offence, either to Jew or Heathen, or to the church of Christ.

Thirty-first of fifth month and first of the week. —We had a meeting in the cabin, with nearly all the ship's company, the whole being near thirty. In this meeting the Lord in mercy favored us with the extending of his love.

Second of sixth month.—Last evening the seamen found bottom at about seventy fathoms. This morning, a fair wind and pleasant. I sat on deck; my heart was overcome with the love of Christ, and melted into contrition before him. In this state the prospect of that work to which I found my mind drawn when in my native land being, in some degree, opened before me, I felt like a little child; and my cries were put up to my Heavenly Father for preservation, that in an humble dependence on him my soul might be strengthened in his love and kept inwardly waiting for his counsel. This afternoon we saw that part of England called the Lizard.

Some fowls yet remained of those the passengers took for their sea-store. I believe about fourteen perished in the storms at sea, by the waves breaking over the quarter-deck, and a considerable number with sickness at different times. I observed the cocks crew as we came down the Delaware, and while we were near the land, but afterwards I think I did not hear one of them crow till we came near the English coast, when they again crowed a few times. In observing their dull appearance at sea, and the pining sickness of some of them, I often remembered the Fountain of goodness, who gave being to all creatures, and whose love extends to caring for the sparrows. I believe where the love of God is verily perfected, and the true spirit of government watchfully attended to, a tenderness towards all creatures made subject to us will be experienced, and a care felt in us that we do not lessen that sweetness of life in the animal creation which the great Creator intends for them under our government.

Fourth of sixth month.—Wet weather, high winds, and so dark that we could see but a little way. I perceived our seamen were apprehensive of the danger of missing the channel, which I understood was narrow. In a while it grew lighter, and they saw the land and knew where we were. Thus the Father of Mercies was pleased to try us with the sight of dangers, and then graciously, from time to time, deliver us from them; thus sparing our lives, that in humility and reverence we might walk before him and put our trust in him. About noon a pilot came off from Dover, where my beloved friend Samuel Emlen went on shore and thence to London, about seventy-two miles by land; but I felt easy in staying in the ship.

Seventh of sixth month and first of the week.— A clear morning: we lay at anchor for the tide, and had a parting meeting with the ship's company, in which my heart was enlarged in a fervent concern for them, that they may come to experience salvation through Christ. Had a head-wind up the Thames; lay sometimes at anchor; saw many ships passing, and some at anchor near; and I had large opportunity of feeling the spirit in which the poor bewildered sailors too generally live. That lamentable degeneracy which so much prevails in the people employed on the seas so affected my heart that I cannot easily convey the feeling I had to another.

The present state of the seafaring life in general appears so opposite to that of a pious education, so full of corruption and extreme alienation from God, so full of the most dangerous examples to young people that in looking towards a young generation I feel a care for them, that they may have an education different from the present one of lads at sea, and that all of us who are acquainted with the pure gospel spirit may lay this case to heart, may remember the lamentable corruptions which attend the conveyance of merchandise across the seas, and so abide in the love of Christ that, being delivered from the entangling expenses of a curious, delicate, and luxurious life, we may learn contentment with a little, and promote the seafaring life no further than that spirit which leads into all truth attends us in our proceedings.

CHAPTER XII.

1772.

Attends the Yearly Meeting in London. — Then proceeds towards Yorkshire. — Visits Quarterly and other Meetings in the Counties of Hertford, Warwick, Oxford, Nottingham, York, and Westmoreland. — Returns to Yorkshire. — Instructive Observations and Letters. — Hears of the Decease of William Hunt. — Some Account of him. — The Author's Last Illness and Death at York.

ON the 8th of sixth month, 1772, we landed at London, and I went straightway to the Yearly Meeting of ministers and elders, which had been gathered, I suppose, about half an hour.*

* There is a story told of his first appearance in England which I have from my friend, William J. Allinson, editor of the Friends' Review, and which he assures me is well authenticated. The vessel reached London on the morning of the fifth day of the week, and John Woolman, knowing that the meeting was then in session, lost no time in reaching it. Coming in late and unannounced, his peculiar dress and manner excited attention and apprehension that he was an itinerant enthusiast. He presented his certificate from Friends in America, but the dissatisfaction still remained, and some one remarked that perhaps the stranger Friend might feel that his dedication of himself to this apprehended service was accepted, without further labor, and that he might now feel free to return to his home. John Woolman sat silent for a space, seeking the unerring counsel of Divine Wisdom. He was profoundly affected by the unfavorable reception he met with, and his tears flowed freely. In the

In this meeting my mind was humbly contrite. In the afternoon the meeting for business was opened, which by adjournments held near a week. In these meetings I often felt a living concern for the establishment of Friends in the pure life of truth. My heart was enlarged in the meetings of ministers, that for business, and in several meetings for public worship, and I felt my mind united in true love to the faithful laborers now gathered at this Yearly Meeting. On the 15th I went to a Quarterly Meeting at Hertford.

First of seventh month.—I have been at Quarterly Meetings at Sherrington, Northampton, Banbury, and Shipton, and have had sundry meetings between. My mind hath been bowed under a sense

love of Christ and his fellow-men he had, at a painful sacrifice, taken his life in his hands, and left behind the peace and endearments of home. That love still flowed out toward the people of England; must it henceforth be pent up in his own heart? He rose at last, and stated that he could not feel himself released from his prospect of labor in England. Yet he could not travel in the ministry without the unity of Friends; and while that was withheld he could not feel easy to be of any cost to them. He could not go back as had been suggested; but he was acquainted with a mechanical trade, and while the impediment to his services continued he hoped Friends would be kindly willing to employ him in such business as he was capable of, that he might not be chargeable to any.

A deep silence prevailed over the assembly, many of whom were touched by the wise simplicity of the stranger's words and manner. After a season of waiting, John Woolman felt that words were given him to utter as a minister of Christ.

of Divine goodness manifested among us ; my heart hath been often enlarged in true love, both among ministers and elders and in public meetings, and through the Lord's goodness I believe it hath been a fresh visitation to many, in particular to the youth.

Seventeenth. — I was this day at Birmingham ; I have been at meetings at Coventry, Warwick, in Oxfordshire, and sundry other places, and have felt the humbling hand of the Lord upon me ; but through his tender mercies I find peace in the labors I have gone through.

Twenty-sixth. — I have continued travelling northward, visiting meetings. Was this day at Nottingham ; the forenoon meeting was especially,

The spirit of his Master bore witness to them in the hearts of his hearers. When he closed, the Friend who had advised against his further service rose up and humbly confessed his error, and avowed his full unity with the stranger. All doubt was removed ; there was a general expression of unity and sympathy, and John Woolman, owned by his brethren, passed on to his work.

There is no portrait of John Woolman ; and had photography been known in his day it is not at all probable that the sun-artist would have been permitted to delineate his features. That, while eschewing all superfluity and expensive luxury, he was scrupulously neat in his dress and person may be inferred from his general character and from the fact that one of his serious objections to dyed clothing was that it served to conceal uncleanness, and was, therefore, detrimental to real purity. It is, however, quite probable that his outer man, on the occasion referred to, was suggestive of a hasty toilet in the crowded steerage.

through Divine love, a heart-tendering season. Next day I had a meeting in a Friend's family, which, through the strengthening arm of the Lord, was a time to be thankfully remembered.

Second of eighth month and first of the week. — I was this day at Sheffield, a large inland town. I was at sundry meetings last week, and feel inward thankfulness for that Divine support which hath been graciously extended to me. On the 9th I was at Rushworth. I have lately passed through some painful labor, but have been comforted under a sense of that Divine visitation which I feel extended towards many young people.

Sixteenth of eighth month and the first of the week, I was at Settle. It hath of late been a time of inward poverty, under which my mind hath been preserved in a watchful, tender state, feeling for the mind of the Holy Leader, and I find peace in the labors I have passed through.

On inquiry in many places I find the price of rye about five shillings; wheat, eight shillings per bushel; oatmeal, twelve shillings for a hundred and twenty pounds; mutton from threepence to fivepence per pound; bacon from sevenpence to ninepence; cheese from fourpence to sixpence; butter from eightpence to tenpence; house-rent for a poor man from twenty-five shillings to forty shillings per year, to be paid weekly; wood for fire very scarce and dear; coal in some places two shillings and sixpence per hundredweight; but near the pits not a quarter so much. O, may the wealthy consider the poor!

The wages of laboring men in several counties towards London at tenpence per day in common business, the employer finds small beer and the laborer finds his own food; but in harvest and hay time wages are about one shilling per day, and the laborer hath all his diet. In some parts of the north of England poor laboring men have their food where they work, and appear in common to do rather better than nearer London. Industrious women who spin in the factories get some fourpence, some fivepence, and so on to six, seven, eight, nine, or ten pence per day, and find their own house-room and diet. Great numbers of poor people live chiefly on bread and water in the southern parts of England, as well as in the northern parts; and there are many poor children not even taught to read. May those who have abundance lay these things to heart!

Stage-coaches frequently go upwards of one hundred miles in twenty-four hours; and I have heard Friends say in several places that it is common for horses to be killed with hard driving, and that many others are driven till they grow blind. Post-boys pursue their business, each one to his stage, all night through the winter. Some boys who ride long stages suffer greatly in winter nights, and at several places I have heard of their being frozen to death. So great is the hurry in the spirit of this world, that in aiming to do business quickly and to gain wealth the creation at this day doth loudly groan.

As my journey hath been without a horse, I have had several offers of being assisted on my way in these stage-coaches, but have not been in them; nor have I had freedom to send letters by these posts in the present way of their riding, the stages being so fixed, and one boy dependent on another as to time, and going at great speed, that in long cold winter nights the poor boys suffer much. I heard in America of the way of these posts, and cautioned Friends in the General Meeting of ministers and elders at Philadelphia, and in the Yearly Meeting of ministers and elders in London, not to send letters to me on any common occasion by post. And though on this account I may be likely not to hear so often from my family left behind, yet for righteousness' sake I am, through Divine favor, made content.

I have felt great distress of mind since I came on this island, on account of the members of our Society being mixed with the world in various sorts of traffic, carried on in impure channels. Great is the trade to Africa for slaves; and for the loading of these ships a great number of people are employed in their factories, among whom are many of our Society. Friends in early times refused on a religious principle to make or trade in superfluities, of which we have many testimonies on record; but for want of faithfulness, some, whose examples were of note in our Society, gave way, from which others took more liberty. Members of our Society worked in superfluities, and bought and sold them, and thus dimness of sight came over many; at length Friends got into the use of some superfluities in dress and in the furniture of their houses, which hath spread from less to more, till superfluity of some kinds is common among us.

In this declining state many look at the example of others and too much neglect the pure feeling of truth. Of late years a deep exercise hath attended my mind, that Friends may dig deep, may carefully cast forth the loose matter and get down to the rock, the sure foundation, and there hearken to that Divine voice which gives a clear and certain sound; and I have felt in that which doth not deceive, that if Friends who have known the truth keep in that tenderness of heart where all views of outward gain are given up, and their trust is only in the Lord, he will graciously lead some to be patterns of deep self-denial in things relating to trade and handicraft labor; and others who have plenty of the treasures of this world will be examples of a plain frugal life, and pay wages to such as they may hire more liberally than is now customary in some places.

Twenty-third of eighth month.—I was this day at Preston Patrick, and had a comfortable meeting. I have several times been entertained at the houses of Friends who had sundry things about them that had the appearance of outward greatness, and as I have kept inward, way hath opened for conversation with such in private, in which Divine goodness hath favored us together with heart-tendering times.

Twenty-sixth of eighth month. — Being now at George Crosfield's, in the county of Westmoreland, I feel a concern to commit to writing the following uncommon circumstance.

In a time of sickness, a little more than two years and a half ago, I was brought so near the gates of death that I forgot my name. Being then desirous to know who I was, I saw a mass of matter of a dull gloomy color between the south and the east, and was informed that this mass was human beings in as great misery as they could be, and live, and that I was mixed with them, and that henceforth I might not consider myself as a distinct or separate being. In this state I remained several hours. I then heard a soft melodious voice, more pure and harmonious than any I had heard with my ears before; I believed it was the voice of an angel who spake to the other angels; the words were, "John Woolman is dead." I soon remembered that I was once John Woolman, and being assured that I was alive in the body, I greatly wondered what that heavenly voice could mean. I believed beyond doubting that it was the voice of an holy angel, but as yet it was a mystery to me.

I was then carried in spirit to the mines where poor oppressed people were digging rich treasures for those called Christians, and heard them blaspheme the name of Christ, at which I was grieved, for his name to me was precious. I was then informed that these heathens were told that those who oppressed them were the followers of Christ, and they said among themselves, "If Christ directed them to use us in this sort, then Christ is a cruel tyrant."

All this time the song of the angel remained a mystery; and in the morning, my dear wife and some others coming to my bedside, I asked them if they knew who I was, and they telling me I was John Woolman, thought I was light-headed, for I told them not what the angel said, nor was I disposed to talk much to any one, but was very desirous to get so deep that I might understand this mystery.

My tongue was often so dry that I could not speak till I had moved it about and gathered some moisture, and as I lay still for a time I at length felt a Divine power prepare my mouth that I could speak, and I then said, "I am crucified with Christ, nevertheless I live; yet not I, but Christ liveth in me. And the life which I now live in the flesh I live by the faith of the Son of God, who loved me and gave himself for me." Then the mystery was opened and I perceived there was joy in heaven over a sinner who had repented, and that the language "John Woolman is dead," meant no more than the death of my own will.

My natural understanding now returned as before, and I saw that people setting off their tables with silver vessels at entertainments was often stained with worldly glory, and that in the present state of things I should take heed how I fed myself out of such vessels. Going to our Monthly Meeting soon after my recovery, I dined at a Friend's house where drink was brought in silver vessels, and not in any other. Wanting something to drink, I told him my case with weeping, and he ordered some drink for me in another vessel. I afterwards went through the same exercise in several Friends' houses in America, as well as in England, and I have cause to acknowledge with humble reverence the loving-kindness of my Heavenly Father, who hath preserved me in such a tender frame of mind, that none, I believe, have ever been offended at what I have said on that subject.

After this sickness I spake not in public meetings for worship for nearly one year, but my mind was very often in company with the oppressed slaves as I sat in meetings; and though under this dispensation I was shut up from speaking, yet the spring of the gospel ministry was many times livingly opened in me, and the Divine gift operated by abundance of weeping, in feeling the oppression of this people. It being so long since I passed through this dispensation, and the matter remaining fresh and lively in my mind, I believe it safest for me to commit it to writing.

Thirtieth of eighth month. — This morning I wrote a letter in substance as follows: —

Beloved Friend, — My mind is often affected as I pass along under a sense of the state of many poor people who sit under that sort of ministry which requires much outward labor to support it; and the loving-kindness of our Heavenly Father in opening a pure gospel ministry in this nation hath often raised thankfulness in my heart to him. I often remember the conflicts of the faithful under persecution, and now look at the free exercise of the pure gift uninterrupted by outward laws, as a trust committed to us, which requires our deepest gratitude and most careful attention. I feel a tender concern that the work of reformation so prosperously carried on in this land within a few ages past may go forward and spread among the nations, and may not go backward through dust gathering on our garments, who have been called to a work so great and so precious.

Last evening during thy absence I had a little opportunity with some of thy family, in which I rejoiced, and feeling a sweetness on my mind towards thee, I now endeavor to open a little of the feeling I had there.

I have heard that you in these parts have at certain seasons Meetings of Conference in relation to Friends living up to our principles, in which several meetings unite in one. With this I feel unity, having in some measure felt truth lead that way among Friends in America, and I have found, my dear friend, that in these labors all superfluities in our own living are against us. I feel that pure love towards thee in which there is freedom.

I look at that precious gift bestowed on thee

with awfulness before Him who gave it, and feel a desire that we may be so separated to the gospel of Christ, that those things which proceed from the spirit of this world may have no place among us.

Thy friend,

JOHN WOOLMAN.

I rested a few days in body and mind with our friend, Jane Crosfield, who was once in America. On the sixth day of the week I was at Kendal, in Westmoreland, and at Greyrig Meeting the 30th day of the month, and first of the week. I have known poverty of late, and have been graciously supported to keep in the patience, and am thankful under a sense of the goodness of the Lord towards those who are of a contrite spirit.

Sixth of ninth month and first of the week. — I was this day at Counterside, a large meeting-house, and very full. Through the opening of pure love, it was a strengthening time to me, and I believe to many more.

Thirteenth of ninth month. — This day I was at Leyburn, a small meeting; but, the towns-people coming in, the house was crowded. It was a time of heavy labor, and I believe was a profitable meeting. At this place I heard that my kinsman, William Hunt, from North Carolina, who was on a religious visit to Friends in England, departed this life on the 9th of this month, of the small pox, at Newcastle. He appeared in the ministry when a youth, and his labors therein were of good savor.

He travelled much in that work in America. I once heard him say in public testimony, that his concern in that visit was to be devoted to the service of Christ so fully that he might not spend one minute in pleasing himself, which words, joined with his example, was a means of stirring up the pure mind in me.

Having of late often travelled in wet weather through narrow streets in towns and villages, where dirtiness under foot and the scent arising from that filth which more or less infects the air of all thickly settled towns were disagreeable ; and, being but weakly, I have felt distress both in body and mind with that which is impure. In these journeys I have been where much cloth hath been dyed, and have, at sundry times, walked over ground where much of their dye-stuffs has drained away. This hath produced a longing in my mind that people might come into cleanness of spirit, cleanness of person, and cleanness about their houses and garments.

Some of the great carry delicacy to a great height themselves, and yet real cleanliness is not generally promoted. Dyes being invented partly to please the eye and partly to hide dirt, I have felt in this weak state, when travelling in dirtiness, and affected with unwholesome scents, a strong desire that the nature of dyeing cloth to hide dirt may be more fully considered.

Washing our garments to keep them sweet is cleanly, but it is the opposite to real cleanliness to hide dirt in them. Through giving way to hiding dirt in our garments a spirit which would conceal that which is disagreeable is strengthened. Real cleanliness becometh a holy people; but hiding that which is not clean by coloring our garments seems contrary to the sweetness of sincerity. Through some sorts of dyes cloth is rendered less useful. And if the value of dye-stuffs, and expense of dyeing, and the damage done to cloth, were all added together, and that cost applied to keeping all sweet and clean, how much more would real cleanliness prevail.

On this visit to England I have felt some instructions sealed on my mind, which I am concerned to leave in writing for the use of such as are called to the station of a minister of Christ.

Christ being the Prince of Peace, and we being no more than ministers, it is necessary for us not only to feel a concern in our first going forth, but to experience the renewing thereof in the appointment of meetings. I felt a concern in America to prepare for this voyage, and being through the mercy of God brought safe hither, my heart was like a vessel that wanted vent. For several weeks after my arrival, when my mouth was opened in meetings, it was like the raising of a gate in a water-course when a weight of water lay upon it. In these labors there was a fresh visitation to many, especially to the youth; but sometimes I felt poor and empty, and yet there appeared a necessity to appoint meetings. In this I was exercised to abide in the pure life of truth, and in all my labors to watch diligently against the motions of self in my own mind.

I have frequently found a necessity to stand up when the spring of the ministry was low, and to speak from the necessity in that which subjecteth the will of the creature; and herein I was united with the suffering seed, and found inward sweetness in these mortifying labors. As I have been preserved in a watchful attention to the divine Leader, under these dispensations enlargement at times hath followed, and the power of truth hath risen higher in some meetings than I ever knew it before through me. Thus I have been more and more instructed as to the necessity of depending, not upon a concern which I felt in America to come on a visit to England, but upon the daily instructions of Christ, the Prince of Peace.

Of late I have sometimes felt a stop in the appointment of meetings, not wholly, but in part: and I do not feel liberty to appoint them so quickly, one after another, as I have done heretofore. The work of the ministry being a work of Divine love, I feel that the openings thereof are to be waited for in all our appointments. O, how deep is Divine wisdom! Christ puts forth his ministers and goeth before them; and O, how great is the danger of departing from the pure feeling of that which leadeth safely! Christ knoweth the state of the people, and in the pure feeling of the gospel ministry their states are opened to his servants. Christ knoweth when the fruit-bearing branches themselves have need of purging. O that these lessons may be remembered by me! and that all who appoint meetings may proceed in the pure feeling of duty!

I have sometimes felt a necessity to stand up, but that spirit which is of the world hath so much prevailed in many, and the pure life of truth hath been so pressed down, that I have gone forward, not as one travelling in a road cast up and well prepared, but as a man walking through a miry place in which are stones here and there safe to step on, but so situated that, one step being taken, time is necessary to see where to step next. Now I find that in a state of pure obedience the mind learns contentment in appearing weak and foolish to that wisdom which is of the world; and in these lowly labors, they who stand in a low place and are rightly exercised under the cross will find nourishment. The gift is pure; and while the eye is single in attending thereto the understanding is preserved clear; self is kept out. We rejoice in filling up that which remains of the afflictions of Christ for his body's sake, which is the church.

The natural man loveth eloquence, and many love to hear eloquent orations, and if there be not a careful attention to the gift, men who have once labored in the pure gospel ministry, growing weary of suffering, and ashamed of appearing weak, may kindle a fire, compass themselves about with sparks, and walk in the light, not of Christ, who is under suffering, but of that fire which they in departing from the gift have kindled, in order that those hearers who have left the meek, suffering state for worldly wisdom may be warmed with this fire and speak highly of their labors. That which is of God gathers to God, and that which is of the world is owned by the world.

In this journey a labor hath attended my mind, that the ministers among us may be preserved in the meek, feeling life of truth, where we may have no desire but to follow Christ and to be with him, that when he is under suffering, we may suffer with him, and never desire to rise up in dominion, but as he, by the virtue of his own spirit, may raise us.

A few days after writing these considerations, our dear friend in the course of his religious visits came to the city of York,* and attended most of the sit-

* During the four months of his labors in England he visited the Quarterly and subordinate meetings of Friends in seven counties, and found time to write essays upon "Loving our Neighbors," "A Sailor's Life," and "Silent Worship." His mind seems to have been greatly exercised by a sense of the intimate connection of luxury and oppression; the burden of the laboring poor rested heavily upon him. In his lonely wanderings on foot through the rural districts (for he did not feel free to use the post on account of the hard treatment of the horses), or in his temporary sojourn in crowded manufacturing towns, the eager competitions and earnest pursuit of gain of one class, and the poverty and physical and moral degradation of another, so oppressed him that his health suffered and his strength failed. It is observable that, in his frequent mention throughout his Journal of inward trials and afflictions, he nowhere betrays

tings of the Quarterly Meeting there; but before it was over he was taken ill of the small-pox. Our friend Thomas Priestman, and others who attended him, preserved the following minutes of his expressions in the time of his sickness.

First day, the 27th of the ninth month, 1772.—His disorder appeared to be the small-pox. Being asked to have a doctor's advice, he signified he had not freedom or liberty in his mind so to do, standing wholly resigned to His will who gave him life, and whose power he had witnessed to raise and heal him in sickness before, when he seemed nigh unto death; and if he was to wind up now, he was perfectly resigned, having no will either to live or die, and did not choose any should be sent for to him; but a young man, an apothecary, coming of his own accord the next day and desiring to do

any personal solicitude, any merely selfish anxiety, for his own soul. His singular conscientious scruples, his close self-questionings, are prompted by a tender concern for universal well-being; an earnest desire that no act or omission of his own should add to the evil and misery under which the creation groans. He offered no prayers for special personal favors. He was, to use his own words, mixed with his fellow-creatures in their misery, and could not consider himself a distinct and separate being. He left all that concerns self to the will of his Father in Heaven, trusting to find a place among the "many mansions," but never asking to see the title-deeds of his inheritance. His last public labor was a testimony in the York Meeting in behalf of the poor and enslaved. His last prayer on his death-bed was a commendation of his "fellow-creatures separated from the Divine harmony" to the Omnipotent Power whom he had learned to call his Father.

something for him, he said he found a freedom to confer with him and the other Friends about him, and if anything should be proposed as to medicine that did not come through defiled channels or oppressive hands, he should be willing to consider and take it, so far as he found freedom.

Second day. — He said he felt the disorder to affect his head so that he could think little and but as a child, and desired, if his understanding should be more affected, to have nothing given him that those about him knew he had a testimony against.

Third day. — He uttered the following prayer: "O Lord, my God! the amazing horrors of darkness were gathered around me and covered me all over, and I saw no way to go forth. I felt the depth and extent of the misery of my fellow-creatures separated from the Divine harmony, and it was heavier than I could bear, and I was crushed down under it. I lifted up my hand, I stretched out my arm, but there was none to help me; I looked round about and was amazed. In the depths of misery, O Lord! I remembered that thou art omnipotent; that I had called thee Father; and I felt that I loved thee, and I was made quiet in my will, and I waited for deliverance from thee. Thou hadst pity upon me when no man could help me. I saw that meekness under suffering was showed to us in the most affecting example of thy Son, and thou taught me to follow him, and I said, 'Thy will, O Father, be done!'"

Fourth day morning. — Being asked how he felt

himself, he meekly answered, "I don't know that I have slept this night; I feel the disorder making its progress, but my mind is mercifully preserved in stillness and peace." Some time after, he said he was sensible that the pains of death must be hard to bear, but if he escaped them now he must some time pass through them, and he did not know that he could be better prepared, but had no will in it. He said he had settled his outward affairs to his mind, had taken leave of his wife and family as never to return, leaving them to the Divine protection, adding, "Though I feel them near to me at this time, yet I have freely given them up, having a hope that they will be provided for." And a little after said, "This trial is made easier than I could have thought, my will being wholly taken away; if I was anxious for the event it would have been harder; but I am not, and my mind enjoys a perfect calm."

In the night, a young woman having given him something to drink, he said, "My child, thou seemest very kind to me, a poor creature; the Lord will reward thee for it." Awhile after he cried out with great earnestness of spirit, "O my Father! my Father!" and soon after he said, "O my Father! my Father! how comfortable art thou to my soul in this trying season!" Being asked if he could take a little nourishment, after some pause he replied, "My child, I cannot tell what to say to it; I seem nearly arrived where my soul shall have rest from all its troubles." After giving in something to be inserted in his journal, he said, "I believe the Lord will now excuse me from exercises of this kind; and I see no work but one, which is to be the last wrought by me in this world; the messenger will come that will release me from all these troubles, but it must be in the Lord's time, which I am waiting for." He said he had labored to do whatever was required according to the ability received, in the remembrance of which he had peace; and though the disorder was strong at times, and would like a whirlwind come over his mind, yet it had hitherto been kept steady and centred in everlasting love; adding, "And if that be mercifully continued, I ask and desire no more." Another time he said he had long had a view of visiting this nation and, some time before he came, had a dream, in which he saw himself in the northern parts of it, and that the spring of the gospel was opened in him much as it was in the beginning of Friends such as George Fox and William Dewsbury, and he saw the different states of the people as clear as he had ever seen flowers in a garden; but in his going along he was suddenly stopped, though he could not see for what end; but, looking towards home, fell into a flood of tears, which waked him.

At another time he said, "My draught seemed strongest towards the north, and I mentioned in my own Monthly Meeting, that attending the Quarterly Meeting at York, and being there, looked like home to me."

Fifth day night. — Having repeatedly consented to take medicine, but without effect, the friend then waiting on him said through distress, "What shall I do now?" He answered with great composure, "Rejoice evermore, and in everything give thanks"; but added a little after, "This is sometimes hard to come at."

On sixth day morning he broke forth early in supplication on this wise, "O Lord, it was thy power that enabled me to forsake sin in my youth, and I have felt thy bruises for disobedience; but as I bowed under them thou healedst me, continuing a father and a friend; I feel thy power now, and I beg that in the approaching trying moment thou wilt keep my heart steadfast unto thee." On his giving directions to a friend concerning some little things, she said, "I will take care, but hope thou wilt live to order them thyself." He replied, "My hope is in Christ; and though I may seem a little better, a change in the disorder may soon happen, and my little strength be dissolved, and if it so happen I shall be gathered to my everlasting rest." On her saying she did not doubt that, but could not help mourning to see so many faithful servants removed at so low a time, he said, "All good cometh from the Lord, whose power is the same, and he can work as he sees best." The same day he had given directions about wrapping his corpse; perceiving a friend to weep, he said, "I would rather thou wouldst guard against weeping for me, my sister; I sorrow not, though I have had some painful conflicts, but now they seem over, and matters well settled; and I look at the face of my dear Redeemer, for sweet is his voice, and his countenance is comely."

First-day, 4th of tenth month. — Being very weak and in general difficult to be understood, he uttered a few words in commemoration of the Lord's goodness, and added, "How tenderly have I been waited on in this time of affliction, in which I may say in Job's words, Tedious days and 'wearisome nights are appointed to me'; and how many are spending their time and money in vanity and superfluities, while thousands and tens of thousands want the necessaries of life, who might be relieved by them, and their distresses at such a time as this in some degree softened by the administering of suitable things."

Second day morning. — The apothecary, who appeared very anxious to assist him, being present, he queried about the probability of such a load of matter being thrown off his weak body; and the apothecary making some remarks implying he thought it might, he spoke with an audible voice on this wise: "My dependence is on the Lord Jesus, who I trust will forgive my sins, which is all I hope for; and if it be his will to raise up this body again, I am content; and if to die, I am resigned; but if thou canst not be easy without trying to assist nature, I submit." After which his throat was so much affected that it was very difficult for him to speak so as to be understood, and he frequently wrote when he wanted anything. About the second hour on fourth-day morning he asked for pen and ink, and at several times, with much difficulty, wrote thus: "I believe my being here is in the wisdom of Christ; I know not as to life or death."

About a quarter before six the same morning he seemed to fall into an easy sleep, which continued about half an hour, when, seeming to awake, he breathed a few times with more difficulty and expired without sigh, groan, or struggle.

APPENDIX.

The TESTIMONY of Friends in Yorkshire at their Quarterly Meeting, held at York the 24th and 25th of the third month, 1773, concerning John Woolman, of Mount Holly, in the Province of New Jersey, North America, who departed this life at the house of our Friend Thomas Priestman, in the suburbs of this city, the 7th of tenth month, 1772, and was interred in the burial-ground of Friends the 9th of the same, aged about fifty-two years.

THIS our valuable friend having been under a religious engagement for some time to visit Friends in this nation, and more especially us in the northern parts, undertook the same in full concurrence and near sympathy with his friends and brethren at home, as appeared by certificates from the Monthly and Quarterly Meetings to which he belonged, and from the Spring Meeting of ministers and elders held at Philadelphia for Pennsylvania and New Jersey.

He arrived in the city of London the beginning of the last Yearly Meeting, and, after attending that meeting, travelled northward, visiting the Quarterly Meetings of Hertfordshire, Buckinghamshire, Northamptonshire, Oxfordshire, and Worcestershire, and divers particular meetings in his way.

He visited many meetings on the west side of this country, also some in Lancashire and Westmoreland, from whence he came to our Quarterly Meeting in the last ninth month, and though much out of health, yet was enabled to attend all the sittings of that meeting except the last.

His disorder, which proved the small-pox, increased speedily upon him, and was very afflicting, under which he was supported in much meekness, patience, and Christian fortitude. To those who attended him in his illness, his mind appeared to be centred in Divine love, under the precious influence whereof we believe he finished his course, and entered into the mansions of everlasting rest.

In the early part of his illness he requested a Friend to write, and he broke forth thus: —

"O Lord my God! the amazing horrors of darkness were gathered around me and covered me all over, and I saw no way to go forth; I felt the misery of my fellow-creatures separated from the Divine harmony, and it was heavier than I could bear, and I was crushed down under it; I lifted up my hand and stretched out my arm, but there was none to help me; I looked round about and was amazed. In the depth of misery, O Lord! I remembered that thou art omnipotent, that I had called thee Father, and I felt that I loved thee, and I was made quiet in thy will, and I waited for deliverance from thee; thou hadst pity upon me when no man could help me; I saw that meekness under suffering was showed to us in the most affecting example of thy Son, and thou taught me to follow him, and I said, Thy will, O Father, be done."

Many more of his weighty expressions might have been inserted here, but it was deemed unnecessary, they being already published in print.

He was a man endued with a large natural capacity, and being obedient to the manifestations of Divine Grace, having in patience and humility endured many deep baptisms, he became thereby sanctified and fitted for the Lord's work, and was truly serviceable in his church. Dwelling in awful fear and watchfulness, he was careful in his public appearances to feel the putting forth of the Divine Hand, so that the spring of the gospel ministry often flowed through him with great sweetness and purity, as a refreshing stream to the weary travellers towards the city of God. Skilful in dividing the word, he was furnished by Him in whom are hid all the treasures of wisdom and knowledge, to communicate freely to the several states of the people where his lot was cast. His conduct at other times was seasoned with like watchful circumspection and attention to the guidance of Divine wisdom, which rendered his whole conversation uniformly edifying.

He was fully persuaded that as the life of Christ comes to reign in the earth, all abuse and unnecessary oppression, both of the human and brute creation, will come to an end ; but under the sense of a deep revolt and an overflowing stream of unrighteousness, his life has been often a life of mourning.

He was deeply concerned on account of that inhuman and iniquitous practice of making slaves of the people of Africa, or holding them in that state, and on that account we understand he hath not only written some books, but travelled much on the continent of America, in order to make the negro-masters (especially those in profession with us) sensible of the evil of such a practice, and though in this journey to England he was far removed from the outward sight of their sufferings, yet his deep exercise of mind and frequent concern to open the miserable state of this deeply injured people remained, as appears by a short treatise he wrote in this journey. His testimony in the last meeting he attended was on this subject, wherein he remarked that as we as a Society, when under outward sufferings, had often found it our concern to lay them before those in authority, and thereby, in the Lord's time, had obtained relief, so he recommended this oppressed part of the creation to our notice, that we may, as way may open, represent their sufferings in an individual, if not in a Society capacity, to those in authority.

Deeply sensible that the desire to gratify people's inclinations in luxury and superfluities is the principal ground of oppression, and the occasion of many unnecessary wants, he believed it to be his duty to be a pattern of great self-denial with respect to the things of this life, and earnestly to labor with Friends in the meekness of wisdom, to impress on their minds the great importance of our testimony in these things, recommending to the guidance of the blessed truth in this and all other concerns, and cautioning such as are experienced therein against contenting themselves with acting to the standard of others, but to be careful to make the standard of truth manifested to them the measure of their obedience. For, said he, "that purity of life which proceeds from faithfulness in following the spirit of truth, that state where our minds are devoted to serve God, and all our wants are bounded by his wisdom ; this habitation has often been opened before me as a place of retirement for the children of the light, where they may stand separated from that which disordereth and confuseth the affairs of society, and where we have a testimony of our innocence in the hearts of those who behold us."

We conclude with fervent desires that we as a people may thus by our example promote the Lord's work in the earth, and, our hearts being prepared, may unite in prayer to the great Lord of the harvest, that as in his infinite wisdom he hath greatly stripped the church by removing of late divers faithful ministers and elders, he may be pleased to send forth many more faithful laborers into his harvest.

A TESTIMONY of the Monthly Meeting of Friends, held in Burlington, the First Day of the Eighth Month, in the Year of our Lord 1774, concerning our esteemed friend, John Woolman, deceased.

HE was born in Northampton, in the county of Burlington and province of West New Jersey, in the eighth month, 1720, of religious parents, who instructed him very early in the principles of the Christian religion as professed by the people called Quakers, which he esteemed a blessing to him even in his younger years, tending to preserve him from the infection of wicked children. But through the workings of the enemy and the levity incident to youth, he frequently deviated from those parental precepts, by which he laid a renewed foundation for repentance that was finally succeeded by a "godly sorrow not to be repented of"; and so he became acquainted with that sanctifying power which qualifies for true gospel ministry, into which he was called about the twenty-second year of his age; and by a faithful use of the talents committed to him he experienced an increase, until he arrived at the state of a father, capable of dividing the word aright to the different states he ministered unto, dispensing milk to babes and meat to those of riper years. Thus he found the efficacy of that power to arise, which, in his own expressions, "prepares the creature to stand like a trumpet through which the Lord speaks to his people." He was a loving husband, a tender father, and was very humane to every part of the creation under his care.

His concern for the poor and those in affliction was evident by his visits to them, whom he frequently relieved by his assistance and charity. He was for many years deeply exercised on account of the poor enslaved Africans, whose cause, as he mentioned, lay almost continually upon him; and he labored to obtain liberty for those captives both in public and in private, and was favored to see his endeavors crowned with considerable success. He was particularly desirous that Friends should not be instrumental to lay burdens on this oppressed people, but should remember the days of suffering from which they had been providentially delivered, that, if times of trouble should return, no injustice dealt to those in slavery might rise in judgment against us, but being clear, we might on such occasions address the Almighty with a degree of confidence for his interposition and relief, being particularly careful as to himself not to countenance slavery even by the use of those conveniences of life which were furnished by their labor.

He was desirous to have his own mind and the minds of others redeemed from the pleasures and immoderate profits of this world and to fix them on those joys which fade not away; his principal care being after a life of purity, endeavoring to avoid not only the grosser pollutions, but those also which, appearing in a more refined dress, are not sufficiently guarded against by some well-disposed people. In the latter part of his life he was remarkable for the plainness and simplicity of his dress, and as much as possible avoided the use of plate, costly furniture, and feasting, thereby endeavoring to become an example of temperance and self-denial which he believed himself called unto; and he was favored with peace therein, although it carried the appearance of great austerity in the view of some. He was very moderate in his charges in the way of business, and in his desires after gain; and though a man of industry, avoided and strove much to lead others out of extreme labor and anxiety after perishable things, being desirous that the strength of our bodies might not be spent in procuring things unprofitable, and that we might use moderation and kindness to the brute animals under our care, to prize the use of them as a great favor, and by no means to abuse them; that the gifts of Providence should be thankfully received and applied to the uses they were designed for.

He several times opened a school at Mount Holly for the instruction of poor Friends' children and others, being concerned for their help and improvement therein. His love and care for the rising youth among us was truly great, recommending to parents and those who have the charge of them to choose conscientious and pious tutors, saying, "It is a lovely sight to behold innocent children"; and that "to labor for their help against that which would mar the beauty of their minds is a debt we owe them."

His ministry was sound, very deep and penetrating, sometimes pointing out the dangerous situation which indulgence and custom lead into, frequently exhorting others, especially the youth, not to be discouraged at the difficulties which occur, but to press after purity. He often expressed an earnest engagement that pure wisdom should be attended to, which would lead into lowliness of mind and resignation to the Divine will, in which state small possessions here would be sufficient.

In transacting the affairs of the discipline his judgment was sound and clear, and he was very useful in treating with those who had done amiss; he visited such in a private way in that plainness which truth dictates, showing great tenderness and Christian forbearance. He was a constant attender of our Yearly Meeting, in which he was a good example and particularly useful, assisting in the business thereof with great weight and attention. He several times visited most of the meetings of Friends in this and in the neighboring provinces with the concurrence of the Monthly Meeting to which he belonged, and we have reason to believe he had good service therein, generally or always expressing at his return how it had fared with him and the evidence of peace in his mind for thus performing his duty. He was often concerned with other Friends in the important service of visiting families, which he was enabled to go through to satisfaction.

In the minutes of the meeting of ministers and elders for this quarter, at the foot of a list of the members of that meeting, made about five years before his death, we find in his handwriting the following observation and reflections: "As looking over the minutes made by persons who have put off this body hath sometimes revived in me a thought how ages pass away, so this list may probably revive a like thought in some when I and the rest of the persons above named are centred in another state of being. The Lord who was the guide of my youth hath in tender mercies helped me hitherto; he hath healed my wounds, he hath helped me out of grievous entanglements; he remains to be the strength of my life; to whom I desire to devote myself in time and in eternity.

"JOHN WOOLMAN."

In the twelfth month, 1771, he acquainted this meeting that he found his mind drawn towards a religious visit to Friends in some parts of England, particularly in Yorkshire. In the first month, 1772, he obtained our certificate, which was approved and indorsed by our Quarterly Meeting and by the Half-Year's Meeting of ministers and elders at Philadelphia. He embarked on his voyage in the fifth month, and arrived in London in the sixth month following, at the time of their Annual Meeting in that city. During his short visit to Friends in that kingdom, we are informed that his services were acceptable and edifying. In his last illness he uttered many lively and comfortable expressions, being "resigned, having no will either to live or die," as appears by the testimony of Friends at York in Great Britain, in the suburbs whereof, at the house of our friend Thomas Priestman, he died of the small-pox, on the 7th of the tenth month, 1772, and was buried in Friends' burial-ground in that city, on the 9th of the same, after a solid meeting held on the occasion at their great meeting-house. He was aged near fifty-two, having been a minister upwards of thirty years, during which time he belonged to Mount Holly particular meeting, which he diligently attended when at home and in health of body, and his labors of love and pious care for the prosperity of Friends in the blessed truth we hope may not be forgotten, but that his good works may be remembered to edification.

Signed in and by order of the said meeting, by

SAMUEL ALLISON, *Clerk.*

Read and approved at our Quarterly Meeting, held at Burlington the 29th of the eighth month, 1774.

Signed by order of the said meeting,

DANIEL SMITH, *Clerk.*

A WORD OF REMEMBRANCE AND CAUTION TO THE RICH.

[First printed in 1793.]

SECTION I.

WEALTH desired for its own sake obstructs the increase of virtue, and large possessions in the hands of selfish men have a bad tendency, for by their means too small a number of people are employed in useful things, and some of them are necessitated to labor too hard, while others would want business to earn their bread, were not employments invented which, having no real usefulness, serve only to please the vain mind.

Rents on lands are often so high that persons of but small substance are straitened in taking farms, and while tenants are healthy and prosperous in business, they often find occasion to labor harder than was intended by our gracious Creator. Oxen and horses are often seen at work when, through heat and too much labor, their eyes and the motions of their bodies manifest that they are oppressed. Their loads in wagons are frequently so heavy that when weary with hauling them far, their drivers find occasion in going up hills, or through mire, to get them forward by whipping. Many poor people are so thronged in their business that it is difficult for them to provide shelter for their cattle against the storms. These things are common when in health, but through sickness and inability to labor, through loss of cattle, and miscarriage in business, many are so straitened that much of their increase goes to pay rent, and they have not wherewith to buy what they require.

Hence one poor woman, in providing for her family and attending the sick, does as much business as would for the time be suitable employment for two or three; and honest persons are often straitened to give their children suitable learning. The money which the wealthy receive from the poor, who do more than a proper share of business in raising it, is frequently paid to other poor people for doing business which is foreign to the true use of things. Men who have large estates and live in the spirit of charity; who carefully inspect the circumstances of those who occupy their estates, and, regardless of the customs of the times, regulate their demands agreeably to universal love, being righteous on principle, do good to the poor without placing it to an act of bounty. Their example in avoiding superfluities tends to excite moderation in others; their uprightness in not exacting what the laws and customs would support them in tends to open the channel to moderate labor in useful affairs, and to discourage those branches of business which have not their foundation in true wisdom.

To be busied in that which is but vanity and serves only to please the insatiable mind, tends to an alliance with those who promote that vanity, and is a snare in which many poor tradesmen are entangled. To be employed in things connected with virtue is most agreeable with the character and inclinations of an honest man. While industrious, frugal people are borne down with poverty, and oppressed with too much labor in useful things, the way to apply money without promoting pride and vanity remains open to such as truly sympathize with them in their various difficulties.

Section II.

The Creator of the earth is the owner of it. He gave us being thereon, and our nature requires nourishment from the produce of it. He is kind and merciful to his creatures; and while they live answerably to the design of their creation, they are so far entitled to convenient subsistence that we may not justly deprive them of it. By the agreements and contracts of our predecessors, and by our own doings, some enjoy a much greater share of this world than others; and while those possessions are faithfully improved for the good of the whole, it agrees with equity; but he who, with a view to self-exaltation, causeth some to labor immoderately, and with the profits arising therefrom employs others in the luxuries of life, acts contrary to the gracious designs of Him who is the owner of the earth; nor can any possessions, either acquired or derived from ancestors, justify such conduct. Goodness remains to be goodness, and the direction of pure wisdom is obligatory on all reasonable creatures.

Though the poor occupy our estates by a bargain, to which they in their poor circumstances agree, and we may ask even less than a punctual fulfilling of their agreement, yet if our views are to lay up riches, or to live in conformity to customs which have not their foundation in the truth, and our demands are such as require from them greater toil or application to business than is consistent with pure love, we invade their rights as inhabitants of a world of which a good and gracious God is the proprietor, and under whom we are tenants.

Were all superfluities and the desire of outward

greatness laid aside, and the right use of things universally attended to, such a number of people might be employed in things useful as that moderate labor with the blessing of Heaven would answer all good purposes, and a sufficient number would have time to attend to the proper affairs of civil society.

Section III.

While our spirits are lively, we go cheerfully through business; either too much or too little action is tiresome, but a right portion is healthful to the body and agreeable to an honest mind.

Men who have great estates stand in a place of trust; and to have it in their power to live without difficulty in that manner which occasions much labor, and at the same time to confine themselves to that use of things prescribed by our Redeemer, and confirmed by his example and the examples of many who lived in the early age of the Christian church, that they may more extensively relieve objects of charity, requires close attention to Divine love.

Our gracious Creator cares and provides for all his creatures. His tender mercies are over all his works, and so far as true love influences our minds, so far we become interested in his workmanship and feel a desire to make use of every opportunity to lessen the distresses of the afflicted and to increase the happiness of the creation. Here we have a prospect of one common interest from which our own is inseparable, so that to turn all we possess into the channel of universal love becomes the business of our lives.

Men of large estates, whose hearts are thus enlarged, are like fathers to the poor; and in looking over their brethren in distressed circumstances, and considering their own more easy condition, they find a field for humble meditation, and feel the strength of the obligations they are under to be kind and tender-hearted towards them. Poor men, eased of their burdens and released from too close an application to business, are enabled to hire assistance, to provide well for their cattle, and to find time to perform those duties among their neighbors which belong to a well-guided social life. When the latter reflect on the opportunity such had to oppress them, and consider the goodness of their conduct, they behold it lovely and consistent with brotherhood; and as the man whose mind is conformed to universal love hath his trust settled in God and finds a firm foundation in any changes or revolutions that happen among men, so also the goodness of his conduct tends to spread a kind, benevolent disposition in the world.

Section IV.

Our blessed Redeemer, in directing us how to conduct ourselves one towards another, appeals to our own feelings: "Whatsoever ye would that men should do to you, do ye even so to them." Now, when some who have never experienced hard labor themselves live in fulness on the labor of others, there is often a danger of their not having a right feeling of the laborers' condition, and of being thereby disqualified to judge candidly in their case, not knowing what they themselves would desire, were they to labor hard from one year to another to raise the necessaries of life, and pay high rent besides. It is good for those who live in fulness to cultivate tenderness of heart, and to improve every opportunity of being acquainted with the hardships and fatigues of those who labor for their living; and thus to think seriously with themselves, Am I influenced by true charity in fixing all my demands? Have I no desire to support myself in expensive customs, because my acquaintances live in such customs?

If a wealthy man, on serious reflection, finds a witness in his own conscience that he indulges himself in some expensive customs which might be omitted consistently with the true design of living, and which, were he to change places with those who occupy his estate, he would desire to be discontinued by them; whoever is thus awakened will necessarily find the injunction binding: "Do ye even so to them." Divine love imposeth no rigorous or unreasonable commands, but graciously points out the spirit of brotherhood and the way to happiness, in attaining which it is necessary that we relinquish all that is selfish.

Section V.

To enforce the duty of tenderness to the poor, the inspired law-giver referred the children of Israel to their own experience: "Ye know the heart of a stranger, seeing ye were strangers in the land of Egypt." He who hath been a stranger among unkind people, or under the government of those who were hard-hearted, has experienced this feeling; but a person who hath never felt the weight of misapplied power comes not to this knowledge but by an inward tenderness, in which the heart is prepared to sympathize with others.

Let us reflect on the condition of a poor innocent man, on whom the rich man, from a desire after wealth and luxuries, lays heavy burdens; when this laborer looks over the cause of his heavy toil and considers that it is laid on him to support that which hath no foundation in pure wisdom, we may well suppose that an uneasiness ariseth in his mind towards one who might without any inconvenience deal more favorably with him. When he considers that by his industry his fellow-creature is benefited and sees that this wealthy man is not satisfied with being supported in a plain way, but to gratify a desire of conforming to wrong customs increaseth to an extreme the labors of those who occupy his estate, we may reasonably judge that he will think himself unkindly used. When he considers that the proceedings of the wealthy are agreeable to the customs of the times, and sees no means of redress in this world, how will the sighings of this innocent person ascend to the throne of that great and good Being who created all, and who hath a constant care over his creatures! He who toils year after year to furnish others with wealth and superfluities, until by overmuch labor he is wearied and oppressed, understands the meaning of that language, "Ye know the heart of a stranger, seeing ye were strangers in the land of Egypt."

Many at this day who know not the heart of a stranger indulge themselves in ways of life which occasion more labor than Infinite Goodness intends for man, and yet compassionate the distresses of such as come directly under their observation; were these to change circumstances awhile with their laborers, were they to pass regularly through the means of knowing the heart of a stranger and come to a feeling knowledge of the straits and hardships which many poor innocent people pass through in obscure life; were these who now fare sumptuously every day to act the other part of the scene until seven times had passed over them and return again to their former states, — I believe many of them would embrace a less expensive life, and would lighten the heavy burdens of some who now labor out of their sight, and who pass through straits with which they are but little acquainted. To see their fellow-creatures under difficulties to which they are in no degree accessory tends to awaken tenderness in the minds of all reasonable people ; but if we consider the condition of those who are depressed in answering our demands, who labor for us out of our sight while we pass our time in fulness, and consider also that much less than we demand would supply us with things really useful, what heart will not relent, or what reasonable man can refrain from mitigating that grief of which he himself is the cause, when he may do so without inconvenience ?

Section VI.

If more men were usefully employed, and fewer ate bread as a reward for doing that which is not useful, food and raiment would on a reasonable estimate be more in proportion to labor than they are at present ; for if four men working eight hours per day can do a portion of labor in a certain number of days, then five men equally capable may do the same business in the same time by working only six hours and twenty-four minutes per day. In proceeding agreeably to sound wisdom, a small portion of daily labor might suffice to keep a proper stream gently circulating through all the channels of society ; and this portion of labor might be so divided and taken in the most advantageous parts of the day that people would not have that plea for the use of strong liquors which they have at present. The quantity of spirituous liquors imported and made in our country is great ; nor can so many thousand hogsheads of it be drunk every year without having a powerful effect on our habits and morals.

People spent with much labor often take strong

liquor to revive them. The portion of the necessaries of life is such that those who support their families by day labor find occasion to labor hard, and many of them think strong drink a necessary part of their entertainment.

When people are spent with action and take these liquors not only as a refreshment from past labors, but also to enable them to go on without giving sufficient time to recruit by resting, it gradually turns them from that calmness of thought which attends those who apply their hearts to true wisdom. That the spirits being scattered by too much bodily motion and again revived by strong drink makes a person unfit for Divine meditation, I suppose will not be denied; and as multitudes of people are in this practice who do not take so much as to hinder them from managing their affairs, this custom is strongly supported; but as through Divine goodness I have found that there is a more quiet, calm, and happy way intended for us to walk in, I am engaged to express what I feel in my heart concerning it. As cherishing the spirit of love and meekness belongs to the family of Jesus Christ, so to avoid those things which are known to work against it is an indispensable duty. Every degree of luxury of what kind soever, and every demand for money inconsistent with Divine order, hath some connection with unnecessary labor. By too much labor the spirits are exhausted, and nature craves help from strong drink; and the frequent use of strong drink works in opposition to the celestial influence on the mind. There is in the nature of people some degree of likeness with that food and air to which they have been accustomed from their youth; this frequently appears in those who, by a separation from their native air and usual diet, grow weak and unhealthy for want of them; nor is it reasonable to suppose that so many thousand hogsheads of fiery liquor can be drunk every year and the practice continued from age to age without altering in some degree the natures of men and rendering their minds less apt to receive the pure truth in the love of it.

As many who manifest some regard to piety in degree conform to those ways of living and of collecting wealth which increase labor beyond the bounds fixed by Divine wisdom, my desire is that they may so consider the connection of things as to take heed lest by exacting of poor men more than is consistent with universal righteousness they promote that by their conduct which in word they speak against. To treasure up wealth for another generation by means of the immoderate labor of those who in some measure depend upon us is doing evil at present without knowing that wealth thus gathered may not be applied to evil purposes when we are gone. To labor hard or cause others to do so that we may live conformably to customs which Christ our Redeemer discountenanced by his example in the days of his flesh, and which are contrary to Divine order, is to manure a soil for propagating an evil seed in the earth. They who enter deeply into these considerations and live under the weight of them will feel these things so heavy and their ill effects so extensive that the necessity of attending singly to Divine wisdom will be evident; and will thereby be directed in the right use of things in opposition to the customs of the times; and will be supported to bear patiently the reproaches attending singularity. To conform a little strengthens the hands of those who carry wrong customs to their utmost extent; and the more a person appears to be virtuous and heavenly-minded, the more powerfully does his conformity operate in favor of evil-doers. Lay aside the profession of a pious life, and people expect little or no instruction from the example ; but while we profess in all cases to live in constant opposition to that which is contrary to universal righteousness, what expressions are equal to the subject, or what language is sufficient to set forth the strength of the obligations we are under to beware lest by our example we lead others astray !

Section VII.

If by our wealth we make our children great, without a full persuasion that we could not bestow it better, and thus give them power to deal hardly with others more virtuous than they, it can after death give us no more satisfaction than if by this treasure we had raised others above our own, and had given them power to oppress them.

Did a man possess as much land as would suffice for twenty industrious frugal people, and supposing that, being the lawful heir to it, he intended to give this great estate to his children ; yet if he found on research into the title that one half of this estate was the undoubted right of a number of poor orphans, who as to virtue and understanding appeared to him as hopeful as his own children, the discovery would give him an opportunity to consider whether he was attached to any interest distinct from the interest of those orphans.

Some of us have estates sufficient for our children, and as many more to live upon, if they all employed their time in useful business, and lived in that plainness which becomes the true disciples of Christ ; and we have no reason to believe that our children will be more likely to apply them to benevolent purposes than would some poor children with whom we are acquainted; and yet did we believe that after our decease our estates would go equally among our children and the children of the poor, it would be likely to give us uneasiness. This may show to a thoughtful person that to be redeemed from all the remains of selfishness, to have a universal regard to our fellow-creatures, and to love them as our Heavenly Father loves them, we must constantly attend to the influence of his spirit.

When our hearts are enlarged to contemplate the nature of Divine love, we behold it harmonious; but if we attentively consider that moving of selfishness which makes us uneasy at the apprehension of that which is in itself reasonable, and which, when separated from all previous conceptions and expectations, appears so, we see an inconsistency in it, for the subject of such uneasiness is future, and will not affect our children until we are removed into that state of being in which there is no possibility of our taking delight in anything contrary to the pure principle of universal love.

As that natural desire of superiority in us, when given way to, extends to such of our favorites as we expect will succeed us; and as the grasping after wealth and power for them adds greatly to the burdens of the poor, and increaseth the evil of covetousness in this age, — I have often desired that in looking towards posterity we may remember the purity of that rest which is prepared for the Lord's people; the impossibility of our taking pleasure in anything distinguishable from universal righteousness; and how vain and weak it is to give wealth and power to those who appear unlikely to apply it to the general good when we are gone.

As Christians, all we possess is the gift of God, and in the distribution of it we act as his stewards; it becomes us therefore to act agreeably to that Divine wisdom which he graciously gives to his servants. If the steward of a great family takes that with which he is intrusted, and bestows it lavishly on some to the injury of others and to the damage of his employer, he degrades himself and becomes unworthy of his office.

The true felicity of man in this life and in that which is to come, is in being inwardly united to the Fountain of universal love and bliss. When we provide for posterity, and make settlements which will not take effect until after we are centred in another state of being, if we therein knowingly act contrary to universal love and righteousness, such conduct must arise from a false, selfish pleasure ; and if, after such settlements, our wills continue to stand in opposition to the Fountain of universal light and love, will there not be an impassable gulf between the soul and true felicity? But if after such settlement, and when too late for an alteration, we attain to that purified state which our Redeemer prayed his Father that his people might attain to, of being united to the Father and to the Son, must not a sincere repentance for all things done in a will separate from universal love, precede this inward sanctification ? And though in such depth of repentance and reconciliation all sins may be forgiven, can we reasonably suppose that our partial determinations in favor of those whom we selfishly loved will then afford us pleasure ?

Section VIII.

To labor for an establishment in Divine love, in which the mind is disentangled from the power of darkness, is the great business of man's life ; the collecting of riches, covering the body with fine wrought, costly apparel, and having magnificent furniture, operate against universal love and tend to feed self, so that it belongs not to the children of the light to desire these things. He who sent ravens to feed Elijah in the wilderness, and increased the poor woman's small remains of meal and oil, is now as attentive as ever to the necessities of his people. When he saith unto his people, "Ye are my sons and daughters," no greater happiness can be desired by them, who know how gracious a Father he is.

The greater part of the necessaries of life are so far perishable that each generation hath occasion to labor for them; and when we look towards a succeeding age with a mind influenced by universal love, instead of endeavoring to exempt some from those cares which necessarily relate to this life, and to give them power to oppress others, we desire that they may all be the Lord's children and live in that humility and order becoming his family. Our hearts, being thus opened and enlarged, will feel content with a state of things as foreign to luxury and grandeur as that which our Redeemer laid down as a pattern.

By desiring wealth for the power and distinction it gives, and gathering it on this motive, a person may become rich; but his mind being moved by a draught distinguishable from the drawings of the Father, he cannot be united to the heavenly society, where God is the strength of our life. "It is easier," saith our Saviour, "for a camel to go through the eye of a needle than for a rich man to enter the kingdom of God." Here our Lord uses an instructive similitude, for as a camel while in that form cannot pass through the eye of a needle, so a man who trusteth in riches, and holds them for the sake of the power and distinction attending them, cannot in that spirit enter into the kingdom. Now every part of a camel may be so reduced as to pass through a hole as small as the eye of a needle ; yet such is the bulk of the creature and the hardness of its bones and teeth, that it could not be so reduced without much labor ; so must man cease from that spirit which craves riches, and be brought into another disposition before he inherits the kingdom, as effectually as a camel must be changed from the form of a camel in passing through the eye of a needle.

When our Saviour said to the rich youth, "Go, sell what thou hast, and give to the poor," though undoubtedly it was his duty to have done so, yet to enjoin the selling of all as a duty on every true Christian would be to limit the Holy One. Obedient children, who are intrusted with much outward substance, wait for wisdom to dispose of it agreeably to His will, "in whom the fatherless find mercy." It may not be the duty of every one to commit at once their substance to other hands, but rather from time to time to look round among the numerous branches of the great family as the stewards of Him who provides for the widows and fatherless ; but as disciples of Christ, although intrusted with much goods, they may not conform to sumptuous or luxurious living ; for, as he lived in perfect plainness and simplicity, the greatest in his family cannot by virtue of his station claim a right to live in worldly grandeur without contradicting him who said, "It is enough for the disciple to be as his Master."

When our eyes are so single as to discern the selfish spirit clearly, we behold it the greatest of all tyrants. Many thousand innocent people under some of the Roman emperors, being confirmed in the truth of Christ's religion by the powerful effects of his Holy Spirit upon them, and scrupling to conform to heathenish rites, were put to death by various kinds of cruel and lingering torments, as is largely set forth by Eusebius.

Now, if we single out Domitian, Nero, or any other of the persecuting emperors, the man, though terrible in his time, will appear as a tyrant of small consequence compared with this selfish spirit; for, though his bounds were large, yet a great part of the world was out of his reach; and though he grievously afflicted the bodies of innocent people, yet the minds of many were divinely supported in their greatest agonies, and being faithful unto death they were delivered from his tyranny. His reign, though cruel for a time, was soon over; and he in his greatest pomp appears to have been a slave to a selfish spirit.

Thus tyranny as applied to a man riseth up and soon has an end; but if we consider the numerous oppressions in many states, and the calamities occasioned by contending nations in various countries and ages of the world, and remember that selfishness hath been the original cause of them all; if we consider that those who are unredeemed from this selfish spirit not only afflict others but are afflicted themselves, and have no real quietness in this life nor in futurity, but, according to the sayings of Christ, have their portion "where the worm dieth not and the fire is not quenched"; if we consider the havoc that is made in this age, and how numbers of people are hurried on, striving to collect treasure to please that mind which wanders from perfect resignedness, and in that wisdom which is foolishness with God are perverting the true use of things, laboring as in the fire, contending with one another even unto blood, and exerting their power to support ways of living foreign to the life of one wholly crucified to the world; if we consider what great numbers of people are employed in preparing implements of war, and the labor and toil of armies set apart for protecting their respective territories from invasion, and the extensive miseries which attend their engagements; while they who till the land and are employed in other useful things in supporting not only themselves but those employed in military affairs, and also those who own the soil, have great hardships to encounter through too much labor; while others, in several kingdoms, are busied in fetching men to help to labor from distant parts of the world, to spend the remainder of their lives in the uncomfortable condition of slaves, and that self is the bottom of these proceedings; — amidst all this confusion, and these scenes of sorrow and distress, can we remember that we are the disciples of the Prince of Peace, and the example of humility and plainness which he set for us, without feeling an earnest desire to be disentangled from everything connected with selfish customs in food, in raiment, in houses and in all things else? That being of Christ's family, and walking as he walked, we may stand in that uprightness wherein man was first made, and have no fellowship with those inventions which men in their fallen wisdom have sought out.

Section IX.

The way of carrying on wars common in the world is so far distinguishable from the purity of Christ's religion that many scruple to join in them. Those who are so redeemed from the love of the world as to possess nothing in a selfish spirit have their "life hid with Christ in God," and he preserves them in resignedness, even in times of commotion.

As they possess nothing but what pertains to his family, anxious thoughts about wealth or dominion have little or nothing in them on which to work; and they learn contentment in being disposed of according to His will who, being omnipotent and always mindful of his children, causeth all things to work for their good; but when that spirit works which loves riches, and in its working gathers wealth and cleaves to customs which have their root in self-pleasing, whatever name it hath it still desires to defend the treasures thus gotten. This is like a chain in which the end of one link encloseth the end of another. The rising up of a desire to obtain wealth is the beginning; this desire being cherished, moves to action; and riches thus gotten please self; and while self has a life in them it desires to have them defended. Wealth is attended with power, by which bargains and proceedings contrary to universal righteousness are supported; and hence oppression, carried on with worldly policy and order, clothes itself with the name of justice and becomes like a seed of discord in the soul. And as a spirit which wanders from the pure habitation prevails, so the seeds of war swell and sprout and grow and become strong until much fruit is ripened. Then cometh the harvest spoken of by the prophet, which "is a heap in the day of grief and desperate sorrows." O that we who declare against wars. and acknowledge our trust to be in God only, may walk in the light, and therein examine our foundation and motives in holding great estates! May we look upon our treasures, the furniture of our houses, and our garments, and try whether the seeds of war have nourishment in these our possessions. Holding treasures in the self-pleasing spirit is a strong plant, the fruit whereof ripens fast. A day of outward distress is coming, and Divine love calls to prepare against it.

Section X.

"The heaven, even the heavens, are the Lord's; but the earth hath he given to the children of men." As servants of God our land or estates we hold under him as his gifts; and in applying the profits it is our duty to act consistently with the designs of our Benefactor. Imperfect men may give from motives of misguided affection, but perfect wisdom and goodness gives agreeably to his own nature; nor is this gift absolute, but conditional, for us to occupy as dutiful children and not otherwise; for He alone is the true proprietor. "The world," saith He, "is mine, and the fulness thereof." The inspired lawgiver directed that such of the Israelites as sold their inheritance should sell it for a term only, and that they or their children should again enjoy it in the year of jubilee, settled on every fiftieth year. "The land shall not be sold forever, for the land is mine, saith the Lord, for ye are strangers and sojourners with me." This was designed to prevent the rich from oppressing the poor by too much engrossing the land; and our blessed Redeemer said, "Till heaven and earth pass, one jot or one tittle shall in no wise pass from the law, till all be fulfilled."

When Divine love takes place in the hearts of any people, and they steadily act in a principle of universal righteousness, then the true intent of the law is fulfilled, though their outward modes of proceeding may be various; but when men are possessed by that spirit hinted at by the prophet, and, looking over their wealth, say in their hearts, "Have we not taken to us horns by our own strength?" they deviate from the Divine law, and do not count their possessions so strictly God's, nor the weak and poor entitled to so much of the increase thereof, but that they may indulge their desires in conforming to worldly pomp. Thus when house is joined to house and field laid to field, until there is no place, and the poor are thereby straitened, though this is done by bargain and purchase, yet so far as it stands distinguished from universal love, so far that woe predicted by the prophet will accompany their proceedings. As He who first founded the earth was then the true proprietor of it, so he still remains, and though he hath given it to the children of men, so that multitudes of people have had their sustenance from it while they continued here, yet he hath never alienated it, but his right is as good as at first; nor can any apply the increase of their possessions contrary to universal love, nor dispose of lands in a way which they know tends to exalt some by oppressing others without being justly chargeable with usurpation.

Section XI.

If we count back one hundred and fifty years and compare the inhabitants of Great Britain with the nations of North America on the like compass of ground, the latter, I suppose, would bear a small proportion to the former. On the discovery of this fertile continent many of those thickly settled inhabitants coming over, the natives at first generally treated them with kindness; and as they brought iron tools and a variety of things for man's use, they gladly embraced the opportunity of traffic and encouraged these foreigners to settle; I speak only of improvements made peaceably.

Thus our Gracious Father, who beholds the situation of all his creatures, hath opened a way for a thickly settled land; now if we consider the turning of God's hand in thus far giving us some room in this continent, and that the offspring of those ancient possessors of the country, in whose eyes we appear as new-comers, are yet owners and inhabitants of the land adjoining us, and that their way of life, requiring much room, hath been transmitted to them from their predecessors and probably settled by the custom of a great many ages, we may see the necessity of cultivating the lands already obtained of them and applying the increase consistently with true wisdom so as to accommodate the greatest number of people, before we have any right to plead, as members of the one great family, the equity of their assigning to us more of their possessions and living in a way requiring less room.

Did we all walk as became the followers of our blessed Saviour, were all the fruits of the country retained in it which are sent abroad in return for strong drink, costly array, and other luxuries, and the labor and expense of importing and exporting applied to husbandry and useful trades, a much greater number of people than now reside here might, with the Divine blessing, live comfortably on the lands already granted us by those ancient possessors of the country. If we faithfully serve God, who has given us such room in this land, I believe he will make some of us useful among the natives, both in publishing the doctrines of his Son, our Saviour, and in pointing out to them the advantages of cultivating the earth ; while people are so much more thickly settled in some parts than others, a trade in some serviceable articles may be to mutual advantage and may be carried on with much more regularity and satisfaction to a sincere Christian than trade now generally is.

One person continuing to live contrary to true wisdom commonly draws others into connection with him, and when these embrace the way the first hath chosen, their proceedings are like a wild vine which springing from a single seed and growing strong, its branches extend, and their little tendrils twist round all herbs and boughs of trees within their reach, and are so braced and locked in that without much labor and great strength they are not disentangled. Thus these customs, small in their beginning, as they increase promote business and traffic, and many depend on them for a living; but it is evident that all business which hath not its foundation in true wisdom is not becoming a faithful follower of Christ, who loves God not only with all his heart, but with all his strength and ability. And as the Lord is able and will support those whose hearts are perfect towards him in a way agreeably to his unerring wisdom, it becomes us to meditate on the privileges of his children, to remember that "where the spirit of the Lord is, there is liberty," and that in joining to customs which we know are wrong there is a departing from his government and a certain degree of alienation from him. Some well-inclined people are entangled in such business, and at times may have a desire of being freed from it; our ceasing from these things may therefore be made helpful to them; and though for a time their business may fail, yet if they humbly ask wisdom of God and are truly resigned to him, he will not fail them nor forsake them. He who created the earth and hath provided sustenance for millions of people in past ages is as attentive to the necessities of his children as ever. To press forward to perfection is our duty; and if herein we lessen a business by which some poor people earn their bread, the Lord who calls to cease from those things will take care of those whose business fails by it, if they sincerely seek him. If the connection we have with the inhabitants of these provinces, and our interest considered as distinct from others, engage us to promote plain living in order to enrich our country, though a plain life is in itself best, yet by living plain in a selfish spirit we advance not in true religion.

Divine love which enlarges the heart towards mankind universally is that alone which stops every corrupt stream and opens those channels of business and commerce in which nothing runs that is not pure, and so establishes our goings that when in our labors we meditate on the universal love of God and the harmony of holy angels, the serenity of our minds may never be clouded by remembering that some part of our employments tends to support customs which have their foundation in the self-seeking spirit.

Section XII.

While our minds are prepossessed in favor of customs distinguishable from perfect purity, we are in danger of not attending with singleness to that light which opens to our view the nature of universal righteousness.

In the affairs of a thickly settled country are variety of useful employments besides tilling the earth ; so that for some men to have more land than is necessary to build upon and to answer the occasions of their families may consist with brotherhood ; and from the various gifts which God hath bestowed on those employed in husbandry, for some to possess and occupy much more than others may likewise so consist ; but when any, on the strength of their possessions, demand such rent or interest as necessitates their tenants to a closer application to business than our merciful Father designed for us, it puts the wheels of perfect brotherhood out of order and leads to employments the promoting of which belongs not to the family of Christ, whose example in all points being a pattern of wisdom, the plainness and simplicity of his outward appearance may well make us ashamed to adorn our bodies with costly array or treasure up wealth by the least oppression.

Though by claims grounded on prior possession great inequality appears among men; yet the instructions of the Great Proprietor of the earth are necessary to be attended to in all our proceedings as possessors or claimers of the soil. "The steps of a good man are ordered of the Lord," and those who are thus guided and whose hearts are enlarged in his love give directions concerning their possessions agreeably thereto, and that claim which stands on universal righteousness is a good right; but the continuance of that right depends on properly applying the profits thereof. The word "right" commonly relates to our possessions. We say, a right of propriety to such a division of a province, or a clear, indisputable right to the land within certain bounds. Thus this word is continued as a remembrancer of the original intent of dividing the land by boundaries, and implies that it was equitably or rightly divided, that is, divided according to righteousness. In this — that is, in equity and righteousness — consists the strength of our claim. If we trace an unrighteous claim and find gifts or grants proved by sufficient seals and witnesses, it gives not the claimant a right; for that which is opposite to righteousness is wrong, and the nature of it must be changed before it can be right.

Suppose twenty free men, professed followers of Christ, discovered an island, and that they with their wives, independent of all others, took possession of it and, dividing it equally, made improvements and multiplied; suppose these first possessors, being generally influenced by true love, did with paternal regard look over the increasing condition of the inhabitants, and, near the end of their lives, gave such directions concerning their respective possessions as best suited the convenience of the whole and tended to preserve love and harmony;

and that their successors in the continued increase of people generally followed their pious example and pursued means the most effectual to keep oppression out of their island; but that one of these first settlers, from a fond attachment to one of his numerous sons, no more deserving than the rest, gives the chief of his lands to him, and by an instrument sufficiently witnessed strongly expressed his mind and will; — suppose this son, being landlord to his brethren and nephews, demands such a portion of the fruits of the earth as may supply himself, his family, and some others, and that these others thus supplied out of his store are employed in adorning his building with curious engravings and paintings, preparing carriages to ride in, vessels for his house, delicious meats, fine wrought apparel and furniture, all suiting that distinction lately arisen between him and the other inhabitants; and that, having the absolute disposal of these numerous improvements, his power so increaseth that in all conferences relative to the public affairs of the island these plain, honest men, who are zealous for equitable establishments, find great difficulty in proceeding agreeably to their righteous inclinations; — suppose this son, from a fondness to one of his children, joined with a desire to continue this grandeur under his own name, confirms the chief of his possessions to him, and thus for many ages there is one great landlord over near a twentieth part of this island, and the rest are poor oppressed people, to some of whom, from the manner of their education, joined with a notion of the greatness of their predecessors, labor is disagreeable; who therefore, by artful applications to the weakness, unguardedness, and corruptions of others in striving to get a living out of them, increase the difficulties among them, while the inhabitants of other parts, who guard against oppression and with one consent train up their children in frugality and useful labor, live more harmoniously; — if we trace the claims of the ninth or tenth of these great landlords down to the first possessor and find the claim supported throughout by instruments strongly drawn and witnessed, after all we could not admit a belief into our hearts that he had a right to so great a portion of land after such a numerous increase of inhabitants.

The first possessor of that twentieth part held no more, we suppose, than an equitable portion; but when the Lord, who first gave these twenty men possession of this island unknown to all others, gave being to numerous people who inhabited the twentieth part, whose natures required the fruits thereof for their sustenance, this great claimer of the soil could not have a right to the whole to dispose of it in gratifying his irregular desires; but they, as creatures of the Most High God, Possessor of heaven and earth, had a right to part of what this great claimer held, though they had no instruments to confirm their right. Thus oppression in the extreme appears terrible; but oppression in more refined appearances remains to be oppression, and when the smallest degree of it is cherished it grows stronger and more extensive.

To labor for a perfect redemption from this spirit of oppression is the great business of the whole family of Christ Jesus in this world.

THE END.

CPSIA information can be obtained
at www.ICGtesting.com
Printed in the USA
LVHW032243100223
739217LV00006B/431

9 783382 106102